love
hunters
series **2**

the RIGHT MAN

CM HAINES

Edited by Heather Dowell
Proofread by Leah Miller
Cover and Formatting by Cait Marie

dedication

To the readers who are tired of running from the pain of the past, it's okay to slow down and look toward the future now. Don't be afraid of happiness.

content warnings

There are some sensitive themes and topics in this book, and while I tried to approach everything gracefully, I do want to let readers know what to expect.

Some of the warnings include: mentions of past parental death, mentions of past suicidal thoughts and ideations, anxiety and anxiety attacks, and implications of past emotional abuse.

If you're concerned or wish to know more about any of the above, please do not hesitate to reach out at cmhaines. author@gmail.com.

ONE

Wyatt

It was never Wyatt's dream job to be a bartender. He'd never planned to do this for long.

But he hadn't planned on a lot of things.

Like his ex-girlfriend convincing him to move to a small town in a different state only to dump him and disappear into the night.

He was still here six years later. Yet, it was only recently that he really started to accept that this was his home. The people he had in his life now were his friends. His coworkers were his new family.

Most of the time, his social anxiety and general dislike of chaos made the job he didn't even want more difficult.

Then, there were days like today.

Almost the entire staff was here, and they were preparing for the evening while also goofing off. They laughed and chatted around The Tavern—cleaning, restocking, and taking care of business. It was early afternoon, so no one else had come in yet. They had the entire bar to themselves at the moment. And despite Becca's arguments, Wyatt took control of the music, which blared over the speakers, putting him in a good mood.

Or at least, as good of a mood as he could be in while waiting for their new manager to arrive.

"Behind you," Owen said just as Becca shouted at

Shawn over the loud music. The latter laughed and tossed a balled-up napkin at her.

Wyatt couldn't help but chuckle too. He might not have planned on working here for long, but he didn't hate his job. In these moments, he actually enjoyed being here. His coworkers were all great. He had no idea how he got so lucky on that front. Even Ryan, who rarely showed up on time and called out more often than not, got along with everyone. They were truly like a family.

And having a new person come in to join them made him nervous.

For weeks now, Jack—their boss and the owner of the bar—had been absent. He'd managed the place for the last two decades mostly on his own and said he needed a break. Except, Jack wasn't coming in at all anymore, and it was starting to worry Wyatt.

In recent years, Wyatt had stepped up to help as much as he could. He owed the man everything for getting him through such a hard time in his life. So, he had no problem running things in Jack's absence. He hadn't expected Jack to call in his daughter to run things instead.

Not wanting to dwell on it too much and start spiraling, Wyatt grabbed a few pieces of ice and crept around the bar toward Owen, who had his back to him. Becca noticed his approach but didn't call attention to it, instead playfully lunging at Shawn. Her on-again boyfriend caught her by the waist and twirled her around. As she squealed in delight, Wyatt made his move. He tugged at the neck of Owen's shirt and dropped the ice inside.

"Are you fucking kidding me?" the man yelled, reaching for his back and wiggling about. His pale blue button-down was tucked into his pants, not letting the cubes fall out. Wyatt laughed, watching him squirm. When Owen finally managed to yank his shirt out, the pieces of ice fell to the tiled floor. One shattered, but that didn't deter him. He scooped it all into his hand and threw it at Wyatt.

Ducking, Wyatt let it fly past him. He knew he would pay for that later. Owen might be the 'responsible' one here, but he was a master at revenge pranks.

As the others went quiet, Wyatt glanced up to find them all staring behind him toward the door. *Shit.* If they hit a customer...

He stood and turned around while Becca ran to lower the music. A young woman in business attire glared at him. Her shoulders were raised, her arms hanging away from her body as her chest heaved. The ice laid scattered around her feet.

It had definitely hit her.

"I'm so sorry, miss." Wyatt grabbed a hand towel from the bar and offered it to her, not knowing if she actually needed it. The front of her white dress shirt was unbuttoned at the top, and with his luck, the ice probably went straight for that little bit of cleavage peeking out. She ignored his outstretched hand. Clearing his throat, he went behind the bar. "How about a drink on the house? We're really sorry. It's been quiet all day, so we were..."

He trailed off when she straightened and clenched her jaw. Her dark brown hair was twisted into a tight bun, emphasizing her sharp cheekbones and incredible dark brown eyes. She was fucking gorgeous, albeit too serious for his liking. He'd sworn off dating after Loren left him six years ago, only having one-nights stands here and there, and he *never* crossed that line with a customer, but he would reconsider for this beauty.

Her dark gaze narrowed. "Are you even listening?"

"I... sorry, what?" No, he wasn't listening. He was far

too distracted right now to even think clearly. Too much blood was leaving his brain to relocate farther south.

"I asked if this is how this establishment normally operates."

So, she was rude and snooty. He could get past that if it meant a night with her. Clearing his throat, he said, "No, miss. Like I said, things were just slow and we were having some fun."

"We do try to keep the atmosphere light though." Owen appeared next to Wyatt with his arms crossed. Ever the parent of the group. He was fiercely protective and took care of them, despite only being thirty.

"Well, then, that's the first thing we're changing," the woman said.

Wyatt's brow furrowed before a sinking feeling coursed through him. It was confirmed when Becca sighed and said, "Olivia, still as delightful as ever, I see."

Shit. This was Jack's daughter? Wyatt clenched his jaw. "Olivia Cartwright?"

"I would say it's a pleasure, but I'm sorely disappointed in this first impression." She crossed her own arms, mirroring Owen's stance as she cocked one hip out. She didn't even acknowledge Becca's statement—the reminder that they went to high school together. "My father has asked me to step in and run things while he takes a break. He has given me full control to make changes as I see fit and has encouraged me to get this place operating more smoothly. It is no secret that it's struggling, and I'm here to fix that."

Becca and Shawn moved closer during her speech. Becca fidgeted, wringing her fingers together in what Wyatt knew was simmering anger. Shawn reached over to hold her hand. The two liked to tease each other, but they had also been dating on and off for years. They were best friends, though they often pretended otherwise. Even when they were off-again, they still very clearly cared about one another. Wyatt took a deep breath. "We're sorry, Miss Cartwright. It won't happen again."

"You're damn right it won't. I didn't work my ass off to get my MBA only to come back and deal with a bunch of reckless townies who couldn't care less how this bar does," Olivia said. "It means too much to my family."

Wyatt shook his head in disbelief. Was she for real? "Just because we were messing around doesn't mean we don't care."

"Right." She rolled her eyes. "We're going to be making a lot of changes, so I hope you weren't too comfortable in your..." She glanced around with a look of disgust. "Lazy working ways."

Wyatt clenched his jaw. He was proud of how well they kept this place running smoothly.

She took in each of them, as if sizing them up. "Starting with uniforms. Apart from you," she pointed at Owen, "you're all dressed way too casually."

Wyatt glanced down at his gray Henley and jeans. It wasn't business attire, but it wasn't sloppy or anything. With a snort, Becca finally broke her silence. "Relax, Ice Queen, this is a small-town pub, remember? Not some ritzy city bar."

Internally cursing, Wyatt watched as Olivia turned. "What did you just call me?"

"It's a pretty fitting name," he muttered, unable to stop himself. Shawn laughed, and Becca grinned, clearly proud of herself. Even Owen chuckled before coughing to cover the noise.

"Enough! That kind of disrespect will *not* be tolerated."

There was practically steam pouring from her ears. "Keep going and I'll start firing."

Mayhem exploded, everyone talking over each other.

"You don't have the authority—"

"Yes, I do," she said, cutting Wyatt off. "This discussion is over. Get back to work."

No one moved.

"Now!"

Becca and Shawn mumbled under their breath. Neither were actually on the clock today, so they headed toward the door. Olivia watched with wide eyes. Before she could get the wrong idea, Wyatt said, "They aren't working today. They only came in to hang out and meet you."

"Fine, then you two get to work. I'm going to my dad's office to settle in." Her heels clacked against the tile floor as she made her way past the bar and through the small hallway.

"I miss Jack," Owen said the moment she slammed the door behind her.

Wyatt sighed and ran a hand through his hair. "Me too."

Jack Cartwright and his brother, Gary, owned The Tavern, but Jack had been running things since before Wyatt moved here. And it had clearly been exhausting him to do so much on his own. He was still calling in to check on things most days while away.

Wyatt really thought Jack was going to promote him to manager soon. But no.

Instead, he brought in his newly graduated daughter to take over. His goddess-looking, brat of a daughter.

How could she be so different from her kind father? The man was beloved in this town.

And how in the hell were they supposed to work together when she treated them so shitty? He was not looking forward to finding out what kind of changes she expected to make.

"That should've been your job," Owen whispered.

Nodding, Wyatt turned to stock more beer. "Yeah, it should've been."

TWO

olivia

Nothing around here ever changed.

Olivia sighed and dropped her purse on the floor as she lowered into her father's chair behind the ancient, worn desk. She was pretty sure it had been old when he bought it two decades ago. It had been years since she sat in this office, yet it looked exactly as she remembered with its gray, wood-paneled walls and a single window looking out at the small back parking lot for employees. Framed photos of her and her mother were scattered around the desk and shelves; a few hung on the walls.

She pulled one closer of the two of them grinning at the lake. Olivia was maybe twelve in the picture, but she already looked so much like her mom. They had the same long dark hair and brown eyes. Even their small button noses matched.

Swallowing past the lump forming in her throat, she set the frame back in its place. The images—the reminders—caused a deep ache in her chest.

The desk was also covered in paper—bills and statements, it seemed. Everything was so unorganized.

"Dammit, Dad," she whispered, rifling through it. No wonder this place was struggling. The entire wall behind her was made up of bookshelves overflowing with binders, boxes of paper records, and who knew what else. She grabbed the binder marked for last year and flipped it open. Handwritten accounts, notes, and order receipts. "What is this, nineteen seventy-five?"

Groaning, she slammed it shut and returned it to its shelf. She snatched her phone out of her purse and called Justin.

Her best friend answered after the first ring. "That bad, huh?"

She snorted, grateful he knew without her needing to say anything. "Worse."

"Miserable already? Want to come back to me?"

"You wish." She smiled, even though he couldn't see her. They had been best friends since they happened to sit next to each other during freshmen orientation, which she knew sounded ridiculous, but it was true. Some people believed in love at first sight; this was friendship at first sight. Or rather, first laugh. The orientation leader had used a ridiculous pun in their introduction, and while most of the room had only smiled uncomfortably, she and Justin chuckled at the same time. They had turned toward each other, and then both started laughing harder.

She often joked that, from that moment, they were destined to be friends. Their appreciation for cheesy comedy demanded it. It helped that they were also both business majors with control issues.

"Seriously," Justin said. "How bad is it?"

"It's hard to tell. I haven't gone through the numbers yet, but it's so unorganized." Olivia shuffled the papers around before looking at the outdated computer. "I don't think any of it is digitized."

"Yikes."

"Yeah. *And* a girl I knew growing up—who hates me—is working here apparently. So, that's going to be fun to deal with." She agreed and clicked the power button on the tower beneath the desk. This thing looked older than her.

"You're really staying there?" His skepticism was understandable. As long as she'd known him, she had made it clear how much she wanted to stay in Chicago. How much she didn't want to come home.

With a sigh, she leaned back in her chair. "My uncle Gary hasn't been around to pick up the slack, and my dad just can't handle it right now. He needs me to take over."

"But Perrington is so far away..." For the last six years, through undergrad and grad school, they had been nearly inseparable. Even dating for the last two years didn't deter their friendship. In the end though, they decided they were better as just that—friends. They got along perfectly, lived together since sophomore year, and the sex was good, but they weren't in love. It always felt like something was missing.

"Only a couple hours. I'll still visit." In truth, she already missed the hustle and bustle of the big city. Her hometown was practically its opposite in every way.

"It's not the same," he said in a mock-whine she knew to be partially real.

"I know." The thought of not living together or even near one another sent a pang of grief through her chest. "I need to do this though. You have no idea what I walked into. It's a literal nightmare, Justin. I know it's still kind of early, but there isn't a single patron in here yet. And the workers... I don't know where my dad found these idiots. They were acting like fucking children when I came in."

Movement caught her attention, and she jerked her eyes up only to collide with a dark gaze.

"Shit. I have to go." She didn't wait for Justin's reaction before ending the call. "Don't you know how to knock?"

The bartender who'd tried to talk to her earlier crossed his arms and stepped into the office. The man was tall, hulking. His muscular arms had tattoos peeking out from the rolled-up sleeves. If she didn't know better, she might have even been intimidated by him. But she'd learned long ago that she couldn't show any sort of weakness in the business world. It was hard enough making her way as a woman; she didn't need to give anyone more of a reason to doubt her.

"The door was open," he said. "I came to apologize again and see if we could start over."

Olivia internally cursed. Pushing to her feet, she said, "I'm sorry for snapping. Things just aren't what I expected here."

"What *did* you expect from a small-town bar?" He smirked, and something about it rubbed her wrong. Sure, he was ridiculously good-looking, but the condescension? She was not here for that.

"A little more respect, for starters." She crossed her own arms and narrowed her eyes.

"Respect is earned, not freely given."

She understood that, truly, but she also believed in offering at least some respect to strangers upon meeting them. "Did you need something..."

"Wyatt," he supplied.

"What do you need, Wyatt?"

His jaw twitched. "Where's your dad?"

If he didn't know the truth, she wasn't going to be the one to share. Her dad could explain things better if he wanted. Instead, she just said, "Taking a break."

"I'm aware of that. Who do you think has been running the place the last couple weeks?" He furrowed his brow. "Is Jack okay?"

It surprised her that he seemed to genuinely care. So much that she gave partial honesty. "He's exhausted."

Wyatt nodded, as if understanding. "I hope he gets the rest he needs. He works hard around here."

Olivia knew he did, but she still couldn't help but glance around at the mess he left her. "If he didn't insist on doing things the hard way, it would help."

"Yeah, he's pretty stuck in his ways," the man said with a deep chuckle that sent a spark through her. "But he's a good guy who really cares about this place."

She knew that too. After all, that was why she was here. This bar meant everything to her dad, and she wanted to help keep it in business. It was all he had left.

"Can we please start over?" The hot bartender held out a hand.

The way he looked at her, the way he made her pulse race just a little too fast wasn't acceptable. She refused to let anything distract her from the reason she was here.

"We can be friends if you just—"

"I'm not here to make friends," she said, cutting off whatever he was about to blame her for. Friends, flings, she wouldn't have any of it while here. This stay was temporary. She would not let anything in that she could get attached to.

Wyatt let out a huff. "Why are you making this difficult? I'm trying to help."

"No, you're trying to take control." Olivia knew she sounded like a bitch, but if this was what it took to keep up those walls protecting her heart, so be it. She rounded the desk to move closer then regretted it. Up close, she could see the gold flecks in his brown eyes, and he smelled so good. Because of course he did. Plus, he was a good foot taller than her. Glaring at him, she said, "The Tavern is struggling; I'm here to make sure it doesn't go under. My dad has given me the all-clear to make whatever changes I deem necessary."

"And you don't think working with those of us who have been here would be beneficial?" He shrugged, slowly shaking his head in clear frustration. "I've worked here for six years and haven't seen you once."

"Because I was in business school!"

"Which is great, but that doesn't mean you understand a damn thing about the day-to-day running of this place," he shouted right back.

She didn't know why she was arguing with this man. It was like she couldn't stop. She couldn't help it. Something about him made her want to stand her ground and fight more than normal. "You don't know anything about me or what I've done the past several years. I'm more than capable of handling a bar in a town with less than ten thousand people."

Wyatt shook his head again and muttered something under his breath as he turned to leave.

"Excuse me? What was that?"

"You're an arrogant brat," he said over his shoulder without missing a beat or stopping.

He slammed the door behind him, and she stared at it with her jaw dropped. How dare he speak to her like that? Clenching her jaw, she stormed after him. She threw the door open and marched out to the main bar area. "Wyatt!"

"What?" He whirled to face her, and she almost ran into him.

Taking a deep breath, she said, "You can't talk to me that way in my own fucking bar."

"It's not *your* bar."

She wanted to scream. Why was he so infuriating?

Instead, she pointed to the front door, ignoring the only other bartender remaining. "Get out."

Wyatt huffed. "You know what? Fine. Have fun handling tonight without me."

He stormed out without so much as looking back.

The room was silent except for the low music that had been turned down. Olivia lifted her chin. She wouldn't let his callous behavior affect her. At least, not in front of the only employee left. She turned toward the man who appeared about five years older. "What about you? Are you staying?"

"Yes, ma'am."

"Good," she said with a nod. "What's your name?"

"Owen."

"All right then, Owen, get back to work and let me know if you need anything."

THREE

Wyatt

Collapsing onto the stool behind the cash register counter, Wyatt let out an exaggerated sigh. He swiveled back and forth, looking around Happily Ever Crafter. Before a few months ago, he'd never set foot in the little arts and crafts shop, and now, he felt like he spent more time here than his own home. It was a cute little store that cousins Charlotte and Violet Powell owned, but they'd also bought the empty shop next door, converted it into a studio and classroom, and then knocked out part of the wall to connect the two buildings. It was genius. And he was so happy his sister had found her way into their little circle after moving here this past spring.

Even if she did drag him into it as well. He was pretty sure that Charlie was somehow now his best friend.

Harper leaned over him to grab a small box from beneath the counter. "No, please, don't move. I'll work around you," she deadpanned.

He poked his sister in the side, and she rolled her eyes. She was so much happier these days. Working here, being independent, and finding a new passion had brought a spark of life back into her eyes that had been absent for too long—snuffed out by her toxic ex-husband.

"Not that I don't love your company," she said, "but

why are you here on a Saturday afternoon? Shouldn't you be at work?"

"I think I got fired..."

She nearly dropped the box as she whipped toward him. "What? Why? How?"

"What's going on?" Vi asked, walking in from the adjoined classroom area with Wyatt's nephew, Elliot, at her side. This was their life now. Whenever Elliot wasn't in school, he was here. As was Wyatt, apparently.

"Uncle Wyatt, look what I made!" The five year old ran over with a ceramic bowl he'd created and painted with Vi's help last week. It was finally dry.

Wyatt leaned down to scoop up his nephew, sitting him on his lap. "Wow! That's amazing." He pointed to the blue squiggles around the middle. "I love the colors you used."

"It's for you." Elliot held it out with a grin, effectively melting Wyatt's entire heart.

He took the bowl and hugged the boy with his other arm. "Thanks, buddy."

"You can put your treats in it!"

"Sounds like a great idea," he said, already thinking of small things he could bake that would fit. With a chuckle, Wyatt lowered the wiggling boy, who then ran to his mom.

Harper knelt in front of him. "What, nothing for me this week?"

"*Mom*, you have to take turns." Five going on sixteen.

"You're right; I'm sorry." Harper kissed his forehead and stood once more.

It still amazed Wyatt to watch her be a mother. Finding out she was pregnant her junior year of high school had rocked quite a few boats, to say the least. But she'd made the best of the situation for as long as she could... until she walked in on her husband screwing another woman in their own bed. Harper had taken a lot of emotional and mental abuse from that asshole for years, ignoring Wyatt's pleas to leave him. When she found him balls deep in his secretary, she finally said enough and moved into their parents' house with Elliot. They weren't much better on the emotional abuse front though. Within a month, she had moved again, this time three hundred miles to live with Wyatt in his minuscule two-bedroom home.

"Why are you staring at me like that?" Harper said, noticing his attention.

He shrugged. "Just proud of you."

She looked away, but not before he saw her smile. "Thanks."

"Seriously, Harps." He stood and went to squeeze her in a hug, rocking from side to side. "You've really taken control of your life, finding a job you love, raising Elliot. I'm so proud of you."

"All right, all right." She squirmed just like her son, playfully pushing Wyatt away.

"As cute as this is, I still want to know what the hel —heck," Vi corrected herself with a glance at Elliot, who now sat in the corner of the shop with his pad of paper and colored pencils. "What the heck did you mean by you *think* you were fired? How can you not be sure?"

He sighed and returned to the stool, glad there weren't any customers at the moment. "Jack's daughter is back from school and taking over for a bit. We kind of... got off on the wrong foot and—"

"And you let your temper get the best of you?" Harper started restocking one of the nearby shelves with markers and pens. "Wyatt..."

"I didn't. She fu-freaking started it," he insisted with a quick glance at his nephew, but the boy was preoccupied. "I tried to apologize and make things better, and I thought it was going to be fine, but then she told me to get out."

His sister turned toward him. "What are you going to do? I can't afford your rent."

"Don't worry about that, okay?" He grabbed her arm to keep her from walking away. "I'll figure it out. I promise."

She worried too much as it was; he didn't want to add to it. He would give it a day or two before returning to see if he was truly fired or not.

"So, Jack's daughter." Harper leaned against the countertop. "Not like her father, then?"

Wyatt scoffed. "Definitely not."

Jack would never pick a fight with anyone. He was too kind for his own good. That was partially why Wyatt had stepped up even before the man said he needed some time off. Jack hated confrontation and would do anything to avoid it, but sometimes it was necessary while running a business. Wyatt wasn't a people person, his social anxiety often made work a struggle, but he could do what was needed most of the time. Even if that meant putting a foot down with vendors or coworkers.

"I haven't seen Liv since high school," Vi said. "She was very... focused on succeeding. She was involved in everything, had the best grades, and was our valedictorian."

That didn't surprise Wyatt one bit. Becca had implied as much in her rant when they found out Olivia was returning. She seemed to really hate the woman, but he still hadn't heard the full story yet.

"She always had to be perfect," Vi went on.

From the little time he had interacted with her, that sounded right. "Well, it doesn't seem like she's changed. She came to the bar wearing a business skirt and shirt, hair up in a tight bun—"

"Oh my God." Harper chuckled. "You're totally into her!"

"Absolutely not." He shook his head. "She is bossy, arrogant—"

"Hot," Vi added.

"So hot," he relented with a groan, hanging his head back. His sister started laughing harder.

Vi grinned. "No, really. Even back then, we weren't friends, but I definitely considered taking a shot there."

He didn't blame her one bit. Not that it mattered; he wouldn't be doing the same. Ever. Except, what came out of his mouth was, "Does that mean she prefers women?"

"I don't think so." Vi shrugged. "She dated the quarterback in high school—shocker, I know—and she was dating some guy throughout college, according to Facebook. Wait, she's going to be working with Becca, isn't she?"

"Yeah. They already got into it before Becca left. What happened there?"

She rolled her eyes. "Teenage girl drama. I don't even know for sure. They were really close friends until we were in high school. All I know is that Liv's boyfriend had dated Becca at one point, and some said he cheated either by going back to Becca or by starting to date Liv before they broke up."

"Sounds like they both should've said good riddance," Harper mumbled.

"I think Liv did break up with him for a while, but she eventually started going out with him again, or was at least sleeping with him until she left for college." Vi smirked at Wyatt. "So, I don't know her preferences, but she has definitely dated men in the past."

He nodded, even as he repeated to himself that it did not matter. It wasn't any of his business. He would work beside her if given the chance, but only because he needed the job. That didn't mean he wanted to get to know her more.

Or see what she looked like if she let that dark hair down and unbuttoned her blouse to reveal those generous curves.

Shit.

He was so screwed.

FOUR

Olivia

Olivia had no idea how she got here.

Okay, that was a lie. It was her own fault for getting into this position, but she would be damned if she admitted Wyatt was right about not knowing anything about this place. She had foolishly assumed the bar didn't get super busy because Perrington was so small. It was nothing like the big cities she'd worked in throughout college.

Yet, here she was helping behind the bar because they were swamped. The only bartender around was Owen, and there wasn't anyone to work the kitchen. Food was off the menu tonight, which didn't bode well for sales on a Saturday night. They'd already heard a lot of complaints and grumbling about it. The other worker she hadn't met yet, Ryan, had called in saying he couldn't make it because his daughter was sick and couldn't go to the sitter, and there wasn't anyone else who could stay with her.

As frustrated as Olivia had been, she also understood.

"Behind you," Owen shouted as she started to turn.

She stilled, waiting for him to pass by, then continued toward the shelf of liquor. Scanning the bottles for the right vodka she needed, she internally cursed. She wasn't a bartender. Beyond the very basics, she didn't have a clue about making drinks. Thankfully, in their small town, most patrons only wanted beer.

Except for the man she was currently serving, of course.

"Where's the Grey Goose?" she asked as Owen ran by again.

He stopped long enough to point to the clear bottle practically in front of her face.

"Sorry..." She grabbed and poured it, making a martini for the guy who kept scanning her with his eyes. With a forced smile, she handed it over.

He took a sip and grimaced. "This isn't right."

"What do you mean?" Her heart raced in her chest. It was so loud in here, with too many people talking over the music. She had moved past anxious straight into sensory overload. And every time someone asked about her dad or mentioned it was about time she came home because they all missed her, it got worse. She appreciated the concern for her father, but she knew no one around here cared that she was gone. She'd made sure of that.

"It's disgusting." The man shoved the glass back toward her.

"Um..." She started to panic. Taking out her phone, she opened the recipe again.

"I've got it." Owen grabbed the glass. "Will you see what he wants at the end of the bar?"

"Yeah." She turned in the direction he nodded and froze. It wasn't a new customer... It was Wyatt, standing with both arms casually braced on the bar top and a smirk playing on his lips. Inhaling deeply, she walked over to him. "What can I get for you?"

"How's it going tonight?"

Gritting her teeth, she said, "Do you want a drink or not?"

"Will you just admit you might not have this completely under control?"

Olivia started to walk away. She didn't have time for this.

"No, wait."

She sighed and faced him, only to find him rounding the counter to join her behind the bar. "What are you doing? I fired you."

"Did you?" Wyatt raised a brow. "Because I wasn't entirely clear on that."

Before she could respond, he stepped closer and continued.

"You're swamped." He angled toward her, as if to keep the rest from hearing. Though, it was too loud for that anyway. "Why don't you let me help? Ryan called in, didn't he?"

Despite wanting to refuse him, she nodded. She might have been stubborn, but she could admit she was in over her head right now. "Fine. You're not fired. Please help us."

"See? Was that so hard?"

She wanted to smack the crooked smile off of his stupidly good-looking face. It was distracting, to be honest. Someone so irritating shouldn't be that attractive. Before she could think of anything to say, he gently eased her aside. It felt like fire where his hands touched her arms, but all too soon he released her to ask the next customer for their order. He slipped into his role with such clear ease, as if nothing had happened.

Then, he pushed his sleeves up to his elbows, revealing tattoo-covered, muscular forearms.

"Of fucking course," she muttered.

"What was that?"

Tearing her eyes from his arms, Olivia met his gaze and

knew she was caught. Clenching her fist, she ignored him and went to one of the patrons who'd been there a while and was lifting a hand to get her attention.

"Another beer?" she asked as she drew nearer.

The older man nodded. "Yes, please, darlin'."

She smiled and whipped around to get it, only to collide with a hard chest. Wyatt's hands went to her waist to steady her, and she made the mistake of breathing in his scent. Heat speared through her, her heart racing in her chest at his nearness.

"Careful." His warm breath stirred the hair that had fallen from her bun throughout the evening. "You okay?"

"Yes," she whispered before realizing he wouldn't be able to hear her.

He leaned down closer to her ear. "First thing you need to learn is to be aware of your surroundings at all times."

To her surprise, it sounded like genuine advice. The snark was gone; he hadn't even lectured her about it. She nodded, barely breathing. His fingers tightened slightly for just a second, and then he let go of her. Without looking away, he opened the small fridge, reached in, and grabbed a bottle of beer.

"Here you go, Walt," he said, finally turning. He cracked it open and passed it over as Olivia attempted to steady her breathing.

This was going to be a long night.

FIVE

Wyatt

The Tavern was usually busy on Saturday nights, but tonight was worse than normal. It worked in Wyatt's favor though. Olivia had looked like a frantic deer caught in the headlights by the time he arrived, especially when George—one of their older regulars—told her she'd made his martini wrong. Wyatt could almost guarantee she did it fine; the man was just picky and liked it made differently than the usual recipe. She couldn't have known that without someone warning her. Luckily, Owen had stepped in to take over and George didn't like to cause trouble.

Truth be told, she wasn't horrible at this. She was holding her own. But she was so... serious. For the last few years, Wyatt had worked to make this a warm, welcoming place. And Olivia was anything but that. Ice Queen, indeed.

"Behind you," he said, putting one hand on her back to let her know he was there. That was another thing she needed to get better at—paying attention to her surroundings. For her first night here though, she wasn't doing too bad. She seemed frazzled, but she hid it well under that cold façade.

Grabbing a chilled mug from the freezer under the bar, he poured a draft and slid it over to another regular. He looked back at the clock on the wall. It was after midnight.

"Last call," Owen shouted, as if reading his mind.

"We're closing?" Olivia asked.

Wyatt shook his head, noting the look of relief in her brown eyes. "Not quite yet. We close at one, so we want people done by then."

She did a little eye roll and nodded, almost like she realized she already knew that. "Right. Sorry, it's been a long night."

"It's also your first night, so how were you to know?" he said before he could stop himself. He could practically feel her glaring at him, but he continued working. Things were slowing down, so he started cleaning a little bit. Shawn had eventually shown up to man the kitchen—at Wyatt's request—but he dipped out as soon as it closed at ten and he'd cleaned back there. Wyatt had tried to get him to stay and help at the bar, but he'd claimed he had plans. He knew Shawn just didn't want to be around their new boss anymore and that he was probably heading to Becca's place.

One o'clock rolled around, and the last of the customers trickled out to an Uber. Owen locked the door and turned off the neon signs in the windows while Wyatt cleaned more and Olivia started restocking napkins, straws, and toothpicks. Wyatt and Owen had a system for closing because they often did it together, so having a new third person in their way was actually slowing them down, but at least she was trying to help.

Until she turned and ran straight into him, dropping her container of toothpicks and knocking a glass out of his hand. It shattered at their feet.

"Dammit," he said as she started to apologize.

They both tried to squat at the same time, resulting in a collision of their foreheads. Olivia teetered on her heels, and he grabbed her before she could fall in the glass. She stumbled into his chest as he hauled her up.

"Shit. Are you two okay?" Owen rushed around the bar from where he'd been wiping down tables.

"Besides the piercing headache, yeah." Wyatt released his new boss to rub at his temple.

Olivia reached toward the mess. "I'm so sorry. Let me—"

His arm darted out around her waist to stop her. "No, stop. Just... help him with the tables. I'll get a broom."

She opened her mouth, as if to argue, but must have thought better of it. Stepping over the mess, she mumbled something as she rounded the bar before disappearing into her office. He rolled his eyes and went to grab the broom from the closet. Normally, Wyatt would have been mad about one of them leaving all the work for the others, but in this case, they were better off.

Besides the music that had been turned down low, The Tavern was quiet. No one spoke as they finished their work. Owen started counting the tip money and split it into three piles. "Rock, paper, scissors for who has to take the ice queen her share?"

"Sure," Wyatt said as he lifted a fist. "Rock, paper, scissors, shoot."

He flattened his hand into the sign for paper. Owen showed scissors.

"Best two out of three?" Wyatt all but begged.

Owen chuckled and said, "Fine."

Wyatt lost again and groaned.

"All right, I'm heading out." Owen tucked his share into his pocket. "I'm off tomorrow, so I'll see you on Monday."

"See ya." Wyatt lifted a hand to wave then turned it around to flip off his friend.

Owen's laughter followed him out the door. Wyatt rolled his eyes and locked it once more. Pocketing his own money, he grabbed the third pile and stared at the short hallway. He counted to five in his head before going to the office and knocking on the door.

"Come in."

He entered and held up the cash. "Your share of the tips."

"What?" Her brow furrowed. She was sitting behind her desk, arms crossed. Something seemed off about her.

Stepping farther into the room, he set it in front of her. "We always split the tips at the end of the night. This is your share."

"But I'm not one of the bartenders."

"You still did the work." When she didn't respond, he sighed and turned to leave.

"Wyatt."

He stopped and faced her.

She stood but didn't uncross her arms. "Next time something happens, don't tell me what to do like I'm a child. I'm the one in charge here."

Surely she wasn't serious.

"You're mad because I stopped you from cleaning up broken glass and toothpicks?"

"I'm mad because you seem to feel the need to undermine me every step of the way, and we've only known each other for a day."

He started to shake his head but stilled as his attention snagged on the paper towel in her hand. The one tinged in red. Furious, he crossed the room and gently eased her arms apart. "How were you cut? Why didn't you say something?"

Without waiting for her to answer, he rushed out to the

bar, snatched the first aid kit from the back of a cabinet and returned to tell her, "Come to the bathroom with me."

"I don't need you to take care of me," she said, even as she followed.

He flipped the fluorescent lights on and set the pack on the sink. "Let me see."

Olivia held out her hand, and he turned on the water. She sucked in a breath as he began rinsing off the blood. It looked like just a small slice along one of her fingers.

"It's not too bad—a small laceration. You don't need stitches." He released her to find some antiseptic and a Band-Aid.

"I know that. I told you I don't need you to—"

"For fuck's sake, just let me help you," he said in a near growl. "I'm not trying to undermine you or whatever the hell you're thinking. Trust me, I get it. You are a fierce, independent woman who doesn't need anyone. I'm not questioning that. I am only trying to help a coworker who got injured."

She clenched her jaw but nodded. As he started applying the cream, she asked, "Laceration?"

Sighing, he glanced up at her. "What?"

"You said laceration, not cut. It sounded... professional, and you don't seem affected by the blood whatsoever."

He did not want to have this conversation, especially with her. Yet, he found himself saying, "I was pre-med before I moved here and started over."

She looked like she was going to ask more, but he couldn't do this. Not tonight. He wrapped the Band-Aid around her finger, threw away the trash, and returned the kit out to the bar. Of course, she trailed after him in a huff.

"We can't work like this, Wyatt. You need to accept that

I'm your boss for the time being," she said. "Would you treat my dad this way?"

"No." He didn't hesitate to answer. Slamming the cabinet, he faced the woman. "Because he wouldn't treat me this way. You came in, acting all high and mighty, as if you're so much better than the rest of us, but you know nothing about running this bar. I don't care what your fancy degrees say."

She started to speak, but he held up a hand and continued.

"It's not your ignorance that caused this; it's your attitude. When I try to explain something to you, you act as if it's a personal attack. None of us give a shit what you do or do not know. If you'd come in here without any knowledge whatsoever but treated us with respect, you would have received it in return, and we would have been more than happy to help you learn how we do things around here."

"Are you done?" Olivia asked, hands on her hips.

He couldn't believe her. Letting out a breath, he said, "Yeah, I'm done." He marched toward the door, flipped the lock, and shoved it open. His heart was pounding too hard. Everything was beginning to spiral, and he needed to get home before he had a full anxiety attack. "You know," he turned toward her again, "if you were a little bit kinder, a little less horrible, people would like you more. You'd get more tips *and* your employees wouldn't call you a fucking ice queen."

With that, he let the door shut behind him.

SIX

olivia

The smell of pancakes woke Olivia far before she wanted to get out of bed. She hadn't left The Tavern until almost three in the morning, staying long after everyone else was gone so she could organize the office and go through more of the books. It was a mess, to say the least. By the time she got home, she'd been dead on her aching feet. Yet, she hadn't been able to fall asleep right away. Not with Wyatt's words playing on a loop in her mind.

Rolling over, she glanced at her phone. It was a little after nine in the morning. She groaned and buried her face into her pillow.

Until she remembered where she was. She sat up and looked around in confusion. Why did she smell pancakes? Pushing her blankets aside, Olivia climbed out of bed. She walked through her familiar childhood home, fighting the nostalgia that made her chest ache. In the kitchen, her father sat at the table with a grin.

"Told you that would wake her," he said to the woman bringing over a bottle of syrup.

Angela smiled and set the bottle down. When Olivia's father started struggling a few months ago, his neighbor volunteered to help him out until he could find a more permanent solution. But as his disease progressed, he needed more and more help. She was in her mid-thirties and worked as a nurse's assistant at one of the doctor's offices part time and at the hospital on alternate weekends—and whenever they needed someone to cover a shift or were short-staffed. Basically, the woman was a superhero. Between working and taking care of Olivia's dad, she was also married with three kids and did a lot of work with one of the churches.

Just thinking about everything she did exhausted Olivia. It was also one of the biggest reasons why she had temporarily moved home. Angela couldn't be here all the time, and she couldn't always drop things and come right over. The possibility of her dad being here alone during an emergency terrified Olivia.

"Good morning," she said, kissing his cheek. "Angela, you didn't have to do this."

The woman waved her off. "I was making them for my family, so I added a few extra. I'm just dropping them off before we head to church."

"Well, thank you."

"Of course." Angela walked toward the front door, and Olivia went with her. "I tried to convince him to go with me, but he still doesn't want people to know."

Olivia sighed and glanced back toward the kitchen. "I'll see what I can do. Maybe next week he'll say yes."

"Everyone misses him," she said. "They're really starting to question his absence, assuming the worst. I've tried to reassure them, but..."

"I get it." Olivia remembered how they were. Caring but nosy. Always wanting to know what was going on. But most of them had the biggest hearts. "I'll talk to him. I think it'd do him some good to return. He needs to get out of this house."

"Agreed." Angela opened the door. "If you need anything, let me know. I'll be home in a couple hours."

"Thank you for everything." Olivia owed the woman so much. She couldn't do all of this on her own.

Angela nodded. "It's no problem. Jack has been there for us a lot the last few years; it's the least I could do."

With that, she left, and Olivia headed to the kitchen, trying to mask the pain those words brought. Everyone in this town loved him and had similar sentiments. Yet, he hadn't been there for her when she needed him most.

Focusing on the present, she sat across from her dad and piled a couple of fluffy pancakes onto the plate Angela must have set out for her.

He'd apparently waited for her and now poured syrup over his. "Did she try to convince you to make me go with her?"

"They miss you, Dad," Olivia said, preparing her food. "You can't sit in your recliner, watching TV, every day for the rest of your life."

"Why not? It might not be that long," he muttered under his breath.

She stilled, her stomach twisting. Every muscle in her body tensed, and she gripped her fork tightly as she whispered, "Don't say that. The doctor said it doesn't necessarily a-affect your life ex-expectancy."

Her throat tightened, cutting off her words.

"I'm sorry." His tone was gentle when he reached for her hand. "I'm sorry, Liv. I wasn't thinking. It's just... frustrating, and sometimes, I..."

She turned her hand over to hold his. "We'll figure this out. And I think getting back out there, returning to your life, will be good for you. Sitting here day after day isn't healthy. It's going to make the depression worse."

"I know." He released her and started eating.

Olivia fought the urge to cry. Not just from grief or fear, but from anger. At him. At the universe. This wasn't fair. Her dad had lived a healthy life, took care of himself, but it didn't matter. No one could have seen this coming.

She ate her pancakes, despite not being hungry. Her appetite had vanished. They sat in silence, like they often did when together. Since her mom passed away eight years ago, it had been like this. It was as if her dad didn't know what to say to her, what to talk about. And she wasn't any better.

After a few minutes, he finally spoke. "How was your first night at The Tavern? Did everything go okay? Find everything you need?"

"Um... it was... interesting." She poked at the remaining food on her plate with her fork. "I think I have my work cut out for me, that's for sure."

"Oh no. I know that look. That's your everyone-is-stressing-me-out face. What happened?"

She wanted to argue that she didn't make that face, but it was definitely a thing. "Fine, you really want to know?" Lowering her fork, she crossed her arms, which only made her remember the cut on her finger. "When I arrived, your employees were goofing off, throwing ice around at each other. As soon as I walked in, I was hit with it. I tried to explain that it wasn't appropriate behavior, that I could've been a customer they hit, but that only backfired. They got mad at me. Two of them stormed out, and I fired a third."

"Wait, what?" Her father's eyes widened. "What the hell, Liv? Who did you fire?"

Groaning, she said, "Don't worry, he came in later for a drink and I gave him his job back out of desperation because Ryan didn't show up, which apparently is a common occurrence? And why didn't you tell me you'd hired Becca? Seriously, Dad? Why her?"

Her dad rubbed at his temple. "Becca was having a rough time a few years ago. She applied, and I knew how badly she needed work. I didn't tell you because I thought you guys would be old enough to move past whatever happened in high school." Her dad sighed. "As for Ryan, he has sole custody of his young daughter and has no one to help take care of her outside of a couple babysitters—one of which is beyond unreliable. So, he wasn't there. I'm guessing the two who stormed out were Shawn and Becca."

She nodded in confirmation.

"You fired Wyatt?" The corner of his mouth curled up.

"How did you—"

"Because Owen is like the dad of the group. He wouldn't have done anything to make you mad enough to fire him." Her dad chuckled. "Wyatt, on the other hand, isn't afraid to speak his mind or stand up for his friends. And I can see how your tempers might clash. You two are a lot alike."

"We are not."

Her dad gave her a pointed look. "Right. But you said he returned later?"

"Yes, for a drink."

"Wyatt doesn't do that. For reasons that aren't mine to share, he doesn't just come in and hang out at the bar. He was alone, right?"

Olivia nodded again, not liking where this was going.

He reached over and squeezed her shoulder. "Wyatt didn't come back for a drink. He returned because it was a Saturday night and he knew you'd need help."

Well, shit. Deep down, she'd figured that, but she didn't

expect anyone to say it out loud. "Fine, but he was still really disrespectful."

"He's worked there for years," her dad said. "And while Owen might act like their dad, Wyatt is the one who takes charge. He is always taking care of things, working extra shifts for people. He's a helper, and it probably threw him for a loop that I brought you in as a new manager instead of promoting him. Especially when he's been doing so much in my absence. Give him a chance to adjust to the change."

She hated that her dad made sense. It was easier to simply hate Wyatt and write him off as a bad worker, but even she'd seen how that wasn't true. Not in the slightest. He worked hard, and everyone else seemed to like him. She could admit that she might have come off a little too strongly in their first meeting, that she overreacted last night. But she'd always had to prove herself so much throughout grad school and during her internship.

The internship that was supposed to end with her being offered a job at Kaiser International, but when it came down to it, they hired Justin and one of the other male interns while letting her go. She was happy for her best friend. He worked hard and deserved it. The other guy though? He was lazy, arrogant, and basically a dick all around. Meaning he fit in perfectly at the office.

Olivia had worked her ass off and accomplished a lot during her internship. She knew the only reason she wasn't picked was because she was a girl. They didn't want her *ruining* their boys' club. It made her sick.

"This isn't the big city," her dad said, as if reading her mind, and took a sip of his coffee. "You don't need to assume the worst of people. I'm not excusing his behavior, but he's not usually a disrespectful person, so my guess is he was having a rough night for other reasons."

"The reasons you can't share?"

He nodded, and she sighed. She really needed him to stop talking about Wyatt. The more he did, the worse she felt. Because she knew how it felt to have things change without any warning, how difficult it was to continue as normal.

"I'll give him another chance," she said. "But we really need to talk about the finances, Dad. Your files are a mess, and almost nothing is updated on the computer."

"I hate the computer," he grumbled.

Despite being frustrated, she couldn't help but chuckle at his dramatic scowl. "I know you do, but it's so helpful to keep records organized and together. It's going to take forever to figure out what's what."

His face softened. "I'm sorry. I thought things were going well. I mean, there's been a slow decline, but I thought it was the economy."

"That's definitely a factor, but some of the numbers don't seem to be adding up."

"Just..." With a sigh, he ran a hand over his face. He'd aged in her absence. Lines crinkled the skin near his eyes, and what had been dark brown hair looked lighter, almost like it was preparing to shift to gray. "Can you call the bank to get our current standing and then work from there? I need you to focus on finding a way to bring in more money and lower costs."

"I can do that, but I still need to organize everything for that to happen." Her head started pounding. They'd gone in circles about this for months over the phone before she even returned home.

"Don't look at me like that, Olivia." He set his mug down and pushed away from the table. "Things might not be going well right now, but I've been running a successful business for twenty years. I know you went to school for this, and I'm so proud of you for that, but that doesn't mean what I know from my hands-on experience is wrong."

The words struck home, making her wince. They were so close to what Wyatt had said last night. She didn't say anything as she stood and took their plates to the sink. He tried to get to his feet and failed.

Olivia closed her eyes and took a deep shaky breath before going to help him. Of course, he groaned and complained, wanting to do it on his own. But more often than not, he couldn't anymore. Once he was settled in his recliner, she brought him a fresh cup of coffee, as well as a glass of water.

"I'm sorry," she whispered, leaning down to hug him.

He squeezed her tightly, and she let out a shaky breath. Growing up, he was always at the bar. It was rough, and she hated it at times because she missed him, but she never questioned his love for her and her mom. He would get out of bed and drive her to school each morning, despite working until well after midnight, and then he'd pick her up before heading back to work. On the weekends, he would spend the day doing whatever she and her mom wanted. He was a great dad, even when he wasn't around much. She had been inspired by his hard work, and she thought it was incredible how upbeat and caring he'd always been, even when working seventy hours a week.

When the accident happened, something changed in him. He became closed off and distant. By then, she could drive herself, get her own food, do what she wanted on her own. She'd always been independent, but she still needed her father, and he couldn't look past his grief to see that.

It tore her apart and drove her away.

Returning here hurt more than words could describe.

"Do you need anything else right now? I'm going to shower and change."

"No, I'm good," he said.

She nodded and headed down the hall to her room before he could notice the tears lining her eyes. It was horrible seeing him like this. She didn't mind helping him at all, but witnessing firsthand how much it was affecting his mentality and attitude was overwhelming. When he'd told her about his falls that led to the doctor visits and testing, she had been concerned but assumed he had something that would get better.

Distal muscular dystrophy did not get better.

His body would continue to weaken the rest of his life. It started in his feet, making it difficult to stand and walk on his own. His hands had lost a little of their dexterity too. He'd explained that he had gradually felt it happening but chalked it up to being exhausted and aging. The tests said otherwise.

And he doesn't want people to know, doesn't want their pity. She understood that, but she still thought he needed to get out of the house and try to get back to some semblance of normalcy.

For most of her life, he'd been a happy, positive man. After her mom died, it was like a dark cloud had settled over him. But now... it was like he'd lost all remaining hope.

It broke her heart.

To add to it, the bar wasn't doing well enough for him to afford the care he needed.

The pressure of needing to handle so much weighed heavily on Olivia's shoulders. She covered her mouth to stifle a sob.

She let herself cry for another minute, then she wiped away her tears and stood. She changed out of her pajamas and into a sports bra and shorts. Throwing a sweatshirt on over the top, she grabbed her phone and earbuds before returning to the living room. "I'm actually going to go out for a bit," she told her dad. "I'll be back shortly. I have my phone."

He gave her a sad, knowing smile and nodded.

Olivia rushed out to the sidewalk and started jogging. The sun was already working to rid the morning chill in the air. Her feet pounded along the cement in time to the beat in her ears.

Running had always been her escape. She loved the feel of her body pushing itself, the rush of adrenaline. It was her way of claiming control.

After all, that was why she ran off to Chicago the first chance she got. To take control of her spiraling life.

And once this was all done and taken care of, she would go back and fight for a job in the business world. Far away from this town that ruined her life.

SEVEN

wyatt

"What are you two doing?" Harper laughed as she and Charlie entered the messy kitchen.

Zoey, their white Maltese puppy, barked and jumped at Harper, wagging her little tail. Harper picked her up and hugged her to her chest.

"Uncle Wyatt had a bad night at work, so we're making cupcakes." Elliot grinned as he continued mixing his bowl of batter.

Wyatt flicked flour at him. "Thanks, buddy."

"What?" His nephew shrugged. "That's what you said."

Harper and Charlie both chuckled as they moved closer to the table. Charlie went to wash her hands, no doubt so that she could help. And by help, he meant eat the frosting. They had only really known each other for six months, but she'd wormed her way into his life so thoroughly that he could predict her moves before she made them. If one didn't know better, it would seem as if they'd been friends for years. He was secretly happy about it. She understood him in a way few ever did.

His sister put Zoey down before sitting in an empty chair and looking around. "How many flavors this time?"

"Three," Wyatt grumbled, not meeting her eyes.

Charlie stepped up beside him and indeed stuck her

finger in the pink frosting he'd made a few minutes earlier. "Yum. Strawberry. So, what happened at work?"

Elliot went to dip his finger in the frosting too. "His boss is mean to him."

Wyatt grabbed the boy's wrist before he could scoop out a whole handful. "Thanks for starting that, Charlotte. We'd been doing so good about not eating it."

His best friend shuffled next to him. "Sorry."

"Wyatt, what happened at work?" Harper said, never letting him change the subject so easily.

He sighed and helped Elliot get a small amount of the delicious strawberry frosting. Then, he grabbed a pan and began putting in liners for the next batch as he told her about the first night Olivia worked with him. The second night went a little better, but only because they barely spoke to one another. The third was about as good as the first, setting the mood for the rest of the week. It was like they couldn't be in the same room without fighting.

"She questions everything I do, and whenever I try to help her or explain anything, I'm suddenly the mansplaining asshole," he said. "There's no winning with her."

"Uncle Wyatt said a bad word," Elliot whispered to his mom.

"I heard. I'll make him put a quarter in the jar later. Why don't you wash your hands and go play for a bit," she said.

"Can I watch *Bluey*?"

Harper nodded, and he ran off to the bathroom with the puppy chasing after him. They all chuckled as his stool scraped along the tile and the water turned on.

Charlie took a seat. "Where's Jack? Is he still not coming in?"

"No, he hasn't been around in weeks." He finished filling the liners with batter and put the pan in the oven. Sitting beside her, he started frosting the lemon cupcakes that had already cooled. "I'm getting worried that something is wrong. Even before Olivia showed up, he would call in and have me run things. That's why..."

"Why you thought he'd make you manager," Harper finished.

It wasn't a question, but he nodded. "I get bringing his daughter in. It's a family business. But she's so fucking infuriating."

"So, what happened last night to cause all this?" She waved a hand around the kitchen. "What'd the ice queen do this time?"

"Nothing specifically worse happened," he said. "I'm just exhausted, and she's making me dread going to work."

His sister reached for a finished cupcake. She unwrapped one side and took a bite. "God, these are so good. You should just quit the bar if you're that miserable and bake all the time. I'd buy these from you."

He laughed and nudged her foot under the table. "Thanks, but I don't think one customer is enough for me to make a living."

She shrugged, looking just like her son in the motion.

"What about the new bakery? Maybe they're hiring," Charlie said.

Wyatt turned toward her. "It's not open yet. Besides, I have no real training or anything. Baking at home with my nephew for fun is not the same thing as working in a bakery."

"Fine," she said. "But it's still something you love that makes you happy. I think you should at least stop by and ask. Even if it's only something part time."

It wasn't a bad idea. Especially with how things were going at the bar.

"Being a bartender wasn't your plan," Harper added. "You got that job after moving here with Loren just to have an income. It was supposed to be a placeholder. If you have a chance to do something you actually care about, you should try."

He sighed and picked up the next cupcake to frost. They were both right. "I'll stop by there the next time I see someone inside."

They beamed at him. Then, his sister said, "In the meantime, we need to figure out this situation with Olivia."

Charlie's smile shifted into something more mischievous. "Sounds like the ice queen just needs a little thawing."

"What the hell does that mean?" Wyatt said with a laugh. The women shared a look, and he knew he would hate whatever was about to be suggested.

"Maybe she just needs someone who... makes her feel appreciated," Harper started.

Charlie rolled her eyes. "She needs to get laid."

He stared at them, shaking his head. "I'm not getting involved in my boss's love life."

"Oh, she should get on Love Hunters." Harper straightened in her seat.

"I don't know. The dates I had from there were all pretty horrible." Charlie shivered, and he wondered if she was thinking of the man with all the cats or the one who verbally assaulted their waitress before storming out of the restaurant. After being left at the altar earlier in the year by her high school sweetheart she was convinced by her cousin to try the app. It did *not* end well. The only good things that came out of that experiment were Colby—who was now their friend—and the fact that it made Charlie confront her feelings for her lifelong best friend.

Wyatt lifted a shoulder. "I've had better luck. It depends on what you're looking for."

"Ew." Harper made a dramatic face of disgust.

Ignoring her, he said to Charlie, "Besides, you were already in love with Aiden, so you didn't want them to work out anyway. And you weren't open to casual. Most of the people on there, in my experience, are just after one thing."

"Please don't go into more detail," Harper said.

Charlie nodded in agreement with him. "That's true, I guess. If you're looking for hookups, it's great. Vi uses it a lot for sex too."

"It's good for that." He lifted one shoulder. "Did I tell you we were matched a while back?"

"Oh my God! No. Did you sleep with my cousin?" She made a face that was somewhere between amusement and disgust.

"Of course not."

"Stop pretending like you can't hear me," Harper said loudly. When no one responded, she groaned and stood. "I'm going to go check on Elliot. I hate both of you."

Wyatt and Charlie grinned at each other. They might have been in their twenties, but he would never pass up an opportunity to torment his little sister. He started frosting again and said, "Seriously though, Olivia could definitely use something to loosen up. It's not a bad idea, but it's not like I can make that happen. What am I supposed to do, go into her office and tell her she needs to get laid so she'll stop harping on us?"

"I mean, I wouldn't do it exactly like that." Charlie dipped another finger into the bowl of extra frosting. "No, you're right. You can't do that. Don't harass the woman."

He would never. "Did you know her in high school?"

"Not really. I mean, I knew who she was; it's a tiny town," she said. "But we never talked or anything."

"Damn. She needs a friend to suggest it."

Charlie patted him on the arm. "Sorry. It looks like you might be stuck with the ice queen a bit longer. Unless..."

"I don't like that tone." He wasn't sure he wanted to hear her next suggestion. Standing, he went to the oven to check on the next batch of cupcakes.

"Relax. I wasn't going to say *you* should hook up with her. Although, that would probably be easier." She shifted in her chair to face him. "I was going to say, unless you tried to befriend her. She was tense throughout school, but she was nice. Maybe figure out what's going on with her dad, why he needed her to return home, and what's making her so irritable. Then, we can try to help and make her less—"

"Controlling?"

"Well—"

"Aggravating?"

Charlie pushed to her feet. "All right, enough. You've made your point."

He grabbed a dish towel to pull the pan of cupcakes out of the oven and set them on the counter to cool. Tossing the towel up next to it, he turned the oven off then leaned against the cabinets and crossed his arms. His friend stared at him, waiting with a knowing look in her eyes, as if she could see his resolve crumbling before he even spoke.

"You're right," he said.

"Of course I am."

Wyatt shook his head with a smile. "I do need to find out what's going on with Jack. Even if it doesn't solve anything with his daughter, I need to know. He's been the greatest boss, and he's genuinely one of the most caring people I've ever met. I can't tell you how many times he's been there for me through one thing or another."

"I believe it." She walked closer. "He's always been that way."

"At first, I thought maybe he really only needed a break, like he said; he was exhausted. But it's been weeks now, and we still haven't seen him. I've talked to him on the phone, but that's it. Something is going on."

And he was determined to find out what it was.

EIGHT
olivia

I t didn't make any sense. Olivia had been going through the numbers for two weeks now, comparing what the bank statements said to what the records at the bar said, and the numbers didn't add up. The same unmarked payment appeared on the statements, coming out every other month, but it didn't say what for, and she couldn't find anything in their costs for that amount.

She rubbed at her temples, closing her eyes. Someone was stealing the money. She just didn't know who or how. She'd told her dad as soon as she found the discrepancy, and he was certain there must have been a mistake, so she took a few days to go through it all once more. When she came to the same conclusion, she talked to him again, and he called her uncle to see if he knew of anything missing.

Her dad and her uncle Gary both owned half the bar. They'd gone in on it together when she was a little kid. Gary didn't have much to do with actually running it though. He'd left that to her to dad while he continued with his job as a supervisor at one of the factories two towns away. So, naturally, he didn't have any answers for her either.

She wondered if there was a way one of the employees was taking money, but she didn't know how they would have pulled that off. According to her dad, none of them had access to the account.

Her phone rang, and she swiped to answer after seeing the name of the bank appear. "Hello?"

"Miss Cartwright? This is Kate from First Bank; we spoke earlier."

"Yes, hi. How are you?" Olivia leaned back in her chair, hoping for good news.

"I'm good. Thanks," she said. "I have some good news and some bad news."

Olivia's stomach twisted. "Okay..."

"We're having trouble tracking those transfers. It looks like the money is going to another bank, but we're unable to find out any more information. There aren't even any notes about who set it up."

Of course not. That would have made things too easy. "So, what can we do about it? Is someone hacking our account?"

"None of our firewalls were triggered, and there haven't been other accounts reporting something like this, so we don't think someone is hacking it," she said.

"So, what do I do? We can't just have money disappearing. That's unacceptable." If there was another bank in their small town, Olivia would have already started the process to switch.

Kate agreed. "I've put an alert on the account. Whoever that third party is will not be able to take out any more unless it's authorized by you, your father, or Gary. We'll also be keeping a close eye out for anything else suspicious."

"Thank you," she said with a sigh. It was better than nothing, she supposed.

"Of course. If I learn more, I will call you right away."

Olivia thanked her again and ended the call. She slumped down in her chair. This was a nightmare. She knew things were bad, but not this bad. At least stopping that automatic withdrawal would help. It wouldn't fix everything, but she could work with what they had so long as it all got back on track.

Someone knocked on the door.

"Come in," she said, straightening in her chair.

Becca opened it with her usual scowl. "We're almost out of stirrers and napkins. The order wasn't put in on time this week."

"Seriously?" She stood and headed toward the main room, pushing past her former friend. She opened the storage closet to see for herself and cursed under her breath. "Who puts in the orders?"

When she turned around, Becca and Ryan were staring at her with pointed looks.

"Okay, who's been putting in orders while my dad has been gone?" She slammed the door and headed to the bar, grateful there weren't any customers yet.

"Wyatt usually takes care of it on Mondays." Becca glared at her.

Olivia clenched her fists, fighting an eye roll. After that first disastrous day, she and Wyatt had made it the rest of the week without killing each other. But this past Sunday, she had temporarily fired him again, and he hadn't worked Monday or Tuesday. By Wednesday, she had given in and called, begging him to return. "No one thought to tell me this?" Her tone grew harsh. "Or took care of it? Why in the hell is he the only person who does it?"

"Because he's basically been the unofficial manager the last couple of years," Becca said. "Until you came in, we all had our duties and system down. We were a well-oiled machine that you decided to fuck up." Quieter, she added, "Like usual."

If they weren't so short-staffed, Olivia would fire her too. Instead, she took a deep breath to try to stay calm. "Look, I get it. You hate me because of what happened with Kevin, but that was high school. Okay? I'm sorry. And I'm sorry for taking away a promotion from your precious king here. My dad called me home to help out, and I said yes. It's not my fault this place is struggling and needed someone to come in and make changes."

"It's doing fine," Ryan finally spoke. Unlike the woman who didn't hold back from spewing her hatred of Olivia, the young man often stayed quiet. He avoided conflict, and she knew it was because of how badly he needed this job.

"No, it's really not," she said.

The door opened, and a few older people walked in. Ryan turned to greet them with a warm smile.

Olivia faced Becca and lowered her voice. "Make a list. I'll go to the store and grab what we need to make it through the rest of the week." She started toward her office but paused beside her. "And don't fucking talk to me like that again or you're done here."

"Or what? You're gonna fire me and then beg me to return a couple of days later like you keep doing to Wyatt?" Becca raised a brow and crossed her arms, popping one hip out to the side. "Step off your high horse, Ice Queen, and look around. Just admit that, for once in your life, you don't know what the fuck you're doing and you need us."

Olivia breathed slowly through her nose, trying to keep her temper from exploding. After counting to three, she said, "Just make the list."

She stormed back into her office and slammed the door behind her. Her chest heaved with shaky breaths. When she agreed to come home, she thought she would be able to avoid most of the people she knew growing up. She figured she would be able to hide in the bar or at the house and avoid everything she'd wanted to leave behind. It was too painful to face the past, and working in such close proximity with Becca was a constant reminder of all that went wrong eight years ago.

Locking the door, she went and snatched her phone.

"Hey," Justin said after the third ring. "What's up?"

"Hi," she whispered, sinking onto the floor against the side of her desk.

"Liv? What's wrong?"

"I don't think I can do this. They freaking hate me, and they're horrible to me."

Concern filled his voice. "Have you told your dad?"

"Yeah. He thinks I'm overreacting or causing it because he never had problems with any of them."

Her best friend was quiet for a moment. She heard shuffling followed by his muffled voice telling someone he'd be back in a few. Even though she had zero romantic feelings toward him anymore, it still did something to her to hear him with another person. She wanted him to be happy.

She just wished she could be too.

"Sorry. I'm here," he said.

"I didn't mean to interrupt."

"You didn't. We were just lying in bed, watching TV."

She nodded even though he couldn't see her. "Anyone I know?"

"Um... Did you ever meet Craig from accounting?"

Her internship at Kaiser International had lasted six months, but she only vaguely remembered anyone's names.

She'd focused on the work, not the other employees. Another probable reason she was picked over. "I think so. Super tall, muscular guy?"

"Yeah." Justin chuckled. "We've been hanging out."

"Ah." After a beat, she had to ask, "Is everything... proportional?"

"Oh yeah. It really is," he said. "But we're not talking about me right now or my new, incredibly hung fuck buddy. Liv, you know I love you, but you can be... a bit intense."

She knew that. It had been her way of keeping people at a distance. Justin was the only one who'd put up with it, and that was because he was almost as bad. She had let him in out of desperation for just one friend after moving away from home. Despite telling herself she wanted to be alone, it had been too much. The loneliness hurt too much.

"I'm not saying this is your fault," he added when she didn't say anything. "But I know how easily you can lose that temper when things don't go exactly how you planned, and there is so much out of your control right now."

Tears welled in her eyes as she whispered, "Yeah."

"Liv," he said in a gentle tone. "You need to slow down and look at things from their perspective. Have you talked to any of your old friends? Are you seeing anyone outside of work besides your dad and neighbor?"

"No." She'd cut ties a long time ago, and the person she'd been closest with was in the other room, loathing her very existence. Tears started rolling down Olivia's cheeks. She bit at her lower lip and leaned her head back.

"You need to let someone in."

I can't, she thought, even while quietly agreeing with him. It was too difficult. Letting someone in meant she would get hurt when they left her.

And everyone always left or moved on.

She was destined to be alone, no matter how much it broke her heart.

NINE

wyatt

The parking lot was almost full when Wyatt pulled in at nearly midnight, but he managed to find a spot. When Ryan texted him, he hadn't hesitated to jump in his truck and take off. He knew what it was like to need to go pick up a kid at the drop of a hat. He'd had to do it for Elliot more than once.

Rushing inside, he made his way behind the bar. It was packed and loud in here tonight, and while it worsened his anxiety, he was able to push through it for his friend. Ryan had just handed over a beer when Wyatt reached him.

"Thank you so much," Ryan said. "I don't know what's wrong, but the sitter is worried it might be the flu or something. Molly has been running a fever for a couple hours, and now she's throwing up. I just want to get her home and into her own bed."

"No worries at all, man. It's no problem." Wyatt patted his shoulder. "We'll see you later. Just make sure she's okay."

Ryan thanked him again. "Oh, and just to warn you, some shit went down with Olivia earlier. She and Becca kind of got into it. She's been locked in her office ever since."

"Awesome. Okay, I'll take care of it." He waved the young man off and took over handing out drinks. Despite the number of people, it wasn't too bad. There weren't many trying to get drinks all at once, so he had time in between orders to breathe.

"Don't start," Becca said the moment he approached her. "It's not my fault she can give it but not take it."

He sighed and grabbed a cherry to eat. "What happened?"

By the time she recapped the situation, he had a headache. This couldn't keep happening. "I don't know what went on between you two in high school, but this has to stop. You can't pick fights with our boss."

"Like you never do?" Becca scoffed. "She's a bitch, and you know it."

He sighed and turned toward her, only to find Olivia behind her. She met his eyes for a second before retreating. Becca spun around to see what had caught his attention.

"Dammit, Becca." He started to follow Olivia, but a few people walked up to the bar. Forcing a smile in place, he took orders instead. He would deal with her later.

He and Becca worked side by side until closing, neither speaking except to customers. After the last one left and he helped Becca clean, he split the tips. "I'll swing by and drop off Ryan's half to him tomorrow."

"Thanks." She pulled on her jacket. Shawn entered to wait for her, lifting a hand in greeting. She walked backward toward the door. "Need me to do anything else?"

Wyatt shook his head. "No, go ahead. I'm just going to check the inventory a bit more and see if there's anything else we need to make it until the next delivery."

"I left a list next to the cash register." She pointed in its direction before taking Shawn's hand and following him outside.

Wyatt went to lock the door after them. The truth was,

he wanted to check on Olivia. He also didn't want to leave her here alone this late. After that first night, he'd felt horrible about doing so. Perrington was a small, peaceful town, but that didn't mean nothing ever happened. So, he started finding ways to linger as long as possible when he closed. The second time he'd waited around, she asked him what he was doing with a suspicious glare. He'd gone to sit in his truck instead until she got in her own car and left. But she'd seen him out there and confronted him again the next night. He'd admitted the truth, albeit reluctantly, and she hadn't mentioned it again. Each night she gave him a subtle nod of acknowledgment, but they never talked about it.

There were a few things he wanted to double check in the bar though, for real. He went to each bathroom to see how they were doing on paper towels, soap, and toilet paper. It looked like enough to get them to Monday—when the late shipment would arrive—but it would be close. He wrote them on the list. The rest they could survive without for one weekend. They just needed those necessities.

As he left the second bathroom, he heard a sniffling noise from the office. He stilled, unable to move. Was the ice queen crying? Stepping closer, he listened carefully. It was too difficult to tell from out here. He debated on whether to go in. Part of their silent understanding about him waiting for her to leave at night was that they avoided each other as much as possible. Because when they didn't, it was like neither could help arguing.

Another sniff came from the other side of the door, and he internally groaned. Wyatt knocked and pushed it open.

Olivia sighed. "I thought I locked that."

She was sitting on the floor with her back to the side of the desk, facing the windows. It was almost disorienting seeing her like this. She was hugging her knees to her chest, and her head was turned away from him. Wyatt stepped inside, unsure what to do.

He set the pen and small pad of paper on her desk. Grabbing the box of tissues, he handed her one and then lowered across from her. She straightened her legs out and wiped at her cheeks. He tried to stretch out his legs as well but was too tall. At his struggle, she let out a breathy chuckle. She so rarely smiled here that it caught him off guard.

Olivia Cartwright, even while crying, was stunning.

Her smile? It was almost too much to handle.

She had unbuttoned the top of her dress shirt, and wisps of her hair had spilled out of its bun. Honestly, she looked like a mess. But it made her appear warmer, more human. He fought the urge to wrap her in his arms and make it all better as big tears rolled down her cheeks.

"Becca can be... a lot," he said instead. "She's got a temper, and it's hard to get on her good side if she decides she doesn't like you for some reason."

"I know. She's always been like that."

He nodded, remembering they were once friends. That was so strange to him, and he imagined it was even worse for her. From what he knew, Olivia had been away for seven years, and it didn't seem like she kept in contact with anyone but her dad. He had practically done the same and knew how weird it would be for him to return to his hometown after all these years.

"Am I finally going to find out what happened?" he asked. "All I've gathered is that you two were close, a boy got between you, and there might have been cheating involved, though no one knows which side it was on."

Olivia rolled her eyes. "It doesn't matter. We were seventeen. Why can't everyone just move on?"

"Well, without knowing the full story, I only have a guess." He crossed his arms and leaned back against the wall. It was oddly peaceful sitting down here in the empty, quiet building. Even with the woman who got under his skin and occupied all of his dreams.

She gave a pointed look, waiting for him to continue.

"You left immediately after high school, right? I'm assuming nothing was resolved before then, so no one got closure. It's hard to move on when you don't understand what happened. Trust me," he added the last part in a whisper. This was hitting too close to home.

"Yeah, she still really hates me." A second passed before she added, "You all do."

Wyatt stared at the ceiling, searching for the correct words. This woman swooped in and made his life hell, and yet, he found himself saying, "We don't hate you."

She made a noise in the back of her throat in clear disbelief then pushed to her feet. He followed suit.

Knowing she would just try to argue, he said, "All right, what's your drink of choice?"

"Excuse me?"

"You look like you could use a drink, and I sure as hell could."

Olivia glared at him. "We're not drinking at work."

"The bar is closed."

"Fine, but I'm not drinking with you so you can find a way to use it against me," she said.

His brow creased. "What are you talking about? I'm trying to offer an olive branch, make peace."

"Yeah, right." She crossed her arms, and he fought to keep his eyes away from where they pushed up her breasts. From where her cleavage was now visible since she'd released the top two buttons of her shirt. Her sadness shifted to anger so fast that it gave him whiplash. "You all want me out of here. What better way than to get me drunk and show my dad how irresponsible I am or whatever?"

Wyatt just stared at her. "You can't be serious. You really think that little of us?"

She didn't say anything as she held his gaze.

"Fine." He held his hands in front of him. "I'm done trying. If you want to be miserable here by yourself and push us all away, I don't care."

He turned and stomped toward the door. This was a waste of time and effort. It was stupid to think he could make things better between them. Clearly, she didn't want to try, so why should he?

He was nearly down the hall when she stopped him in his tracks with a single word.

"Wait."

TEN

olivia

"I'm done trying. If you want to be miserable here by yourself and push us all away, I don't care." Wyatt stormed off, but his words repeated in her head.

Just like they did her first weekend here.

Had she really fallen so low that she now assumed the worst of everyone? Her dad had mentioned it too. She didn't know how it had come to this. Before she could overthink it, she said, "Wait."

Wyatt stopped in the hall but didn't face her. She slowly approached his broad, muscular back. When he still didn't move, she stepped around him and walked backward toward the bar.

"You're right. I'm sorry."

The corner of his mouth twitched as he followed her out. "How much did that hurt you to admit?"

She rolled her eyes. "You have no idea."

He chuckled and went behind the bar. Actually chuckled. And she hated how the sound stirred something in her gut.

Wyatt held out a hand toward the wall of liquor. "What will it be, Miss Ice Queen?"

Olivia clenched her jaw, bracing her arms on the bar top.

"Too soon?" When she nodded, he said, "Okay, then, Olivia, what would you like to drink? I recommend something with a high alcohol percentage because you desperately need to relax."

"I have to drive home, so no. Just a—"

"I'll drive you home." He cut her off and grabbed the tequila and whiskey, setting both before her. "Pick."

She sighed. "Vodka."

He smirked and returned the bottles before grabbing the Grey Goose. Snatching glasses, he poured two shots. He lifted one, and she mirrored him with a resigned sigh. They clinked them together then gulped it down. Wyatt poured another for her but not himself, and she hesitated only a moment before knocking it back too.

"There you go," he said, washing his glass. "See, you need to relax more. It's not good to bottle everything up so much."

"I don't bottle things up."

"Yes, you do, and then you explode on me every few days." He crossed his arms, drawing attention to the tattoos and muscles under his white T-shirt that made her mouth water. Did he purposely buy them a size too small so they would be that tight?

She scowled. "You literally walked in on me sobbing on the floor. That's not bottling things up."

His smile slipped, his features softening a fraction. "Well, in your defense, you didn't know I was working tonight, so you didn't get a chance to take it out on me before hearing Becca."

"Ah, so it's *your* fault."

"Are you always this difficult?" His tone was lighter than before, more teasing.

Olivia shrugged. "Yes."

Wyatt laughed harder. "At least you're honest."

She returned the smile. The alcohol wasn't quite working through her system yet, but she blamed it anyway. Pulling out his phone, Wyatt unlocked the screen and started playing some rock band she'd never heard. She shook her head and rounded the bar. "No. Nope." She grabbed for the phone, but he held it over his head. "I have to listen to your guys' music every fucking day. It's my turn."

"God, you're short," he said as she reached for his arm.

"I'm well aware." She was also overly aware of how her body was plastered against the front of his as she continued reaching.

As if he realized it too, he lowered his arm and offered her the phone. She took it and turned around. His breath warmed her cheek as he watched over her shoulder. Finding The Lumineers, she clicked on her favorite song then hit shuffle.

"*That's* what you've been wanting to listen to?"

Olivia whirled. "Don't start with me. They're wonderful."

Taking his phone back, he set it on the bar without turning it. "I know. I like them too."

Her jaw dropped, and she made an exaggerated face of disgust. "We have something in common?"

"Terrifying, right?"

She walked to the end of the bar, needing a bit of space. Nodding her head to the beat, she smacked her hand down. "Barkeep, another shot please."

"As you wish, Your Majesty."

She didn't even berate him for the reference to her nickname this time. Taking the shot, she sighed again. "Okay, I have two things to admit."

"What?" He leaned one hip against the bar.

"I like you more with alcohol." She grinned for a second before shaking her head. "Wait, no, that was supposed to be the second confession. The first one was that you were right. I needed this."

Wyatt put a hand over his heart. "Telling me I'm right twice within ten minutes? You're cut off."

"I'm not drunk," she said.

He lowered his arm, but his smile stayed in place. "I know. I'm kidding. See, I told you that you just needed to relax, let off some steam. And the best ways to do that are with sex and alcohol."

Everything in her tensed. The slight buzz she'd been feeling vanished. The ulterior motive she'd worried about reared its ugly head. "*That* was your plan?"

A second later, Wyatt's dark eyes widened and he shook his head. "No, I didn't mean—I wasn't suggesting that *we*—"

"Unbelievable."

He grabbed her by the wrist as she started to turn away. "No, wait. It was just a general statement, not a suggestion. Or at least, it wasn't a suggestion to include me."

Seeing the man flustered and rambling made her pause.

"And technically, it came from a friend, who said it sounded like that's what you need because you're so angry all the time," he went on. "She even told me I should get you on Love Hunters, the dating app, but I said it wasn't my business. I wasn't trying to get in your pants myself."

Olivia stared at him in shock. He reminded her of how she was when her anxiety got bad.

"Fuck! I didn't mean—I wasn't trying to…"

Remembering what her dad had said about Wyatt

having reasons not to hang out at the bar outside of work and why he might have been struggling, she wondered if that was what he meant. Did Wyatt have anxiety? *Social* anxiety? Surely not. If that was the case, how could he be such a good bartender with charisma coming out of his ass? Never toward her, but she couldn't deny it was there with customers. Everyone loved him.

A slight flicker of guilt rushed through her. He was still apologizing, but she had already stopped listening. It dawned on her that, once again, he was being sincere. She was the one who'd made a snap judgment. Why did he constantly make her do that? It was like she couldn't help it around him.

There was something other than guilt lingering within too—fear. She had moved away from this small town for a reason, and she didn't plan on staying. As soon as she got the bar back on its feet and found her father the care he needed, she would return to Chicago.

She had retreated to her old mentality of locking everyone out because she didn't want to grow close with anyone here. It was how she managed to get through college without making a lot of friends. The few she did have weren't deep relationships. They were people she studied with or went to the occasional party with, but she hadn't kept in touch with any of them. Justin was always the one exception. He'd pushed past her barriers and inserted himself into her life.

Olivia realized Wyatt had stopped talking. He stared at her, waiting. His hand still circled her wrist, and his thumb started brushing her skin. It didn't seem like he was even aware of the motion.

Maybe he—or his friend—was right. Maybe she needed to let go for once.

She didn't have to let people in, but she didn't need to fight them. She didn't need to fight *him*.

His dark eyes bore into her, probably expecting her to fire him again.

Instead, she shocked them both by grabbing the front of his shirt, tugging him closer, and kissing him.

ELEVEN

wyatt

O livia was kissing him.

Wyatt's boss was kissing him.

And he didn't hate it.

Quite the opposite, actually. He released her wrist to cup her cheek, but she pulled back before he could.

Her eyes were wide in clear concern. "I... I'm so sorry."

He had about half a second to process everything. She started to step away, but he reached out to stop her. His hand hooked around her waist. Their mouths collided, his other hand going to the back of her neck to hold her close. She gasped, and he took the opportunity to sweep his tongue in against hers.

Sliding his hand up, he found her hair clip. He broke the kiss just long enough to watch her reaction when he removed it and threw it behind her. Her dark hair tumbled around her shoulders, and he brushed his fingers through the silky strands.

"You have no idea how long I've wanted to do that." He pressed his lips to hers again. "This hair has been taunting me for two weeks. I love it down."

Her own hands explored, roaming higher on his chest and linking behind his head as she stood on her toes. Chuckling, he lowered both arms to cross beneath her ass and lifted her. Her hair draped around them as the kiss deepened.

Wyatt turned to sit her on the end of the bar. He tried to stand between her legs but couldn't. Groaning, he glanced down. "This fucking skirt."

With a soft laugh, she pulled at the hem, revealing her thighs one tantalizing inch at a time. He strained against his own pants. The second it was high enough for her to spread her knees, he stepped closer to kiss her. He trailed his lips along her jaw to the curve of her neck. Pushing her shirt aside, he moved down to her collarbone.

"Wyatt," she whispered, and he stopped to meet her gaze. "This... this doesn't mean anything."

He nodded in full agreement. "I'm not looking for a girlfriend."

"Good. You're just a means to an end right now."

It took everything he had not to laugh. "Happy to be of service."

She stared at him for a moment, as if deciding whether she really wanted this. Sighing, she shoved against his chest and hopped down from the bar.

Dammit. For a second, he really thought she would go through with it. That he could get her off and maybe catch a fucking break at work. Taking another step back, he apologized. Though, he wasn't sure why. She had initiated this. She had kissed *him* first.

He was about to say something but forgot all words as she reached for the zipper at the side of her skirt. His heart hammered in his chest, sending all of his remaining blood south. She shimmied out of the skirt, letting it fall to the floor. As she stepped out of it, she began unbuttoning her shirt.

Scowling, he swore she was going as slow as possible

just to watch him squirm. Finally, it fell open, and she slipped it off to hang over the nearest stool.

Olivia stood before him in nothing but her heels and underwear. Her matching black lace thong and bra. Because of course even that had to be flawless. She was perfect, and it was infuriating as hell. He wanted to taste every inch of her. Her curves, her warm-toned skin, all of it.

He wanted to bury himself so deep inside her that she screamed his name in pleasure.

But right now, this wasn't about him. He fought his own carnal needs to focus on her and the reason this started: she needed to let out that pent-up anger and relax.

One step at a time, he erased the distance between them, never breaking eye contact. He didn't stop until those gorgeous breasts brushed against his shirt. She had to tilt her head back to see him. But not for long.

He kissed her cheek once then lowered to his knees. Placing one hand on each of her hips, he leaned in to brush his lips along her lower stomach. Her hip bone. Her inner thigh. He paused before continuing. "Are you sure?"

"Just a release?" she whispered.

Wyatt echoed her words. "Just a release."

She nodded, but he shook his head.

"No, I want to hear you say it. Tell me what you want."

Her hand laid over his, guiding it to the edge of her underwear and pushing the fabric down on one side. "I want you to..."

He stilled his hand when she hesitated. "Say it. You know you love bossing me around."

She lifted a brow, worry morphing into a smirk. "I want you to get me off." She spread her legs more. "With your tongue. Finally put it to good use instead of arguing with me all the time."

Grinning, he said, "Yes, Your Majesty."

Wyatt dipped his head in a mock bow. He lowered her underwear the rest of the way to the floor. She was so fucking beautiful.

Leaning forward, he pressed a kiss to one inner thigh then the other, working his way higher until he reached the spot they both wanted him in. He lightly sucked on her clit before circling it with his tongue. Olivia's fingers made their way into his hair, holding his head to her. She was already wet.

He darted his tongue out to tease her entrance, and the whimper she let out made his dick twitch. Shifting, he pulled one of her legs over his shoulder to get a better angle.

"Fuck," she hissed when he finally pushed his tongue in deeper. Eventually, he replaced it with his middle finger. He looked up to see her face, but her head was tilted back. It was hot as hell. For two weeks, he'd dealt with the uptight, tense woman. To see her let go like this...

Wyatt added a second finger, eliciting another moan. He continued sucking on that little bundle of nerves as he pumped in and out. Her breathing grew more ragged, the noises coming from her throat spurring him on faster, harder.

When he felt her getting close, he curled his fingers the way he knew would do the trick.

"Oh God!" she screamed, her grip on his hair tightening as she continued grinding against his hand. "Wyatt—fuck."

He scraped his teeth against the sensitive area. The sounds escaping her nearly made him come in his pants like he was a fucking teenager again. She shook a little, and he reached up with his free hand to squeeze her ass before holding on to her hip to steady her.

"Wy-Wyatt," she said between breaths. "I'm... I'm going to..."

Against her skin, he said, "Let go, baby. Come for me."

She moaned loudly, all but ripping at his hair as she climaxed. Wyatt slowed his motions but didn't stop while she rode out the waves of pleasure, spasming around his fingers. He waited until her orgasm subsided, gave her a couple extra gentle pumps for good measure, then kissed the top of her sex as he slid out of her and lowered her leg.

Her hand brushed against his head softly, and he sat back on his heels to smile at her. She met his gaze, chest heaving. Without breaking eye contact, he licked his fingers clean. She visibly swallowed.

He still had a hold of one hip as he stood. She looked about two seconds away from losing her balance.

Olivia narrowed her eyes. "Did you call me *baby*?"

"I..." His brow furrowed. Did he? He shrugged. "I don't know."

She let out a quiet snort and lifted her hands to cross behind his neck. "You did."

Wyatt couldn't help but smile. Then, her words registered. It was like an instant cold shower.

When she started kissing his jaw, he stopped her. This couldn't happen. Not only because she was his boss and Jack's daughter, but because he didn't do relationships. Not anymore.

Having meaningless sex while hating each other was one thing. Getting along, joking afterward? No.

He had to get out of here.

Her own smile fell as he stepped away. He grabbed her underwear and handed them over.

"You... you don't want more?" she asked, giving his hard

cock a pointed look. While she dressed, he went to grab the hair clip he'd tossed.

"This was about you, not me. Remember?" He approached slowly as she yanked on her skirt. Guilt rushed through him. She was clearly upset. He set the clip on the bar beside her. "I was just helping you find a release. I didn't expect more."

She stilled and glared at him. "No, you just wanted to make me the vulnerable one and have something on me. If you use this to... to..."

"What?" The guilt was quickly fading into anger again.

"I don't know. Get promoted as manager? Get my dad to fire me?"

Wyatt shook his head. "Unbelievable. I told you I wasn't going to do anything like that. Why the hell do you think so low of me?"

Now dressed, she crossed her arms and whispered, "I don't know."

"Well, whatever shitty person made you so on guard... They're not here, Olivia. I'm not that kind of man, despite what you think." Before she could respond, he lifted both hands and backed toward the hallway. "I'll still drive you home. Just tell me when you're ready."

"Wyatt."

He turned and headed toward the bathroom. After washing his hands, he braced himself on the sink, head hanging low. He would *not* get involved with Olivia Cartwright. Her trust issues weren't his problem. She was here to help her dad, and then hopefully she would go back to wherever she came from. He would never have to deal with her again.

Though, he doubted he would forget the way she tasted, the way she shouted out his name, any time soon.

TWELVE

Olivia

For the third time, Olivia hit snooze on her alarm. She rolled over, facing the wall and hugging her extra pillow to her chest. The last thing she wanted to do today was go into work and see people. She didn't even want to see her father.

At twenty-five, she was far from being 'innocent'. Her dad knew that—he'd once picked her up in the middle of the night from her high school boyfriend's house after they got in an argument and she couldn't find another ride—but that didn't mean she wanted him knowing when these things happened. And even though she knew no one had seen her and Wyatt, somehow, her dad would be able to tell. He read her too well, could always see right through her.

At least, he could before her mom's accident.

Last night had been humiliating, and she couldn't stop thinking about it. The way Wyatt pushed her away made her stomach churn.

Olivia had meant what she said about not wanting a relationship, but the rejection still hurt. She didn't want a boyfriend, especially one who was an annoying bartender from her hometown, but she hadn't expected him to stop things mid-sex. The drive home had been so awkward.

Sighing, she sat up. She needed to get her mind off of

this. It was bad enough she would have to deal with him tonight; she didn't want to think about him all day too.

She got out of bed and dressed in black leggings and a sweater. Thankfully, she had showered this morning after getting home. She didn't want the temptation of remembering how his tongue and fingers felt on her. As she went to put her hair in her usual bun, she paused. Wyatt had said he loved her hair down. He'd admitted it, along with the fact that he thought she was beautiful... An idea flickered in her head, and she chewed on her bottom lip while staring in the mirror.

What if she left it down? Made him regret not fucking her when he had the chance?

Determined to do just that, she changed into a quarter-length-sleeved burgundy shirt that dipped lower in the front than was strictly professional. She may have also put on a better bra that pushed everything up on display. Then, she spent more time on her makeup than usual.

She did not dress *for* him. She would never dress for a man she liked, let alone one who angered her so much.

No, this was for her. This was to show that his rejection meant nothing to her. She didn't care if he had to leave with a hard-on.

At least she got off before he changed his mind.

Satisfied with her appearance, she slipped into a pair of cute flats and headed to the living room. Her dad was napping in his chair, reclining back with the TV on. She went over and kissed his cheek. When he stirred, she said in a soft voice, "I'm going out for a bit. Do you need anything before I go?"

He shook his head. "Everything okay?"

Of course he sensed something was wrong. She gave her best false smile. "Yeah. I just want to head downtown.

It's been a while since I visited the shops and stuff. I might go to the café for coffee. Want me to bring you a muffin?"

"Blueberry, please. Be careful."

She patted him on the shoulder and said goodbye. Only to freeze the moment she stepped outside. Her car was still at the bar. She'd completely forgotten. Groaning, she looked in her purse to make sure her keys were inside before taking off on foot. Perks of living in a small town—nothing was far. Her childhood home sat a few blocks away from Main Street.

Olivia had meant what she said about wanting to visit the shops. She and her mom had loved going to support local businesses when she was a kid and teenager. It had been too hard to go back after her mom died, but now that Olivia understood the struggles of owning a business first-hand, she thought it was time.

The sun hovered high in the sky, but it barely fought off the chill in the air. They were a couple of weeks into autumn now. That didn't mean much in Indiana though. The weather in October was never predictable. It could jump from sunny and warm to snowing within a day. She'd seen it happen.

Main Street was their version of busy. It was nearing noon, which meant the church crowds were out and about. Some were heading home; others were going to lunch or to shop. With the birds chirping overhead, the entire scene held such serenity. It made her chest ache. She missed her mom so much. That was why she'd avoided all of this for so long.

She saw familiar faces down the street, and she ducked into the closest shop. Braving the town itself and facing her mom's old friends were two very different things. She didn't have it in her to do the latter. Especially when one of them was Becca's mom.

To her pleasant surprise, Olivia found herself in the arts and crafts store—Happily Ever Crafter. She hadn't intended to come here specifically, but maybe it was what she needed. After all, she'd wanted a distraction. Perhaps she could start a DIY project. She used to love crafting with her mom.

"Welcome," a voice said from the counter. "Is there something I can help you find?"

Olivia turned toward the young blond woman at the counter and shook her head. "No. Well, not yet. I don't really know what I want. I'm hoping looking around will spark... something."

Her voice trailed off as she heard chatter coming from an open doorway near the back of the store. She peeked around the corner and was surprised. It connected to the next building, it seemed. To a classroom currently filled with adults painting canvases. She recognized Violet Powell in the corner, painting pottery with a little boy instead. Olivia hadn't seen her since graduation, but Vi still looked very much the same, albeit with a different hair color. Even back then, she had changed it frequently though. Right now, the long bob was pale blond with a pinkish hue. Her younger cousin, Charlotte, was walking around, talking to the students like a teacher.

"That's new," she whispered to herself.

"What?" the woman from the counter asked as she moved closer.

"It's been a while since I was last here." Olivia pointed to the room in general. "None of this was here before."

The woman nodded. "Oh, yeah. Charlie and Vi bought the store two or three years ago from Ms. Barnes and renovated it. They hold classes in the evenings and on weekends, and throughout the week, they open it for kids as an after-school program."

"Wow." Olivia walked away from the door, wandering along the wall on the store side. "That's incredible." She hadn't been close to either of the Powell girls in school, but in such a small town, everyone knew each other. They had run in the same circles once in a while when she dated Kevin. The two were always with the Barnes brothers, who both played baseball, and in a school as small as theirs, it didn't matter what sport they were in, all of the jocks hung out together most of the time.

She hadn't kept in touch with anyone after leaving, but she was still friends with most of them on social media. Not that she checked it often. She knew there was a big debacle regarding Charlie and the Barnes boys—apparently one had left her at the altar and then she got together with the other —but Olivia thought she'd seen something about everyone being fine now.

"You said it's been a while since you were here. Did you used to live here?" the woman asked.

Olivia nodded. She absently touched a box of fake flowers as she passed it. "I grew up in Perrington. I graduated with Vi but haven't seen her since. It's strange seeing them here, owning a business, Vi with a son."

"Oh, no, that's my son. We just moved here, and he loves to paint. He hangs out with her while I work in the store."

That made more sense.

"I know you don't know me, but is everything okay?" she asked, following Olivia. "You look kind of lost."

Olivia stopped and faced her. The truth was, she was quickly getting overwhelmed by everything again. Seeing them with their lives figured out reminded her that all of her plans had a massive hole in the center. "Yeah, just got a lot on my mind."

"Guy trouble?" She quickly added, "Or girl trouble?"

With a sigh, Olivia gave in. "Guy trouble, but that's only part of it. I thought finding something to do in here might distract me from... him."

"Come with me." The woman headed toward the counter and said over her shoulder, "I'm Harper, by the way."

"Liv." She wasn't sure why she gave the nickname. Harper seemed nice though, and right now, she could use a friend. She'd been tempted to call Justin, but despite being her best friend, he was also her ex. At the moment, she wanted to talk to someone who didn't know her, didn't know her past. Someone who didn't know the *intense* person she was usually. Right now, Olivia could just be a random woman whose biggest trouble was a guy who made her feel some sort of way.

"Nice to meet you." Harper went to one of the shelves, pulled out a box, and set it on the countertop. "Diamond art painting. It takes enough focus to keep you occupied, but the beginner ones aren't super difficult, just time consuming. It's pretty fun, and it's relaxing."

Olivia turned the kit over to read more. It did look like something she would enjoy, but she didn't exactly have a lot of time to spare. Maybe she could set it up and work on it a little bit at a time.

"Want to talk about the guy?" Harper took a seat on the stool behind the cash register. "I mean, I know I'm a stranger, but—"

"That actually makes it easier," she mumbled before she could help it.

Harper chuckled, and Olivia lowered the box to meet her gaze. There was a familiarity about her, but she didn't think they'd ever met before. "Look, I've had my share of crappy man problems," the woman said. "If it makes you feel better, I'm a newly divorced twenty-two year old with a five-year-old son who just moved in with her brother because she had nowhere to go except to her uptight parents' house."

Olivia's eyes widened.

"Yes, I had him at seventeen. So, really, whatever is going on? No judgment here."

Damn. She liked this girl. She didn't want to make friends here—that was the whole point of moving away—but maybe she could make an exception. It would be nice to talk to another woman about this kind of stuff for once.

When she didn't respond fast enough, Harper said, "Sorry. I tend to overshare. You should ask Charlie about the day we met. I actually hugged her."

Olivia couldn't help but let out a breathy laugh. She appreciated blunt honesty. "Okay, fine." Leaning against the counter with her elbows, she took a deep breath. "So, there's this guy... Long story short, saying we don't get along is the understatement of the century, but every once in a while, we have a moment, and it's like..."

"Like none of the fighting matters?"

"Exactly!" Olivia shocked herself with the outburst and lowered her voice. "Exactly. And last night, we had one of those moments that led to..."

Harper raised a brow, grinning like she already knew. "To?"

"I... We kissed, and he... I let him..." How much detail should she give? "Sorry, I don't know how to do this. I've never really had girlfriends to share stuff like this with."

"It won't leave this room if that's what you're worried about."

Olivia nodded, though, in truth, that was only part of her hesitation. *Screw it.* She glanced around to make sure they were still alone. "He went down on me—while in a somewhat public place—got me off, and then pushed me away when I tried to reciprocate. He literally stopped us from having sex after giving me one of the best... Let's just say it's been a while since I've had any attention of that sort."

"Wow. What an asshole." Harper crossed her arms, looking angry on her behalf. "Maybe it doesn't work and he didn't want you to know?"

"He was as hard as a rock when grinding up against me, so I don't think that's the case," she said with a scoff. "And it didn't feel like size was a concern either. I considered these things. I've done nothing but think about them all night. It's so frustrating." She lowered her voice to a whisper, just in case. "Why go down on me like that if he didn't want to fuck me after? I was ready to go. He could've bent me over and—"

The bell over the door chimed, and she stopped abruptly, not wanting to be overheard.

She turned and met a pair of dark eyes. Her jaw clenched, and her lungs fought to work properly. This wasn't happening. There was no way her luck was this bad.

"What are you doing here?" Wyatt asked, striding toward her.

THIRTEEN

wyatt

Wyatt stopped in his tracks as Olivia turned toward him. Her wavy hair was down around her shoulders, and her tight shirt made him lick his lips. He'd never seen her like this. Even her makeup was more prominent than usual. He wanted her so badly. Last night, he shouldn't have stopped them.

He worked to clear the emotions from his face and crossed the store. "What are you doing here?"

The shock in her eyes hardened to anger. "Shopping. Is that okay with you?"

Harper glanced back and forth between them, her jaw slightly dropped. Then, as if realization struck, she gasped and slapped a hand over her mouth. From behind it, she said, "You're Olivia."

"Yeah?"

"Uncle Wyatt!" Elliot ran out of the classroom.

Wyatt put a hand on his head when he reached his side. "Hey. Ready to go home?"

"Uncle..." Olivia whispered. Horror flashed in her eyes, and she turned toward Harper. "You're his sister?"

The color drained from Olivia's face as Harper bit her lip, clearly fighting a smile. Wyatt bent down to his nephew. "Can you go sit with Vi or Charlie? I need to talk to your mom for a minute."

Elliot nodded and took off. As soon as he was in the classroom, Wyatt moved closer to Harper and Olivia. "What the hell is going on?"

Olivia looked like she was about to be sick. "N-nothing. I have to go."

"Wait, Liv," Harper said, but it was too late. His boss was already rushing past him and out the door.

"Harps?" Wyatt needed answers. Now.

She grabbed the art kit on the edge of the counter and put it back on a shelf. "Um... so, I met your boss."

"And?"

Sighing, she sat down again. "And she looked upset, so I asked her what was wrong. I asked if it was guy problems, and she admitted it was." Harper narrowed her eyes on him. "She didn't want to open up to a stranger, but I told her she could and then summarized my own problems to show her I wouldn't judge."

Wyatt was used to his sister's rambling. It was part of what made her so loveable and easy to open up to. Her meaning hit him, and he groaned. "Oh God. What did she tell you?"

"More than I ever wanted to know about my own brother."

"Dammit." He brought both hands up to swipe down his face. "Fuck me."

"Isn't that what should've happened last night with Liv?"

He scowled at his sister. "Don't."

"Sorry," she said with a chuckle. "Couldn't resist. I don't have as much willpower as you, apparently." When he slammed a hand onto the counter, she raised both of hers in front of her. "Okay, okay. I'm sorry. I'm done."

"I can't believe she just *told* you. She made a huge deal

of being worried *I* would tell someone to get her in trouble, yet here she is spilling the details to a fucking stranger?" He seethed.

His sister's features softened. "She seemed... lonely and hurting. I kind of pushed her into telling me."

Wyatt stared at her for a second, shaking his head slowly. Another thought hit him. "That's going to make this even worse."

"Why?"

He summed up how Olivia freaked out last night. How she'd assumed the worst of him and thought he was trying to use her and take her job. Shifting uncomfortably, he scratched the back of his neck. "And now, of all the people in this town to get her to talk, it was my sister. She's going to think I had you do it on purpose."

Harper's brow furrowed. Elliot joined them again, and she picked him up. But she still glowered at Wyatt.

"What?" he asked.

"That doesn't make any sense. *She* came into the shop. I didn't seek her out."

"I know, but her logic hasn't made sense since I met her." He held his arms out for Elliot. The boy laughed as she passed him over. It made Wyatt smile. Few people eased his anxiety like his nephew did. Harper knew that. She often handed him the boy to help ground him and make him focus on something else.

She stood and rounded the counter. People from the classroom started trickling out, and she waved in greeting. Her attention returned to him though. "Not that I want to think about it more, but why did you stop last night? Liv seemed to enjoy it, and she was upset you didn't..." She eyed Elliot. "Go through with things."

He looked down at the floor. The reason sounded

stupid in his head the more he thought about it.

"Wy?"

"Because we were getting along," he said, lowering Elliot to stand next to him. The boy wandered over to where Vi was talking to Mrs. Davis—the older woman who served as the town's biggest gossip. And everyone's biggest supporter. "Because it wasn't supposed to mean anything, but it felt... real."

Harper tilted her head to the side with pity bright in her eyes. "It's been six years. You can't hold on to this anger forever. What Loren did was horrible, but that doesn't mean every woman out there is terrible."

"It doesn't matter. I'm never giving anyone control over me again."

"Which is why you and Liv keep fighting. She likes control too."

He clenched his jaw. "Would you stop calling her Liv? Just because she told you intimate details about our night doesn't make the two of you friends."

"Whoa," Charlie said as she joined them. "What did I just walk into? Intimate details? With whom?"

"His boss," Harper said before he could say anything.

"You slept with Olivia?"

"No—" he started, but his sister cut him off.

"Not entirely. He was very generous to her, but then he pushed her away because they were *getting along*."

Charlie sighed. "Wyatt." She dragged his name out, like he exhausted her.

"He's scared because his ex ruined his life, and he refuses to move on."

Wyatt huffed out a breath, smacking his hands on the sides of his legs. "Seriously? I'm the bad guy because I *didn't* sleep with my boss? What the hell?"

"No one is calling you the bad guy," Harper said, her voice full of sass that reminded him of their frequent arguments growing up. "I'm just saying it's not healthy to keep using Loren as an excuse to push people away."

"Really? You want to go there?" He crossed his arms.

"All right, children," Charlie said, trying to stop things from escalating.

Harper ignored their friend though. "What's that supposed to mean?"

"You're doing the same thing to Colby," he said.

"That is *not* the same thing," she hissed, stepping closer. "It's only been a few months since my divorce was finalized. I'd been with David since we were sixteen. I'm sorry if I'm not eager to jump right into someone else's bed the first time another man shows me attention. I was with him for *years*; he wasn't a random guy I changed my life for."

Wyatt ran a hand over his hair. "Are you fucking serious?" He couldn't believe her. "That's *exactly* what you did. You got pregnant almost immediately after you two started hooking up, and then you wanted to keep the baby, so you married the asshole the second you graduated because he manipulated you and got Mom and Dad to convince you it was the right thing to do. You gave up *everything* only to end up right where I am."

He regretted the words as soon as they were out. Not because they weren't true. Every bit of it was true, and it was an argument they'd had before. But when her lips pursed, her cheeks turning pink as tears rimmed her eyes, he knew he'd crossed a line.

"I changed my life for Elliot," she whispered. "And I would choose that path every single time. *Everything* was for him. Because I love him."

"I know." He reached for her, pulling her into his arms

even when she tried to fight against it. "I'm sorry." He met Charlie's gaze over his sister's head as he hugged her. She put a hand on Harper's back.

"What's wrong with Mom?"

Harper sniffled and turned her head away from the rest of the shop as she wiped at her cheeks. Wyatt released her to pick up Elliot. "Nothing, buddy. Everything is okay."

He felt like shit, but the five year old didn't need to know that. Shifting Elliot to hold with one arm, he draped the other around his sister.

"Sorry," he whispered with a soft kiss to the top of her head.

"Me too." She leaned back and gave him a sad smile.

Squeezing his nephew into a tight hug, making him giggle, Wyatt said, "For the record, I'm glad you chose this path. I hate what you went through, but I'm happy it brought the two of you here to me."

He didn't know how he'd been living here alone for so long. He couldn't imagine returning to that loneliness without the two of them. Not to mention the friends he also now had because of them.

Charlie met his gaze with a sympathetic nod. Because of course she understood what he was thinking. She knew exactly how much it meant to him to have people he cared about in his life.

She seemed... lonely and hurting. His sister's words about Olivia echoed in his mind. Maybe he needed to apologize and try to make things right. After all, he knew how it felt to be alone in this town. And he'd never seen her chatting or hanging out with anyone. Maybe she really didn't have friends here. Just like he hadn't all those years.

FOURTEEN

olivia

It was probably considered childish to hide like this, but Olivia didn't care. She came to work like she was supposed to; no one said she had to stay out on the floor with everyone. So, she was avoiding Wyatt. She was still mortified from her conversation with his sister a couple of days ago. And she had already been humiliated before that.

Now, she wanted to crawl under a rock and never see either of them again.

Or she wanted to run back to Chicago. To the invisibility a large city provided.

She'd considered firing him again, but that would cause even more problems at this point. They didn't need a lawsuit on top of everything else.

Her phone rang, and she smiled at the photo of her and Justin that popped up. She swiped to answer and held it to her ear. "Hey."

"Hey, Liv. Sorry I missed your calls," he said.

She rolled her eyes, wondering what his excuse would be this time. Her favorite had been when he'd claimed to be on Navy Pier and the wind got so strong that it threw his phone into Lake Michigan.

"I spent the weekend with Craig, and we agreed to keep phones off the whole time."

Oh. That actually sounded legit. "No worries. How was it?"

"Nice," he said with a contented sigh. "Relaxing. We spent a lot of time in his rooftop hot tub."

"Ugh, jealous. Sounds so much better than my drama." She slid down in her seat and rested her head on the chair's backrest.

"What happened this time?"

She didn't appreciate his tone. As if he was exhausted by her because she was always the problem. Instead of going straight into the issue, she decided to throw him off. "Well, I had the best orgasm of my life on Saturday with the irritating bartender, who then rejected me. And I accidentally vented about it to his sister the next day."

It was silent for a long moment before Justin laughed. "What the fuck? Start from the beginning."

"That was pretty much all of it." She pinched the bridge of her nose.

"Okay, well, first off all, I take offense to the best orgasm comment."

"As you should," she said with a genuine smile.

She could practically hear his eyes rolling as he asked, "What do you mean he rejected you? You want to date the guy now?"

"Hell no. He went down on me in the bar after closing but didn't want sex after. And no, before you ask, nothing seemed wrong. He seemed in perfect working order physically." She let out a slow breath. "It was like he got freaked out."

"You mean he got freaked out and *didn't* want to screw around more with the woman who signs his paychecks?"

"When you say it like that..."

Her best friend knew her too well. "Oh, Liv. Wait, how do you *accidentally* vent to the dude's sister?"

She told him about her trip into town and talking with Harper. For a few minutes there, it had been nice to consider she might have been friends with the woman. They'd clicked fast, and that never happened. Because Olivia didn't let it.

Justin was quiet again for a minute. He'd stopped laughing after she explained how she ran off and had been avoiding Wyatt ever since. "His rejection really hurt, didn't it?"

Olivia didn't answer.

"It wasn't just for a release," he said. "You wanted to have sex with him. Because you like him."

"I do not." Even she didn't believe the words though. Clearing her throat, she tried again. "I don't like him. I can barely be in the same room without wanting to strangle him."

"Maybe he's into that," Justin teased.

"Oh my God." She chuckled and shook her head. "It doesn't matter. I'm never finding out."

He made a noise of disbelief.

"I'm not. Just because I wanted to have sex with the man doesn't mean I want anything more. Besides, I'm heading back to Chicago as soon as I figure things out with my dad."

"But if you weren't?"

She groaned. "It doesn't matter. I'm still not dating him, or anyone in this town."

"Fine, don't date him. I think you should continue what you started though."

"Oh God. Please stop." She rubbed her forehead with one hand, not wanting him to say more. "I'm actually glad we didn't have sex. I don't care how hot he is or how good he is with his damn tongue."

"Liar."

Except, it wasn't Justin who spoke.

"You've got to be kidding me." She lifted her head to glare at Wyatt. "Don't you ever knock?"

"What?" Justin asked.

"I have to go."

"Tell your boyfriend I say hi," he said as she hung up and set her phone down.

She straightened in her chair. "I'm not a liar."

"Really? Because according to my sister, you seemed pretty upset. Seems like you *do* care that we stopped." Wyatt shut the door behind him.

"I was upset because you made me look like a fool." She pushed to her feet.

He stepped farther into the room, his brow furrowed. "Why? Because I had the good sense to stop, and you were practically begging for more?"

Olivia huffed out a breath and walked around her desk. "I don't beg. And if I did, it's because I literally needed more, as in you weren't doing a good enough job."

"Well, we both know *that's* a lie. What did you tell your friend? That it was the best orgasm you've ever had?"

"God. How long were you eavesdropping?" She shook her head. "It doesn't matter. I was lying to make him jealous."

At that, Wyatt stilled. He took a small step backward, and she realized how close they'd been standing. The brief flash of uncertainty in his gaze was replaced with a mischievous look. "You also said I was good with my fingers and tongue. Even if you were lying to whoever that was, there's no faking the way you screamed my name and came on my fingers. I can practically still taste you, *Liv*."

"Don't call me that. Only friends get to call me that."

"Ouch. We're not friends?" He put a hand over his heart. "I've seen you naked, for the most part, and had my tongue inside you. That's about as friendly as I get."

"Yeah, well, friends don't continuously try to humiliate each other." And she'd had about as much as she could handle at the moment. "Are you about done? Or am I going to need to fire you again?"

To her surprise, his features softened. "I wasn't trying to humiliate you. That was never the goal."

"Right." She rolled her eyes.

"I swear," he said. "I actually came in to apologize and to make sure you didn't think..."

"What?"

He sighed and sat on the arm of the nearest chair. "That night, you thought I was trying to get something on you to take your job. And then, yesterday... I didn't want you to think I had anything to do with Harper getting you to talk."

It had crossed her mind. She'd hoped it wasn't true though. Instead of questioning it, she said, "Fine, but you still keep putting me in vulnerable positions. It's not exactly fair."

"I didn't make you vulnerable," he said in a softer tone than she'd ever heard him use before. "I just gave you a safe place to *be* vulnerable. And at least some part of you must trust me. Otherwise, we wouldn't be here."

She hated that he was right. "We're still not even," she said as a plan started to form. "Why did you stop the other night?"

"Because it felt too real, and I don't want that."

The honesty surprised her, but she welcomed it. "Is that the only reason? You weren't... turned off or anything?"

He let out a bark of laughter. "Seriously? That was probably the hottest thing I've ever done. It physically hurt to walk away."

"Good." She smiled and walked around him to the door. "Where are you going?"

Flipping the lock, she turned and said, "Just making sure no one walks in since none of you know how to knock."

His smirk infuriated her. But she also wanted to kiss those tilted lips. He stood when she stopped in front of him. "And why don't you want anyone to walk in on us?"

"Because it's time we got even." She turned the chair and then pushed against his chest until he took a seat. With one hand, she let down her hair. "I told you I didn't want a relationship. That night was supposed to just be sex."

Grateful she wore pants today, Olivia climbed onto his lap, straddling his waist. His hands went to her hips. She paused with her lips millimeters from his, and their breath mingled as the anticipation built.

Brushing a single kiss across his mouth, she said, "You had me naked and vulnerable. And yes, you were good with your tongue."

Hers darted out, sweeping in to touch his as she kissed him harder and rocked her hips. And then, she leaned away enough to tug his shirt up and toss it aside. None of them—besides Owen—had listened to her about wearing business apparel or a uniform. In this moment, she was grateful. It made undressing him quicker.

He was so good-looking. With his tattoos sprawled up his muscular arms, and his stupid fucking abs. She traced a finger along the ridges, wishing it was her lips, and reached for his belt as she stood.

"If you don't want this, tell me now," she said, kneeling in front of him.

He chuckled and lifted up enough to lower his pants and boxers in one motion, his dick springing out, already hard. Her mouth watered at the sight. Stroking himself a few times, he sat back down, seemed to think better of it, and stood while shoving the chair away.

Olivia sat on her knees, waiting. With a raised brow, she asked, "You done?"

Wyatt used his free hand to tilt her chin up. His thumb went to her lower lip. "Did you wear this red lipstick for me?"

"No."

He bent down to kiss her once more. "Liar."

Straightening, he moved closer, and she replaced his hand with hers, sliding it along his length. And there was a lot of length. There was no way it was all going to fit in her mouth, but she would sure as hell try. Leaning forward, she pressed a soft kiss to the tip before licking along the sensitive underside.

Wyatt tensed as she enclosed her lips around him, taking him deeper and deeper. She fought the urge to gag. Bobbing back and forth, she used her hands to cover the area she couldn't take. The next time she tried to go deep, he hit the back of her throat. Her gagging only seemed to turn him on more.

"Fuck, Liv," he hissed, his hand sweeping into her hair and gripping tightly.

She pulled off of him and glared up at his face. "Don't call me that."

"You are literally on your knees, choking on my cock, and you still won't admit we're friends?"

"Do you really want to question the woman who *liter-*

ally has you by the balls right now?" She reached back and gave them a squeeze.

"Okay, okay. Fuck."

Olivia laughed then continued, sucking him into her mouth. She might have confessed he was good with his tongue, but she was determined to show him that she was better.

FIFTEEN

wyatt

Wyatt stared down at Olivia in wonder as he fought to catch his breath. He'd blasted down her throat, clenching his jaw to stifle his groan, and she'd swallowed every drop. She sat back on her heels now with a grin and wiped the corner of her mouth with a delicate finger. Leaning down, he gripped her chin and kissed her again. He couldn't resist. She was so fucking gorgeous.

Releasing her, he reached to pull his boxers and pants up. "If that's your idea of humiliating me, I'm all for it."

When he offered his hand, she took it and got to her feet. He slid an arm around her waist to draw her in, but she put a palm on his chest and shook her head.

"No, this isn't happening. We're even now." She stepped back, and he chuckled. "What?"

"If that's how you get even, I should make you mad more often."

She scowled at him. "You know what I meant."

Wyatt stepped closer, following her as she backed away, until she was against the shelves behind the desk. He towered her, but she still managed to look down her nose at him. Not touching her, he said in a low tone, "I do, but that doesn't make what I said any less true."

He wanted to kiss her so badly, but he wouldn't cross that line. Not unless she wanted him to. Her eyes darted to his lips, and he knew she was considering it. Then, she turned her head. "Just go."

Sighing, he gave her space. "You're right. We're even now. Let's just... pretend it never happened. Okay, Ice Queen?"

The words were out before he could stop them. He regretted them instantly. Despite all their arguing, he didn't want to hurt her, and he knew that nickname did. She tensed and shook her head slightly.

As she went to grab her hair clip, she said, "Get out, Wyatt."

"I'm sorry."

"I don't care." She twisted her hair into a bun and clipped it in place. "Get out of my bar. I'm done with these games."

His jaw dropped. "Seriously? You're firing me again?"

Olivia took her seat, a clear dismissal as she went back to working on the computer.

"Unbelievable. You can't keep doing this."

"I just did." She didn't even look up at him.

Storming toward the door, he said, "Fine. I'll see you next time it gets busy and you're desperate."

She didn't respond.

He unlocked the door and threw it open. She said she was done playing games? So was he. For weeks, he'd gone back and forth with Olivia. It was exhausting.

Out in the bar, Owen asked, "Everything okay?"

"No." Wyatt shook his head. If he wasn't so angry, he might have laughed. "Fired again."

"You've got to be kidding me," Becca said.

"I'm not." He sighed. "Call me if it gets too busy. I'm sure I'll be back in a couple of days."

They waved as he headed toward the door.

He wandered down the street toward Happily Ever Crafter, wanting to vent to Charlie or Harper. At this twilight hour, most of the shops along Main Street had their lights on, giving the town a cozy feeling. This was why its residents loved it here so much.

Wyatt paused before he reached the door, his eyes lingering on the bakery across the street and down a couple buildings. Tapping his thigh with his fingers, he took a deep breath while deciding whether to follow his sister and Charlie's advice. He glanced toward the bar. Olivia or Owen would call him to return, he had no doubt about that, but he was sick of this. Maybe it was time to move on and try to find something else that didn't make him want to rip his hair out.

Decision made, he crossed the street and made his way to The Sweet Tooth bakery. Through the window, the lights illuminated the nearly empty shop. They were still setting things up, but it looked like they finally had tables and chairs. A young woman was hanging a painting on one of the striped pastel walls. Wyatt tried the door, but it was locked. She noticed him and came over to open it.

"Can I help you?" she asked in a wary tone, staying partially behind the door.

"Hi, my name is Wyatt. Are you the new owner of this shop?" He attempted to look less intimidating; he knew what kind of picture he painted. To help, he took a step back.

She shook her head. "I'm their niece. I'm just helping to set things up and decorate."

"Oh." He scratched the side of his neck. "Are they around? Or will they be soon?"

"They're visiting family a few hours away. Is there something you need?"

Licking his lips, he said, "I was just hoping to talk to them about possibly working here. I didn't know if they'd be hiring or running everything themselves."

Her gaze softened, and she opened the door a little more. "Really?"

When she looked him up and down, he chuckled. He shrugged. "Really. I currently work at The Tavern down the street, but baking is my guilty pleasure. If there's a chance I can do it for a living, I have to try."

"Well, I don't know what they have planned exactly." She leaned against the doorframe. "Like I said, I'm just helping out with the interior design stuff. I'm only here for the weekend. But I will let them know you stopped by to ask. You said your name is Wyatt?"

"Yeah, Wyatt Clarke." He gave her a smile.

She nodded and added, "If you want to come back next week, they should be around."

"Thanks. I appreciate it."

"No problem. Have a good night."

He lifted a hand in a small wave. "You too."

As she closed the door, he started across the street, feeling lighter than he had in a while. Granted, his heart felt like a fucking hummingbird in his chest. He got paid to serve and talk to strangers, but that was behind a bar, and they approached him. Initiating a conversation with someone he didn't know was an entirely different thing.

He quickened his pace until he made it to the art shop. There was a small pottery class this evening with Vi leading it, which meant Charlie sat behind the cash register. Harper must have already gone home.

Charlie grinned at him when he entered, but her smile faltered when she took in his nervous energy. "Hey. You okay?"

"Yeah, I just... I need a moment." He stopped beside her counter, bracing his hands on the end and lowering his head to focus on his breathing. Thankfully, no one else was on this side of the shop, and the class was fairly quiet.

She slid off of her stool and moved to his side. Putting one hand over his, she gently squeezed, as if to reassure him she was there with him. But she knew he needed silence. This wasn't the first time she'd seen him on the verge of an anxiety attack.

After a few minutes, it started to ease. He sighed and lifted his head. "Sorry. It came on fast."

"Don't apologize," Charlie said, keeping her tone soft. "Do you want a water or something?"

"No, I'm fine. Thank you." He placed his other hand over hers.

"What happened?"

"I, um... went to the bakery to ask about a job."

Her eyes lit up. "Really? What'd they say?"

"They weren't there." He recapped everything as she took her seat again.

"Wait, what triggered this? I thought you were going to go apologize to Olivia."

Wyatt leaned against the counter. "I did."

"And?"

The corner of his mouth twitched. He could still picture her on her knees, the way she looked with her red lips around him. Clearing his throat, he shifted on his feet. "It was going well for a few."

"Oh my God." Charlie groaned. "What did you do?"

"I did nothing." He pointed at her. "It was all Olivia. She wanted to... get even for the other night."

With a mischievous grin, Charlie said, "Did this happen at the bar?"

"In her office..."

"Wyatt!" She laughed and playfully smacked his arm. She lowered her voice. "You can't keep sleeping with your boss *at work* and expect it to end well."

"I didn't sleep with her."

She waved him off. "Semantics."

"And besides, it already ended badly," he said as if she hadn't spoken. "Well, it ended amazingly, but then it went south real fast. We started arguing after, and she fired me again."

Charlie rolled her eyes. "Of course she did. And that led to you going to Sweet Tooth, I'm assuming. What was the argument over this time?"

He let out a huff of breath. "I don't even know. She told me to get out, and then I called her Ice Queen, which made her angrier. But before that moment, I don't know what was wrong. Her ups and downs give me whiplash, yet she's the one who said she was done playing these games. It's fucking ridiculous."

"You like her so much," Charlie said with another grin.

"No, I really don't." He was tired of people saying that. Sure, she was gorgeous and made him come harder than he had in a long time, but he couldn't be with her without fighting. It didn't matter that she'd filled his fantasies from the moment they met. "Ice Queen isn't an accurate nickname for her. She's too hot and cold for that."

"Maybe she has a good reason. Did you ever find out what's going on with her dad?"

He shook his head.

Charlie grabbed one of the pencils from beneath the counter and began tapping it. She always kept a box with them and pads of paper down there. "Mrs. Davis said he hasn't been at church and that someone has seen his neighbor—who's a nurse's aide—going over there a lot. They think he might be sick."

Wyatt's stomach twisted. He knew it was true deep in his soul. "That's why she came home."

Charlie nodded. "She already lost her mom back in high school. If her dad is sick, she's probably struggling to deal with everything. She might be taking it out on you just because you're there."

And because she knew by now that he would still keep showing up. The moment she called, he was there, regardless of how much they fought.

Pushing off the counter, he whispered "dammit" as he headed toward the door.

SIXTEEN

Olivia

When her dad had called Olivia, asking her to come home, her concerns about Wyatt and the bar fled from her mind. She raced to the house, even though he'd assured her it wasn't an emergency. Except, when she pulled into the driveway, another car already sat there. Gritting her teeth, she parked and went inside to find her dad and uncle in the living room.

"Please tell me you didn't call me away from work just to lecture me," she said the moment she entered.

Her dad lifted a hand. "No, of course not. I was going to ask for your help walking to the bathroom and making dinner. Gary arrived just a couple minutes ago. I was going to call you, but—"

"But we figured this would be a good opportunity to check in with how things are going at the bar," her uncle cut in.

She glared at him. "You know, you can stop by and check on things *at* the bar."

"Liv," her dad said with a sigh.

"I need to get back to work. Thursday nights get busy, and we're short-staffed tonight."

"Why?"

The last thing she wanted to do was talk to him about what was going on with Wyatt. She went with a partial truth instead. "Ryan called in again. I'm working on finding someone to cover, but in the meantime, I need to help out." She had reluctantly texted Becca before heading this direction. "So, do you still need me? Or is Gary going to get you settled?"

"I already helped him with the bathroom," Gary said in a disbelieving tone, as if it was absurd to think he hadn't. "I'll stay for dinner. You can go."

She nodded, but before she could take even a step toward the door, he continued.

"The bank called. Said you found an account automatically withdrawing money each month and that you couldn't figure out what it was for?"

Olivia sighed and crossed her arms. "Yeah. I can't figure out if it was for a vendor or what—something that never got canceled. I had the bank stop it from happening more in the future, but it did a good amount of damage already."

"I thought you had this under control. How can you not know where money was disappearing to?" Gary asked. "It sounds like one of the employees got access somehow."

She had considered that a lot, but she didn't know how that could have happened. "I'm working on figuring that out, but that's not the priority at the moment. I've stopped it from continuing, so now, we need to figure out a way to bring in more customers and try to make up the difference. The goal is to build the business back up."

"How?"

"I... don't know," she admitted. "I haven't figured that out yet."

Gary shook his head with a scoff.

It was her dad who said, "It's been weeks, Liv. Surely you have some ideas, right?"

Not really. The words coming from him hurt significantly more than when Gary nagged at her. The disappointment in her dad's brown eyes made her chest ache. It was the same look he had the last time he'd visited her in Chicago when she told him she wasn't coming home.

"I'm trying," she whispered, gripping her elbows tighter.

"You went to school all these years, getting two fancy business degrees, and you can't even figure out the issues of a small-town bar?" Gary said. "What was the point, then? How do you think you're going to make it in the city at some big business?"

She couldn't take any more of this. "It's your fucking bar, Gary." She stormed toward the door when her father didn't step in. "Why don't you actually go in and try to do something instead of blaming the only person attempting to help?"

Olivia didn't wait for a response. Slamming the door behind her, she returned to her car and took off. How dare he try to put this on her? For twenty years, her father had done almost everything for The Tavern. Gary had been around in the beginning, according to her mom, but as soon as the money started coming in and they could hire more help, he returned to his other job. He'd left all the actual work to her dad.

As she drove back to the bar, she fought to keep her breathing steady. She'd never liked her uncle much. Not that he was around a whole lot. But he'd always seemed angry at the world and aggressive with his words. The last straw had been when he insinuated that the car accident eight years ago had been her mom's fault. They hadn't even buried her yet, and he was joking about her bad driving.

That was the first time Olivia ran away. She had overheard him and didn't want to tell her dad about the hateful accusation. He was already struggling to function. So, she took off. She'd driven around for an hour before ending up at Kevin's house. At the time, she had wanted to forget, to feel anything other than grief. He didn't argue with her asking for sex or try to stop her, despite them breaking up a few months earlier... and despite him dating Becca instead. He had just snuck her up to his room.

Of course, that had ruined her friendship with Becca. Olivia had started dating the quarterback again, only for him to graduate a couple of months later and break up with her the week before leaving for college. But throughout those five months, she'd spent a lot of time in his bed and in the back of his car. She had loved him, loved how he made her feel. He was the one good thing in her life at the time. He was the one person who could get her to forget the pain for a while and make her smile.

And then, he left her too.

She'd started her senior year feeling used up and utterly alone.

The same feelings coursed through her now.

Parking behind the bar, she tried to clear her mind of the memories. She tried not to think about her dad's disappointment, her uncle's harsh attitude, or the ache in her chest from her mom's absence. The boy she gave up everything for, betrayed her best friend for.

She tried to pretend that when she walked in and saw Wyatt behind the bar, her heart didn't beat a little faster and the weight didn't lighten the slightest bit.

"What are you doing here?" she asked, joining him and Owen. There were a dozen or so people here, but she knew it would get busy soon.

Without looking at her, he said, "I came back to apologize and to see if you wanted my help tonight since Ryan can't make it."

"Apologize? You never apologize. You say you're going to and then never do."

Wyatt finally turned, and she saw it—the pity in his dark gaze.

"I fired you," she said. "You shouldn't be here. I've already texted Becca to see if she can cover for Ryan."

"I'm already working, just let me help."

Curling her hands into fists, she said, "No, Wyatt. I told you to go."

"What's going on with your dad?" he said, as if she hadn't spoken.

The back and forth was giving her a headache. "He was overworked and needed a break. I already told you that."

"Liv, I—"

She turned to go to her office. "Don't call me that."

"Oh joy, the ice queen is in a good mood again." Becca arrived and moved behind the bar. "So glad I came in for this." Pointing at Olivia, she added, "To be clear, I'm not here for you. I'm only here because I didn't want Owen to be by himself on a Thursday night. You're practically useless serving drinks."

Olivia was going to be sick. Her anxiety tended to nauseate her.

"Enough, Becca." To her surprise, it was Wyatt who spoke up.

Becca rolled her eyes. "Please. You know it's true. You complain about her more than anyone."

The world was closing in around her. She couldn't take any more of this. Not tonight. Not after hearing the same shit from her uncle. Normally, she would argue with them, stand up for herself, but she couldn't right now. She was done.

Spinning on her heel, she rushed for the hallway, tears blurring her vision as she ignored someone calling after her. Like she usually did, she ran.

SEVENTEEN

wyatt

"**O**livia!"

She didn't stop. She kept running toward the door in the back near her office.

At the sound of Becca chuckling, Wyatt whipped around to face his friend. As he walked backward, he said, "You have to stop, Becca. That's enough. I don't care what happened nearly a decade ago; stop picking fights just to upset her."

He didn't wait for a response. Her look of shock was enough. Wyatt turned and raced after Olivia. She was almost to her car when he caught up.

"Wait, Olivia," he tried again.

"Leave me alone." She pulled out her keys and hit the fob button, but her fingers shook as she reached for the door.

Wyatt put a hand against it to keep it from opening.

"Move," she whispered.

"No, hold on."

Her eyes snapped up to his, glistening in the streetlights that illuminated the parking lot. For the second time—that he knew of—the crew had made her cry and want to disappear. He hated it. Even with how frustrating she was, he didn't want to hurt her.

"Move, Wyatt."

"No," he repeated in a gentle tone as he eased between her and the car.

"W-Wyatt, I can't do this right now." Her voice cracked on his name, and he couldn't stand it anymore.

"I know." Sliding an arm around her waist, he pulled her into a hug. The fact that she didn't fight it told him more than anything. He held the back of her neck as she cried against his shoulder. Before he could stop himself, he pressed a kiss to the top of her head. "I'm sorry."

Her fingers fisted his shirt. It took a couple of minutes, but her tears slowed. She sniffled and said, "I can't stay here. I need to go."

He rubbed her back. "You can't drive like this. Let me at least take you home."

"I can't go home. That's almost worse right now."

"Where do you want to go?"

She hesitated. "I don't know."

It was almost too quiet to hear her, but he caught the words. Her pain practically radiated from her, and even though he didn't know exactly what was going on, his heart broke for her all the same. Thinking through options, he realized the most obvious. "Come with me."

"Where?"

"Just trust me."

Olivia leaned back to stare at him. That was a big request from someone she hated. He swiped at her damp cheeks, ridding them of the remaining tears. Her small nod surprised him, but he tried not to show it. Instead, he gave her a smile, took her hand, and led her to his truck a few spots away.

He helped her into the passenger seat then pulled out his phone as he rounded to his side.

Can you and Becca handle things tonight? I'm going to take Olivia home and try to figure out what's going on. Maybe find a way all of us can work together better.

OWEN

Yeah, no worries. Is she okay? Becca's mad you took her side...

Becca will get over it. Olivia's pretty upset. I didn't want her driving like this.

OWEN

I wouldn't either. I get it. We've got things covered here. I'll drag Shawn out of the kitchen to help on the floor if needed.

Thanks.

"Owen has things under control here," Wyatt told Olivia as he started his truck and reversed from his spot.

She stared out the window. "Thank you."

He drove down Main Street in silence, waiting to see if she wanted to talk. If she didn't yet, he wouldn't push it until they got home. Bringing her to his house probably wasn't the best idea, but she needed somewhere to go. Somewhere she could vent and break down. Harper had taken Elliot to a friend's birthday party, so the house was dark when they arrived.

Turning off the truck, he went around to open Olivia's door. Her brow furrowed at the gesture, but when he offered his hand, she took it and let him guide her inside. He flipped on the lights and smiled as barking greeted them. Zoey ran out and jumped up, her little paws landing on his shin. He reached down to pet her and grabbed the leash from beside the door.

"Make yourself at home. I'm going to take her out really

quick," he said, hooking the leash to the white Maltese's collar.

Olivia didn't move right away, but by the time the puppy did her business and they came back inside, she was sitting on the edge of the futon. Freed from her leash, Zoey went straight for the quiet woman.

"Hi." Olivia slid to the floor.

Wyatt took a seat on the futon beside them. "Her name is Zoey."

"Hi, Zoey." She smiled as the dog climbed into her lap and licked her chin. Lifting the puppy, Olivia hugged and kissed her. No one could resist Zoey. Not even the ice queen, it seemed.

He stopped that line of thinking. That nickname needed to end. It was hurting her more and more; he could see that every time it was used.

Watching her play with the puppy reminded him that she was still just a twenty-five-year-old woman. He lowered to her side, sitting with his arm against hers. She didn't pull away, but she tensed slightly.

"Olivia," he said in a soft tone. "Do you want to talk about it?"

She shook her head, but then she lowered her hand between them, lacing their fingers together. "Thank you for bringing me here. I just... I know you hate me, so I appreciate you doing this."

"I told you, I don't hate you." His thumb brushed her knuckles.

A small snort escaped her. "Right."

"I mean, I could do with less of the superior attitude, and I wish you'd stop firing me, but I don't hate you."

She finally turned her head toward him, her red-rimmed eyes meeting his. "My dad is sick."

Even though he'd started to suspect as much, he hated hearing it. Jack had taken him under his wing and given him a chance. He'd been more of a father figure to him the past several years than his real dad. Releasing her hand, Wyatt wrapped his arm around her shoulders and waited for her to continue.

"This past spring, he went to the doctor because he'd started falling. His feet were dragging, making it hard to walk." She leaned into Wyatt's side. "They eventually diagnosed him with distal muscular dystrophy. It tends to set in later in life, so we had no idea."

"Shit." That was not what he expected at all.

"He's... physically, he's struggling; it's progressive. But his actual health is fine at the moment. People live with this, and they can have full lives."

Wyatt ran a hand along her arm, unsure what to say as they watched Zoey curl up on her lap. "That's good to know. It still sucks, I'm sure, but at least he's not..."

He couldn't bring himself to say it.

"It's not killing him," she whispered. "But it's not only taking a physical toll on him. He won't leave the house except to go to the doctor. He stopped going to work, obviously, but he also hasn't been going to church or to the store or to see his friends. And I get that this is a massive change to his life—it's not going to be easy to adapt—but he doesn't want anyone to know. He's acting as if his life is already over, and I... I can't..."

Wyatt's heart shattered. Olivia wasn't one to ramble. She always seemed to have her shit together. Well, at least when she wasn't overwhelmed by the gang at work.

"That's why you came back to take over for him," he said in understanding.

With a short nod, she said, "Yeah. And to help him

around the house. He can't really walk on his own anymore, and he hates using his wheelchair. Our neighbor has been coming by a lot to help out. She can't always be there though." Pausing for a moment, she took a deep breath. "I didn't want to come home... I haven't been here since I left for college, and I had no intention of returning or taking anyone's job. I'm just trying to help him."

Guilt wracked, Wyatt tightened his hold on her, wishing he could make things better. Silently, he vowed to try harder to make it a more welcoming place. He would talk to the others about backing off, and he would stop taking things personally.

"I know," he whispered. "I see that now."

He saw so much now.

EIGHTEEN

Olivia

Warmth surrounded Olivia as she came to. She didn't open her eyes right away, wanting to savor this moment between being asleep and awake. The heavy weight over her waist shifted, and she realized with a start that it was Wyatt. She was in his room. In his bed.

Opening her eyes, she tried to look over her shoulder at him. His arm tightened around her. "Five more minutes."

She didn't bother hiding her grin. He couldn't see her anyway. Instead, she settled back in, letting herself enjoy the feeling of lying with him. She couldn't remember the last time she was this comfortable and relaxed.

It terrified her.

At least they still had their clothes on.

Actually, that seemed worse.

As soon as his breathing slowed again, she slipped out from under his arm and carefully stood from the bed. She made sure he was asleep then headed to the bathroom across the narrow hallway. Once inside with the light on, she shut the door and leaned back against it with a sigh.

She'd lost it last night for the first time in a while. If it weren't for Wyatt running after her, stopping her, she didn't know what might have happened. She likely would have taken off for Chicago straight into Justin's bed. Except, he was now dating Craig, so that wouldn't have worked.

But it didn't matter. Wyatt was there, apologizing and holding her, keeping her from falling back into that cycle. He'd brought her to his home without hesitation. She wanted to hate the man, to keep her distance, but he was making that impossible.

No one ever ran after her...

Freshening up, she checked her reflection. She'd been so tired, that she had fallen asleep fully dressed with her hair still in a bun. Letting it down, she combed through the long dark waves with her fingers until it sat around her shoulders.

She chastised herself for even caring. Nothing was going to happen. Wyatt hadn't even attempted to have sex with her last night. They did nothing but sleep cuddled up together.

Olivia took a deep breath and opened the door, only to come to an abrupt stop. Elliot stood just outside the bathroom, staring up at her with big brown eyes.

"Hi." She placed a hand on her pounding heart. "You scared me."

The little boy tilted his head. "You're Uncle Wyatt's friend."

It wasn't a question, but she said, "Yes, I am."

"Are you his boss?"

"I am." She chuckled.

Elliot fidgeted, rocking back and forth. "The mean one who made him sad?"

Olivia's eyes widened in shock. "What?"

"He said his boss was mean." The boy shrugged. "He was sad and made a bunch of cupcakes."

What the hell kind of *Twilight Zone* had she walked into? Nothing about that statement made sense. There was no way Wyatt was upset after one of their fights. Mad, probably, but not sad. And what did cupcakes have to do with anything? She had very little experience with small children and had no idea how to talk to them. "I don't think he was sad. He just doesn't like having a new boss because he wants to be in charge."

Elliot seemed to consider that, then he nodded like it made sense. His anger on behalf of his uncle was adorable, but it faded, replaced by a smile. "So, *you're* in charge?"

She grinned. "Yep."

"Why are you here before school and work?"

"Um..."

"Did you have a sleepover?"

"All right," Wyatt cut in, appearing in the hallway. "Enough with the questions." He scooped up his nephew, making the boy giggle. "How about we make breakfast for my friend?"

Elliot nodded enthusiastically. "Waffles?"

"Sure, buddy." Wyatt's gaze finally landed on her. "What do you say, Livvy? Want some waffles?"

Her heart stuttered in her chest.

He was making waffles? And *Livvy*.

No one had called her that in a long time. Her mom had called her that, and after she died, Olivia had insisted no one else could use the name.

For some reason, she didn't correct Wyatt. She gave him a small smile, trying to keep her voice steady. "Sounds great."

She followed them down the hall, watching as Wyatt playfully held his nephew upside down. Elliot's laughter was contagious, but Wyatt quickly hushed him. "Your mom's still sleeping. We need to be quiet."

Indeed, Olivia spotted Harper curled up on the futon before they went into the kitchen. Setting Elliot on one of the chairs, Wyatt opened the pantry and began pulling out ingredients.

"How can I help?" Olivia asked.

"Can you grab the milk and eggs out of the fridge?" Wyatt nodded toward the corner of the room.

"Sure." She opened the stainless-steel refrigerator with shaking fingers and grabbed both then set them on the table where he'd put the flour, salt, and baking powder. Memories of the last day her mom was alive assaulted her. "You're making them homemade?"

"Of course," he said with a shrug, as if there weren't any other options. "Oh, the butter." As he went to the fridge to get it, he pointed to one of the cabinets. "Can you get a mixing bowl?"

Olivia went to where he indicated and looked up. And up. She tried to grab it, but the shelf was out of reach. Even standing on her toes didn't help. Her fingertips barely brushed the glass. At home, she would have climbed onto the counter, but she didn't want to do that at someone else's house.

"Sorry." Wyatt moved in behind her, reaching over her head for it. His low chuckle vibrated against her back. "Forgot you're so tiny."

"I'm five-three. That's perfectly average, thank you very much."

His other hand gripped her waist, and to her surprise, he pressed a kiss to the side of her head. "Whatever you say."

The gesture was so natural.

Something had shifted between them last night. It both terrified her and made her feel better. She was pretty sure the latter was why it scared her.

"Waffle time?" Elliot asked, reminding them both that they weren't alone.

Wyatt squeezed her side once. They joined him at the table, and he told her, "Sit, pretty lady. Let the men cook for you."

She wouldn't argue with that. On top of the grief bombarding her, the casualness of this morning freaked her out, but she couldn't help but enjoy it. Especially while watching Wyatt cook with Elliot. He was so good with the boy, teaching him what to do with such patience. His smile never faltered.

Olivia didn't think she had ever seen him so light and happy. Not that they had known each other that long. But he was like an entirely different person here in his comfort zone. His love of cooking and baking was as clear as day, especially since Elliot had mentioned him making cupcakes when upset. It made her wonder why he didn't pursue this as a career path.

The boys worked together, pouring the batter into the two waffle makers. Almost as soon as they started cooking, the delicious scent filled the air. Watching the two of them together warmed her heart. Wyatt obviously adored his nephew.

Eventually, they had half a dozen huge waffles made and sitting in the middle of the table.

"They look so good," she told Elliot.

Wyatt put the butter and syrup near her. "Help yourself."

As she started to plate a waffle, Elliot asked, "Chocolate chips?"

Olivia couldn't help but chuckle. It was barely seven in the morning. The sun hadn't even fully risen yet. Did

Wyatt do this a lot—get up early with Elliot after working so late?

Like her dad had done for her...

"A few, but only if you don't tell your mom." Wyatt grabbed a bag from the pantry.

"Mom already knows," Harper said as she walked by and snatched the chocolate out of his hand. She plopped into a chair, her blond hair a mess and a blanket around her shoulders. With a yawn, she put a waffle on the plate in front of her and poured the chocolate chips over it before handing the bag to her son, who bounced up and down and followed suit.

Wyatt took the last open chair beside Olivia. He stopped Elliot from dumping the entire bag then offered it to her. It was as if her smile was permanently etched into her face here. She couldn't stop.

She sprinkled a few across her breakfast before adding syrup. The chocolate slowly melted—Wyatt had placed the finished waffles in the oven to stay warm while making the others since he could only cook two at a time—and she took a big bite.

"Oh my God." She let out a moan, and Wyatt choked next to her. Lifting a hand to cover her mouth, she gave him a knowing look.

"See. It's the best like this," Elliot said in a pointed tone directed at his uncle, who hadn't put any chocolate on his like the rest of them.

Harper made a *harrumph* of agreement, and Olivia bit the inside of her cheek to keep from laughing. The woman obviously wasn't a morning person.

Shit. Olivia liked this family. Loved being here with them. It was so different than what she was dealing with back home with her dad and uncle. It reminded her of how it had been growing up, before her mother passed. Another pang of sorrow hit her hard, and she blinked away the stinging in her eyes as she stared down at her food.

Someone nudged her foot gently beneath the table. She glanced up at Wyatt, who tilted his head, silently asking what was wrong. As subtly as she could, she shook her head. She didn't want to bring down the mood of the morning.

"Okay, monkey, finish your waffle so you can brush your teeth and get ready for school," Wyatt said to Elliot.

He kept his foot pressed against hers. She stayed quiet as they finished breakfast, soaking in the joy and love this family had for one another. When Elliot was done, he tried to stall, but Harper stood and picked him up.

"Time to get dressed. You're going to be late for school," she said, carrying him away.

"But Mom..."

His words trailed off as they disappeared into his bedroom.

Suddenly, Olivia and Wyatt were alone again. Alone in his warm, inviting home she found she didn't want to leave.

NINETEEN

wyatt

Wyatt watched Olivia poke around the last couple bites of her waffle, wondering what was going through her head. She had gone quiet earlier, and though she still looked at peace here with his family, something had changed in her. There was grief in her eyes that he didn't quite understand.

"What's wrong?" He placed a hand over her wrist.

She smiled at him and shook her head, but he could still see the sadness.

"Livvy, talk to me." They hadn't yet discussed what had happened the night before, what had triggered her and upset her. "Why didn't you want to go home last night?"

"Why'd you start calling me Livvy?"

"You said not to call you Liv... I don't know. Livvy just felt... right."

With a deep breath and then a sigh, she turned her hand over to lace their fingers together. "My mom used to call me Livvy."

All at once, her behavior this morning made sense. Her grief was for her mother, for the family she hadn't been a part of in years. And now, to be with his... He lifted their clasped hands to kiss her knuckles. "She passed away when you were in high school, right?"

"Junior year," she whispered with a nod.

"I'm so sorry." He couldn't imagine losing a parent like that, let alone when so young. His own may have lived in the next state, but they were always just a phone call away. And he knew that, despite their disagreements and different ways of life, they loved him and Harper. They would drop everything for them if needed.

"No one has called me that since..."

Oh. "I... I'm sorry. I won't—"

"No," she said, cutting him off with another sad smile. "I like it." She looked down, as if embarrassed by the confession.

In other circumstances, he might have teased her about it. Instead, he squeezed her hand in understanding.

"This morning, eating with you guys and watching you... it reminded me of how it used to be with her and my dad," Olivia said.

Wyatt wanted to pull her into his arms and take away her pain. But they didn't have that kind of relationship. Last night had been an exception. He rubbed his thumb across the back of hers, hoping to give some comfort. "What's it like now with everything going on?"

"Stressful." She took the last bite of her waffle with her free hand and set the fork down. "On top of his health issues, The Tavern isn't doing well."

He knew that. He'd worked there for six years and often wondered how they stayed afloat in such a small town with slow business. Sure, they had their busy nights a couple times a week, but it didn't seem like enough to make up for the rest of the quiet days.

"If we don't figure out something major to help it, we're going to have to shut down."

"Shit," he whispered. How had Jack hidden this from them?

Olivia nodded and swept her fingers through her hair, which she'd let down at some point this morning. "And now, my uncle Gary is coming in, acting like he knew this was going to happen and that we should listen to him. Except, he doesn't want to put in the work or give real suggestions. He hasn't helped in that bar in over a decade; he knows nothing about how it operates."

It was so similar to what he'd told her when they first met.

"He's showing up more and more at our house, and my dad won't stand up to him," she went on. "It's awful there right now. It's always tense."

Wyatt had only met Gary a few times, but he never got good vibes from the man.

"Our bank account statements and records don't match. Someone has been taking money, and we can't figure out who. I thought it was a supplier or something that wasn't being recorded, or maybe one that was supposed to be canceled but was still charging us, but I can't find anything that matches," she said. "The bank didn't have answers either."

His brow furrowed. "Wait. Seriously? Surely they can figure it out."

She shrugged. "They're trying, but so far, they haven't been able to. I got them to stop it from happening again in the future. That alone won't save the bar though."

"Damn." He released her hand when Harper and Elliot reappeared.

It wasn't fast enough. His sister gave his hand a pointed look and raised an eyebrow. When he gave a subtle shake of his head, she rolled her eyes. Thankfully, she didn't say anything about it. Instead, she said, "We're leaving. I'm heading to the shop right after I drop him off at school. Can you still pick him up later?"

"Yeah, no problem."

"Thanks." To Olivia, she added, "It was nice seeing you again. I'm sorry about... before. I had no idea."

Olivia's cheeks blushed. "I didn't either."

Harper waved and tried to usher Elliot out. The little boy ran around the table to give Wyatt a hug then yelled, "Bye, Livvy!"

"Bye," she said with a smile, but he was already racing out the door. "He's adorable. You two seem close."

"He is, and we are." Wyatt stood to clear the table. "He's kind of my best friend."

Olivia helped put away the syrup and then stood beside him as he rinsed a plate. "She told me their story the other day—at least part of it. It's great that they have you." She let out a huff.

"What?"

"You just take in anyone who needs a place to go, don't you?"

He turned toward her. That wasn't sarcasm in her tone; it almost sounded like awe. "Why the shock?"

She groaned. "You're supposed to be an asshole."

"Sorry to disappoint." He chuckled and turned off the water before leaning against the counter and crossing his arms.

"No, it just makes it harder to hate you." Her words were quiet as she looked away from him. "How can I hate someone who took in his sister and nephew, who bakes with them, who drives home emotionally unstable women who continue to yell at him?"

He bit the inside of his cheek. "Sometimes, the yelling is good. Or rather, sometimes, it leads to good things."

Olivia tucked a piece of her long hair behind her ear and went to sit again.

Wyatt joined her at the table. "For what it's worth, I'm sorry."

"Me too." She took a deep breath. "Yesterday was bad. I didn't expect to... I didn't expect what happened between us. Nor did I expect a confrontation with my dad and uncle. It triggered a lot of bad memories. Being back here is hard. I miss my mom so much, and yesterday really brought back all of that grief and anger."

"What happened? How did she..."

Olivia visibly swallowed. "Car accident. Someone ran a red light and hit her side of the car. They said she died on impact. I... I never got to say goodbye."

"I'm so sorry." He couldn't imagine. He might not get along with his parents, but the thought of losing them still churned his stomach.

"I was so mad, but I couldn't even take out my anger on the other driver because they passed too," she said, staring at her hands. "So, I found other ways of coping." She lifted her eyes to his. "The same way I still cope with things, apparently."

Ah.

"I shouldn't have used you like that."

He wanted to reach for her hand but thought better of it. "It's okay. Really. I get it. Plus, it's not like I didn't enjoy it. I told you yesterday that you're more than welcome to *get even* like that as much as you want."

She snorted and covered her mouth with a palm.

Wyatt smirked and watched her for a moment before saying, "So, can we call a truce? Maybe start over and try to get along at work?"

"You think we can actually manage not to fight?" she asked, her tone full of disbelief.

"Okay, how about this." He leaned forward, putting both arms on the table. "We don't fight at the bar. It's a neutral zone. Outside of it is fair game though."

Olivia narrowed her eyes. "That implies we'll be together outside of work."

"I just mean we save it for after work. If we want to fight, it has to happen before or after. You can come here and yell at me if needed—as long as Elliot isn't around, please." Before she could respond, he added, "You can also come here if you ever need another break from home."

She licked her lips. He tracked the movement, knowing how they tasted and wanting more. That was a horrible idea. One he shouldn't pursue...

"All right, well," Wyatt pushed to his feet, "I'm getting in the shower. Then, I'll drive you home."

Her eyes widened at the abruptness. His words seemed to register. "You can't take me first?"

He shook his head, fighting the urge to laugh at her pouty face. "I feel gross. I need to shower before leaving this house."

She audibly sighed.

When he reached the doorway to the hall, he glanced over his shoulder. "You're welcome to join me."

TWENTY

olivia

Running a hand through her hair for what felt like the hundredth time, Olivia continued pacing the kitchen. She chewed on her other hand's thumbnail. This was ridiculous. She knew it was stupid. They were grown-ass adults who'd already gone down on each other. Jumping in the shower with Wyatt shouldn't have been a big deal.

Then, why did it feel like it was?

If she went in there, they would have sex. There wasn't any doubt about it. The question was, did she want that? Or rather, *should* she do that? Because she definitely *wanted* to climb that man like a damned tree. Her body was screaming for her to follow him.

But her brain kept shouting that it was a bad idea.

Wyatt was her employee. More than that, despite her best efforts, she was pretty certain they were now friends as well. Did she want to risk that for potentially great sex?

And she knew it would be great. He'd performed pure magic with his fingers and tongue, and she knew how perfect his cock was after yesterday...

"Fucking hell," she whispered, marching out of the kitchen and down the hallway. She hesitated only a moment before opening the bathroom door quietly and sneaking inside. Steam billowed out of the running shower, and she could slightly make out his silhouette through the curtain.

She began slipping off her clothes, her heart racing.

"Olivia…"

She stilled. Had he heard her? He hadn't moved the curtain.

"Shit," he hissed, followed by a soft grunt.

She bit her cheek, realizing what was going on. Taking off the last of her underwear, she approached the curtain and gently put a hand on the edge. "Want the real thing?"

As she stepped into the tub in front of him, he let out a breath and nodded. He continued to stroke himself, already hard. When she lowered to her knees and replaced his hand with her own, he whispered, "Livvy."

That was enough to convince her this was the right choice. The genuine desire in his voice, in his eyes as she looked up at him and stuck out her tongue to taste him.

His fingers went to her hair. She took him in her mouth as far as she could. Over and over, she bobbed, his grip on her hair tightening as he began fucking her face.

"Baby, if you don't stop, I'm going to come right now."

She paused long enough to say, "That's kind of the point, *baby*."

He smirked, and she suddenly wanted that mouth on hers more than anything. Well, more than almost anything.

Standing up, she nodded in understanding and consent. "I want you inside of me."

"Thank fuck." He gripped her hips. "Don't move; I'll grab a condom."

She held on to his arm. "I'm clean and on the pill."

Visibly swallowing, he said, "I'm clean too. I don't hook up often, especially since Harper and Elliot moved in. But they're exactly why I don't take the chance. I know what an unplanned pregnancy looks like, and I—"

Olivia nodded, interrupting his rambling. "I get it."

Kissing her cheek, he jumped out of the tub and didn't even bother wrapping a towel around him as he left to get a condom, presumably from his bedroom.

"Fuck!"

Olivia pulled the shower curtain aside in time to find him gripping the doorframe. He'd clearly almost slipped and fell in his rush to get back. She was still laughing when he shut the door and ripped open the foil as he joined her again.

"Shut up," he whispered, rolling the condom on.

She shook her head and twisted her arms up around his neck. Standing on her toes, she pulled him down to kiss him. He stepped closer, pushing her back against the cold wall.

"I want you," she whispered as she raised a palm to his cheek.

His answering smile brightened the room. He lifted her up, and she wrapped her legs around his waist. She was already wet for him, but the water would help too. Holding her, he shifted his hips to rub his erection along her slick entrance. Back and forth.

"Wyatt." She needed him now.

"Uh-uh. That's another rule. You might be in charge at the bar, but here? When we're like this?" He kissed the side of her jaw. "I'm in charge, *baby*."

Oh, fuck. She was in so much trouble with this one. Nodding, she silently agreed. She would probably agree to anything he asked right now if it ended the teasing. He pushed against her harder but still wasn't inside her.

"Are you going to be a good girl and let me have control

for once?" His lips brushed the other side of her neck as his tip pressed into her.

She tried to wiggle, needing to relieve this building pressure, but it was no use. "Fine! Yes. The control is yours. I just need more. Now."

"Ask nicely."

"I hate you," she hissed.

Wyatt chuckled and pulled out of her, making her whimper.

"Okay, fine. Please, Wyatt?"

"Please, what?" he asked, pushing an inch or so into her.

A shudder ran down her spine. "Please make me come. Fuck me until I see stars or I'm screaming your name, whichever happens first."

Slowly, he thrust all the way into her, stretching her, filling her. "Oh, sweetheart. It's hilarious that you think it's an either-or-situation." He leaned in to whisper against her ear, "You'll be screaming my name *while* you see the stars, Livvy."

As he began moving, he finally—*finally*—brought his mouth to hers, devouring her with the most perfect kiss.

TWENTY-ONE

Wyatt

Wyatt had never been one to have *friends*. At least, not in the sense that he chilled with people outside of work, or school back in the day. Yet, here he was, standing in Aiden Barnes's apartment, drinking a beer with the man and his brother.

"I don't understand why we're arguing about this," Aaron said, leaning on the bar top across from the kitchen sink. The open window in the wall peeked from the living room to here, lending the appearance of a bigger space.

"Because you're stubborn and won't admit I'm right," Aiden said, as if it were simple.

To be honest, Wyatt didn't even remember what they were fighting over. He couldn't stop thinking about Livvy in the shower the day before. The way she'd responded to his touch, gasping his name.

"Right, Wyatt?"

He snapped his attention to his friends. "Um... what?"

Aiden chuckled and shook his head as his younger brother asked, "What's got you so distracted?"

"His new boss." Aiden took a pull of his beer. "Elyse said she saw you two leaving the bar together the other night."

"It wasn't like that." Not at first, at least. "She was

upset, and I didn't think it was a good idea for her to drive home like that."

Aaron smirked. "So, you didn't take her to your house and cook her waffles the next morning?"

"Dammit, Harper." He sighed and ran a hand over his hair. His sister had a big mouth. "Fine. Yes, I did."

"And?"

"And what?" Wyatt set his empty bottle on the counter. Opening the fridge, he searched for ingredients out of habit. He needed something to occupy his hands. Grabbing the eggs and butter, he silently thanked Charlie for making Aiden stock his kitchen. She'd bought items specifically for this reason when he started hanging out here more and more. As he searched for a few other ingredients in the cabinets, as well as a mixing bowl, he gave in. "We've been... fooling around a little bit this past week. It's not a big deal."

"You're sleeping with your boss?" Aiden brought him some measuring cups without needing to be asked. They might not have been friends long, but Wyatt had to admit it was nice having someone who got him. He hated explaining that baking helped his anxiety.

"Sounds like a pretty big deal," Aaron said.

Wyatt shook his head and began pouring dry ingredients together. "Not until yesterday. Before that it was just... I don't know what it was. She's so cold and infuriating ninety-five percent of the time."

"And the other five percent?" Aiden asked.

She's choking on my dick. He couldn't say that though. Instead, he shrugged and said, "She's different."

Glancing over his shoulder, Wyatt saw the brothers share a look. One he didn't want to understand or accept. He knew he was in deep with Livvy, but it didn't mean anything. It never would.

"We're just using each other to relieve some tension," he said. "That's it. We figured it's better than constantly arguing."

"Right." Aaron stood and rounded the wall to stand in the kitchen doorway.

"I'm serious," Wyatt said, mixing the cookie dough a little harder than necessary. "I've been down that road before. Never again. I don't care how fucking beautiful she is or how good she—It's not happening."

Aiden went to grab another beer and handed it over. "Bad ex?"

Wyatt narrowed his eyes. "The worst."

"That doesn't mean this woman's going to be the same."

"You're right; she'd be worse," he conceded. Then, he realized what he was admitting. "I mean because she's so distant and... and..."

"And because you've already fallen harder for her than the other one?" Aaron asked.

Shit. He had. And it would hurt so much more when this ended badly. He could already tell. Somehow, Livvy had found a way into his heart. "Fuck."

The Barnes brothers laughed behind him, and Aiden clapped him on the shoulder. "Welcome to the club, man."

"I can't be here." Wyatt turned to face them both. "Not again."

The front door opened before he could say more. Charlie waltzed in, oblivious to the conversation she'd interrupted. She hadn't even looked up to notice them as she kicked off her shoes and dropped her purse on the coffee table. Walking toward the hall, she reached for the bottom of her shirt. "Aiden, you better be in that bed. It's been a long day, and I want to try out our new—"

"Charlotte," her boyfriend cut her off, pushing past

Aaron to grab her by the waist and stop her from stripping. "We have company."

Her eyes rounded at the sight of Wyatt and Aaron in the kitchen. "Oh, um..."

Aaron shook his head, no doubt tired of their nonsense. Wyatt didn't know how the three lived together after everything, but they seemed to make it work. When Aaron left Charlie at the altar this past spring, after dating since high school, she was devastated. But it turned out the older brother had been in love with her all along, and she felt the same, which Aaron knew. He was stepping aside so they could be together, but he didn't tell them why exactly. The whole situation was messy, but they'd all moved on and were happy now. Aaron had even moved in with Aiden. But if Wyatt had to guess, he wouldn't be here much longer, especially with Charlie spending most nights here. How could he? Living with his brother and ex-fiancée had to be difficult. Especially in times like this.

Clearing her throat, Charlie said, "I thought you were heading to Summersville for the weekend, Aaron."

"I am. I just haven't left yet." He shrugged. "I'm grabbing pizza for Lars and the girls on the way."

She nodded. "Gotcha. And Wyatt, it's nice to see you."

He laughed; he couldn't help it. "No, it's not. It's fine. I get it. Let me just wrap up this cookie dough that you can make later, and then you two can try out whatever new toy you got."

Her face turned a deeper red. Aaron groaned and walked out of the kitchen, yelling, "I'm leaving now."

"You don't want to hear what they got?" Wyatt teased.

"I hear enough, thank you very much," he called from down the hallway. He reappeared a moment later with a bag and headed toward the front door. "I'll text before coming home tomorrow. If you do anything in a room that's not your own, clean it up and never tell me."

They all chuckled as he slammed out of the apartment.

"Glad to see that's going well," Wyatt said.

"Some days are better than others." Aiden wrapped Charlie in a hug from behind. "He may have walked in on us last week in a... compromising position."

Wyatt was curious as to how compromising. The couple seemed so calm and collected beyond these walls, but he knew they were adventurous in the bedroom—and other places—because of the little things Charlie had let slip in the past. He didn't dare ask questions this time though. He just turned and started looking for plastic wrap. Charlie moved closer, opened a drawer, and pulled out a box of it. "What's wrong? Why'd you make cookies?"

"He's freaking out because he's in love with Olivia," Aiden said oh-so-helpfully.

"I'm not in love with her." Wyatt scooped the cookie dough onto the wrap. "I've known her for less than a month."

Charlie snatched a piece of dough and popped it into her mouth. "A lot can happen in a month. Trust me."

Sighing, he faced his closest friend. "That's not fair. You and Aiden had known each other your whole lives; it's not the same."

"Fine, but I stand by the statement." Putting a hand on his arm, she said in a gentler tone, "She's not Loren."

He knew that. Honestly, he did. But it was so hard to separate his ex who'd destroyed his heart from the rest of the world. She'd made him a pessimist, a loner, someone who would rather fight on his own than chance being hurt again.

As if sensing where his thoughts had gone, Charlie

wrapped her arms around his middle. Smiling, he returned the embrace.

"I know it's hard to let someone in after that, but you'll be miserable the rest of your life if you don't even try," she whispered.

Hugging her close, he nodded in agreement. He knew it was the truth. Hell, just thinking about locking out Livvy forever made his chest ache.

For too many years, he'd sat by in this town, acting like it wasn't his. He spent his time working at a job he didn't care for and keeping everyone away out of fear.

But he longed for so much more in this life.

And maybe, he could start by letting Livvy in.

TWENTY-TWO

olivia

There were no words to accurately describe Olivia's exhaustion. She stared up at her dark ceiling, thankful for blackout curtains. Once again, Ryan had called out, so she had stepped in last night to help. She took back everything she'd ever thought about things being boring around here. She would give anything for boring right now.

Rolling over, she grabbed her phone from the bedside table. It was almost eleven in the morning, which she'd always considered late. But after closing and cleaning up the bar, she hadn't made it home until after two, and of course, she couldn't fall asleep immediately. Not with thoughts of a certain bartender running on a loop in her head.

He hadn't been at work last night either, and try as she might, she couldn't help but miss him. The way he took charge and handled situations. The way his strong arms would sometimes cage her in on the pretense of reaching for something and then press up against her just enough to remind her that she had now seen every inch of that glorious body.

It had been over a week since their rendezvous in the shower, but she couldn't stop thinking about it. She couldn't stop wishing Wyatt would just grab her one day, drag her into the office or a fucking storage closet, and have his way with her.

She groaned and pulled her pillow over her face. Feeling like a lovesick teenager was not part of her plan. She was here to save her dad's bar; that was it. Once she did that, she would be out of here. There was a reason she'd picked a big-city school. She didn't want to be stuck in a small town the rest of her life. Especially this one.

Olivia tossed her pillow aside and climbed out of bed. She needed to get up and go about her day, not lie around dreaming of a man she'd known for mere weeks. Even if it was the best sex she'd ever had.

Deciding she needed a good run to rid herself of this tension thrumming through her, she changed into a sports bra and leggings, tied her hair into a high ponytail, and slipped on her tennis shoes. She grabbed the armband for her phone from a drawer then put in earbuds. Her dad was sitting in his recliner when she went out to the living room, and she bent to kiss his cheek.

"Morning, sweetheart," he said with a smile that warmed her heart. A good day, then. He still refused to leave the house, but he seemed in better spirits than when she first arrived. It was progress. She could almost believe he was returning to the man he was before her mom's accident.

"Good morning. Do you need anything before I go for a run?"

He shook his head and pointed to the little table beside him. "Angela set me up. I have my coffee, water, and remote. I'm fine for a while."

She needed to do something for Angela. There was no way Olivia could do all this on her own. "I'll be back to make us lunch. Or I can bring us something. Feel like anything special?"

"You know I'd never turn down pizza."

With a chuckle, she grabbed her hoodie from the front closet to tie around her waist. "Sounds good. I'll grab some on my way back."

"Be careful," he said, just as he always did.

"Love you."

She headed out into the morning sunlight. Turning on her running playlist, she stretched her arms and legs, and then she was off.

Her feet pounded along the sidewalk in time to the beat for one block, two, three. To keep from thinking about Wyatt, she started mentally listing her five-year plan.

First, she needed to save The Tavern. She had to find a way to turn the numbers around before it completely went under.

Second, her dad needed full-time care, even if he denied it. Which meant he needed better insurance.

Actually, this should be number one, she thought.

Next, she would convince him to sell the bar, or at least a portion of it, to someone who knew what they were doing. In reality, this would help with the first two, but she knew bringing a partner onto an already-sinking ship would be nearly impossible. The only option would likely be an investor or businessperson who would want to change everything. And despite her own initial plans to do the same, she now understood what this place meant to the people of this town. To her father, who put his life and soul into it.

So, this part of the plan would wait. But once that was settled, she would return to Chicago or another city to find a job that valued her skills.

The problem was, she didn't know what that job should be. Her entire life, she had been a planner. She'd scheduled her life down to the minute and had known since she was in middle school that she wanted a business degree. But she never got past that. She never figured out exactly what she wanted to do with it. Every time she pictured herself in the future, she was this bigshot businesswoman, living in a high-rise apartment downtown in a big city with a husband and two-point-five kids. In those visions, she had everything she wanted. Except, the job was always fuzzy. It was too vague.

A car stopped in front of her as she waited on the corner to cross the next street, and her brow furrowed. She'd been so lost in her thoughts that she hadn't realized she'd made it to Main Street. The passenger window lowered. Olivia turned off her music and pulled out an earbud, thinking they needed directions.

She almost tripped when she finally registered the face staring back at her. "Justin?"

Grinning, he threw his door open and climbed out as she ran around the front of the car. In such a small town, someone stopping like this wasn't a big deal, and she was so grateful. She all but jumped into her best friend's arms.

"I've been driving alongside you, shouting your name," he said when they broke apart.

Oops. "I was in the zone. What are you doing here?"

"I had the day off, so I thought I'd come down and surprise you, maybe take you to lunch." His familiar smile made her homesick. Seeming to sense her shift in demeanor, he said, "Whoa, hey, what's wrong?"

She wrapped her arms around him, resting her head on his shoulder. "I'm really glad you're here. I missed you so much."

"I missed you too." He held her tightly, knowing what

she needed after years of friendship.

They stood like that another minute or two before she pulled away. "We should probably move your car."

He laughed and agreed. "Want a ride home?"

"Sure, but we need to make a stop first." She got into his silver Lexus and pointed him toward the pizza shop down the street. The car should have given it away. It was rare to see one that expensive around here. They walked in and put in an order to go then stood near the windows. Olivia had always loved A Little Slice of Heaven, with its old-fashioned décor that made it look like a restaurant from the fifties.

"How's your dad doing?" Justin asked.

"He has his good days and bad," she said, grateful to have someone here who already knew what was going on. "He'll be excited to see you."

Justin nodded with a smile. "It's been too long since I've seen him."

"You've been busy. He understands that." Her dad had visited them in Chicago once in a while, but Justin hadn't been around the last couple times.

"Still..." After a moment, he said, "And the hot bartender?"

Her cheeks heated, and she lowered her eyes.

"Oh my God," he whispered.

"Don't," she begged, afraid of whatever he saw on her face.

He slipped his hand into hers. "Babe, it's only been a few weeks."

She groaned and leaned in to press her forehead to his upper arm. "I know."

His soft chuckle vibrated through her.

"Liv?" a voice cut in before she could say more.

Her heart halted in her chest. This was not happening. *Please don't be with her. Please don't be with her.*

She slowly turned toward Harper and let out a breath when she realized Wyatt wasn't with her. Except, instead of relief, a tinge of disappointment rang through her. Putting on a smile, she said, "Hey, Harper."

"How's it going?" She glanced at their clasped hands. It was quick, but Olivia still caught it.

"Pretty good. This is my best friend, Justin. He drove down from Chicago to surprise me." Olivia pulled her hand from his as nonchalantly as she could. She didn't know what was going on with Wyatt, but she did know that she didn't want Harper to think she was sleeping around with other men. Not that she thought the woman would judge her.

Harper gave a little wave. "Nice to meet you. Are you staying for long?"

"Um... we haven't really talked about it." He glanced at Olivia. "I was hoping until tomorrow but hadn't invited myself to crash with Liv yet."

"That's fine." Then, because Olivia couldn't stop herself, she added, "There's a spare room you can take anytime."

He raised an eyebrow. Likely wondering why she was being so weird, why she would clarify that they weren't sharing a bed. Especially when they usually did, even after breaking up. A few times, they had hooked up again, but mostly, it was platonic cuddling. Neither liked sleeping alone very much.

"Oh, I was only asking because a bunch of us are getting together this evening. Charlie's parents host these Friday night family dinners, and we're all invading for a cookout since the weather is nice. I was going to say you two should come," Harper said with a look of suspicion. "But if you have other plans—"

"That sounds fun," Olivia blurted.

"You two don't want to avoid—"

"No. It's fine." Was it hot in here? She was starting to sweat.

Justin shifted beside her, crossing his arms. "Okay, what the hell is going on?"

Olivia sighed. "This is Harper... Wyatt's sister."

"Wyatt?" His eyes widened. "Oh!" His confusion turned to amusement. "*Ohh.* So, I get to meet the guy you're—"

"Yes," she said, hoping he'd stop.

Of course, he didn't. He leaned against one of the beams near the wall and asked Harper, "Do you know what's going on with them? Getting anything from this one is almost impossible."

"Justin," Olivia hissed.

Harper laughed. "Not really. My brother's just as stubborn and won't share his feelings. But I think they're both falling hard."

Olivia's eyes snapped to her new friend. "You think he's falling hard?"

"I do," she said with a knowing look. Like she could see exactly how much Olivia both wanted that and dreaded it. "But he's been so guarded since his ex really messed him up. He doesn't let anyone in."

He let me. Or started to, at least.

This was getting too serious. She wasn't supposed to know this, feel this. It didn't fit into her plan, and that scared the shit out of her. There was no denying the fluttering in her stomach though. It was one thing for her to ignore her own growing attachment and move on after the bar was taken care of. But if Wyatt was feeling the same...

She didn't want to hurt him.

So, where did that leave her?

"What do you think? Dinner tonight?" Harper asked.

She took a deep breath and nodded. "Yeah. We'll be there."

TWENTY-THREE

wyatt

Wyatt really wasn't in the mood for a big dinner with all his friends, but Charlie had convinced him it was the first time they could all be together since Aiden's mother had returned from her road trip painting around the country. Charlie had gone with her for a good portion of the summer, but she had come back in August while Ms. Barnes continued for another two months. It was strange how much he missed Charlie during those weeks she was gone. That was when it hit him how important she was in his life. So, for her, he would do this.

He stared at the wall across from the couch, trying to get the motivation to stand and leave. That was usually his biggest hurdle—just getting out of the house. Most of the time, once he made it to where he was going, he was fine.

Then, there were the days when he would rather do just about anything other than be around people. Today was one of those days.

Eventually, he forced himself out to his truck and drove over to Charlie's parents' house, where he faced the same dilemma of not wanting to get out and join everyone. It didn't matter if it was only a small gathering of his friends and family. He still didn't want to be here. He had no desire to put on a smile and talk.

Groaning, he climbed out of the truck and slowly made

his way past all the other cars in the driveway. It seemed like everyone else was already here. Music and laughter came from the backyard, so he went around the side of the nice two-story home. He loved the Powells' house, with its dark gray-blue siding, white accents, and stonework along the base. The landscaping was so clean and vibrant, reminding him of what one would see in a magazine. It even had the cliché white picket fence around the decent-sized yard. Wyatt longed to have a home like this someday. His tiny two-bedroom had seen better days, and while it had been fine when it was just him, it was way too small for him, Harper, and Elliot. He wanted to have plenty of space for them *and* his future family.

He stilled at the corner of the house. *Where the hell had that thought come from?*

Sure, once upon a time, he had dreamed of settling down and having kids of his own. But when Loren left and shattered his heart, she'd taken those wishes with her.

Elliot's giggles pulled him back to the present. Stepping forward, he peeked around the house to prepare himself for everyone. Charlie's dad stood at the grill, talking to Vi. Charlie sat on Aiden's lap at the picnic table with Aaron, their mothers, and another man Wyatt didn't recognize. Harper was nowhere in sight.

The scene was so warm and welcoming, everyone enjoying this nice fall day, but what held his attention was his nephew. Or rather, the woman sitting with him. Livvy—the uptight, never-a-hair-out-of-place ice queen—was on her knees in the grass, playing with Elliot and his plastic dinosaurs. She looked so casual, light. Her smile beamed as Elliot roared and jumped toward her. She caught him and set him on her lap, nodding as he held up his T-Rex and undoubtedly spewed facts at her.

Wyatt couldn't stop staring. She had her dark hair loosely curled and falling over one shoulder, and she wore a sundress. A fucking pink sundress. And she was barefoot, laughing and talking to Elliot, moving around one of his other dinosaurs to make it 'walk'. It was like seeing a whole new side of her.

"Are you going to keep standing there like a creeper or join us?" his sister said, appearing beside him.

He jumped at her voice. He'd been so focused on Livvy and Elliot that he hadn't even seen Harper walking toward him. "I'm not a creeper," he mumbled as he followed her to the others.

"Uncle Wyatt!" Elliot ran at him, and Wyatt lifted him into his arms. "Livia is playing dinosaurs with me."

"I see that," he said with a chuckle at the mispronunciation of her name. Elliot always made him feel at least a little bit better.

The stranger from the picnic table stood and offered Livvy a hand, pulling her to her feet. When he playfully brushed grass off the back of her dress and she grinned at him, Wyatt clenched his jaw. Who was this guy? They were clearly familiar with one another. He was still holding her hand.

She finally turned toward Wyatt, and her smile softened. Much to his chagrin, Harper took Elliot and went to chat with Vi, leaving him without anything to occupy his hands. Livvy moved closer with the blond guy in tow. "Hi."

"Hey." Wyatt shot a look at her friend then down at their joined hands.

She immediately withdrew hers. "This is my best friend, Justin. Justin, this is Wyatt, my..."

When she trailed off, Wyatt met her gaze. "Employee."

"And friend," she added.

He raised a brow. Was she finally admitting as much?

"Ahh, *this* is the infamous Wyatt," Justin said, amusement clear in his tone that sounded familiar. He stuck out a hand.

Wyatt reluctantly shook it. "You were the one she was talking to that day on the phone. You told her to..."

"You're welcome." The man laughed. "Though, I admit, I didn't think it would lead to all of... whatever the hell it is you two are doing."

"Okay, I think that's enough." Livvy elbowed him in the side. "Why don't you go see if you can help with the food."

"Fine. Fine. I can take a hint." He walked off, shaking his head and leaving them somewhat alone.

Wyatt was distinctly aware of how quiet the others had become. When he glanced at the picnic table, all but Charlie quickly acted as if they were having a conversation. She winked at him before joining in. Wyatt cleared his throat, trying to figure out what to say to his boss—the woman he hadn't stopped thinking about in weeks.

She beat him to it. "How have you been?"

It had only been two days since they saw each other at work, but it felt like longer. He hated that he'd missed her. "Fine." After a beat, he added, "You?"

"I'm okay."

They stood in awkward silence for a moment before both trying to talk again at the same time.

"Go ahead," he said, wishing he knew what to do with his hands. He crossed his arms.

"I was just going to explain that we ran into Harper earlier, and she invited us," Livvy said, her own fingers tapping against her thigh. "I hope this is okay."

He jerked his eyes back up to hers, realizing he was staring at her bare legs. "Yeah. Of course."

"Liv, you want cheese on your burger?" Justin called over.

She turned and nodded.

"So, your friend..." Wyatt said in a hushed tone, unable to contain the ridiculous jealousy flowing through him.

Livvy faced him. The corner of her lips twitched, as if she knew what he was thinking. "Yes?"

He didn't want to say it, didn't want to ask. So, instead, he said, "Never mind. I'm gonna grab a drink. Want anything?"

"A water, please."

Without another word, he headed to the cooler by the backdoor. He lifted the lid and pulled out two water bottles, but he hesitated to return. This entire situation made him want to leave even more. He had no right to be jealous. It wasn't like he and Livvy were dating or anything. They fooled around a few times; that was it.

But why the fuck would she bring another man, knowing Wyatt would be here?

Thoroughly pissed off, he returned to the group. He handed her one of the drinks in silence before going to the extra folding table that had been set up for more seating. Sitting in the farthest chair from everyone, he cracked open his bottle and gulped down some of the cold water. He was picking at the label when someone took a spot next to him.

He couldn't look up.

"Wyatt?" A hand covered his, and he froze. He'd expected his sister to come berate him or Charlie to comfort him.

The last person he expected to approach, especially so gently, was *her*.

"What's wrong?" Livvy whispered.

"Nothing." He still wouldn't raise his eyes.

She scooted closer. "Liar. Talk to me."

"I don't want to." He sounded like a damn child throwing a fit. He knew that, but he couldn't stop. His mood had gone from bad to worse.

"Why?" She squeezed his hand.

Wyatt finally lifted his gaze as he said under his breath, "Because I don't want to talk to *anyone* right now. Especially the woman I'm sleeping with, who brought another man to dinner with *my* fucking friends."

To her credit, she didn't flinch away from the harsh words. But she had always gone toe to toe with him without blinking.

She stared at him for a long minute. Then, she stood and walked away. To Justin.

Wyatt grit his teeth as he tried to steady his breathing, but his chest heaved. His anxiety built, overwhelming him. He was certain that at any second, he would explode.

"Hey." Charlie took the chair Livvy had vacated. "What's going on?"

He shook his head, the words caught in his throat. *I shouldn't have come here.*

"What do you need?" Concern filled her blue eyes. "Wyatt?"

He opened his mouth and closed it. The others were watching him now. He could feel their stares like a spotlight.

Someone grabbed his hand. "Come with me."

Wyatt stood and followed, even as his vision blurred. They made it to the driveway, to his truck, and he leaned against the passenger door. Where was his water? Had he dropped it? Why was it so hot?

"Breathe," a voice said a second before the person gripped both sides of his face. "Look at me."

He met dark chocolate eyes, and his heart beat faster. He shook his head again.

"Wyatt, I need you to breathe." Livvy took one of his hands and placed it on her chest. "With me. In. Out."

He mirrored her, but his breath stuttered unevenly.

"Good. Do it again," she said. "Just breathe, baby."

It was the nickname that finally brought him down enough to focus. He wrapped his other arm around her and hugged her to him, leaning in to bury his face against the side of her neck. The scent of her lavender shampoo filled his senses. She held on to him tightly, whispering soothing words.

He didn't know how long they stood like that. It could've been minutes or hours. At some point, she asked for his keys, guided him into the passenger seat, and climbed in to drive him home. The next thing he knew, he was sitting on his bed with Livvy handing him a glass of water. He took a drink, then another, before setting it on the nightstand.

When she sat beside him, he whispered, "It wasn't because of—"

"I know."

With a deep, steady breath, he looked at her. "How?"

"Because you looked miserable walking into the backyard," she said. "I knew something was off."

"You... you could tell that? I was trying to hide it." He'd been smiling, holding his nephew. How had she known?

She licked her lips. "I saw it in your eyes. You didn't want to be there."

How could this woman understand him so well? "No, I didn't. But I told Harper I'd go, and she's always insisting that the more I do, the easier it'll get."

"That's not how anxiety works," Livvy said with a sad tilt to her head.

"I know." He wanted it to work that way, but it didn't. "How did you know what to do to help me?"

"Because I get that way too. Not often, but I do. I was diagnosed with generalized anxiety in middle school."

"High school," he said, lifting a hand. "Social anxiety."

"And you still manage to work in a bar?"

He nodded. There were always days when it was near unbearable to be around others. When the world was just too much. Even with his meds, the bad days didn't fully disappear. They became more manageable. They made it possible to work. But they didn't get rid of the struggle altogether.

"I know it's not my place, but have you tried therapy?"

He shook his head.

"Maybe that's something to consider?"

He didn't bother telling her he couldn't afford it. Definitely not while supporting his sister and Elliot as she worked part time. Not that he wanted her to go out and work more. He loved being able to help her get on her feet.

Livvy slipped her hand into his, entwining their fingers and drawing him back to the present. "Either way, I'm here if you want to talk."

"Thanks... but talking is kind of the issue right now. I... I can't..."

"That's fine," she said. "We don't have to talk. Do you want me to leave? Do you need to be alone?"

Yes. That was what he'd wanted from the start—to be alone, left to hermit until it passed. But the second he nodded again and she stood, he wanted to take it back.

"No, wait." He jumped up and reached for her. When

she faced him, he whispered, "Stay. Please. I... I do need quiet alone time, but... I want you to stay."

She stepped closer.

"Unless you need to get back to blondie." He couldn't keep the words in.

A snort escaped her, and she slapped a hand over her mouth and nose. The noise broke through the tense moment, making him chuckle, which should have been impossible right now. He gently took her wrist and lowered her hand to see her grinning.

"Justin is only a friend." She closed the last of the space between them. "We do have a past." He must have made a face because she added, "But we decided we were better as friends a while ago. Nothing is going on with us. I promise."

"You don't owe me an explanation," he managed to say.

At that, her smile softened. "I know, but I wanted you to know."

Before he could second guess himself, he pressed a kiss to her forehead. She sighed in his arms.

"It hasn't been this bad in a while," he said, hugging her.

"You don't owe me an explanation," she mirrored his sentiment, and he smiled against the top of her head.

He ran a hand along her back, content to stand here in silence with her forever.

After a few moments passed, she whispered, "Want to watch a movie? I can order us food. No talking necessary."

How much he wanted that terrified him. He was getting far too attached to this woman. But instead of pushing her away like his brain screamed for him to do, he nodded and kissed her temple. "Sounds perfect, *baby*."

TWENTY-FOUR

olivia

Olivia nearly slipped on whatever had spilled on the floor as she rushed to grab the bottle of tequila. She caught herself, pausing to take a deep breath before returning to the task at hand. Thankfully, she hadn't been carrying an open drink yet.

She made a margarita for one customer and then grabbed a beer for the next. Once again, they were slammed. Ryan had come in though, so she was grateful. He was really good at this when he managed to make it, but even with him and Becca, they struggled to keep up tonight.

"What can I get you?" she asked the next person before even looking. When she did, she smiled. "Hi."

Wyatt shook his head with a grin. "Need some help?"

"Please."

His eyes widened, and she remembered the first time this happened. She'd been so determined to say no. Now, she didn't even bother pretending she didn't need him.

"Shut up," she said, turning to another patron.

Wyatt laughed as he rounded the bar. They worked in tandem, side by side. He made it better, not just by helping them serve faster but by being his usual charming self. It was like a switch had been flipped since the other day. Seeing him have a full-blown panic attack had scared the shit out of her, but as soon as she realized what was happening, she knew he needed to get out of there. Justin had understood, insisting it was fine to leave him at the cookout with a bunch of strangers. She still felt guilty about that, which was the *only* reason she had eventually gone home that night. She and Wyatt had sat in his bed, watching movies and eating, curled up together for hours. Nothing more had happened. And despite worrying about them growing too close, she enjoyed simply being with him when they weren't fighting and they could ignore the rest of the world for a little bit.

She glanced at him now, wondering how he worked this job when struggling like that.

"Why are you staring at me?" he asked without even glancing her way.

"I'm not." She went back to serving.

Wyatt stepped behind her and leaned down to grab a new towel, using the movement to run a hand along her hip. When he straightened, he said against her ear, "Liar."

She couldn't help but chuckle. Rolling her eyes, she bumped him backward so she could continue working. She headed toward a man who looked to be in his thirties and asked for his order. Of course, he wanted some drink she'd never even heard of. She pulled out her phone to Google it.

"Seriously?" he said. "You're checking your phone now?"

"I was looking up your drink."

"You're a bartender and you don't know basic cocktails?" he scoffed.

She shoved her phone in her pocket. "Actually, I'm not a bartender. I'm the owner's daughter trying to help out, and I think we're done here."

Needing a break, she walked away, not caring if he had to wait a while for one of the others. She went out to collect empty glasses and bottles instead. That was easy not to mess up.

Before she could reach the first table, the rude customer blocked her path.

"Why the hell did you walk away when I was ordering?"

"Because I don't serve assholes who speak to me like that." She crossed her arms and stared down her nose at him, which was difficult because he stood almost a foot taller than her, but she'd become a master at it.

He looked at her like she was nothing more than dirt beneath his shoes. "You're the owner of this place? How the fuck is it still open?"

Olivia Cartwright was not easy to intimidate. Hell, she used to walk home at night downtown Chicago without fear. At least, most nights. But this hulking man had a menacing look about him, and despite not being served yet, he already reeked of alcohol. When he took a step forward, she moved back.

She didn't want to need a man's help, but she started looking for Wyatt. The moment she turned, the guy grabbed her by the arm.

"I'm not done talking to you." The corner of his mouth curling in disgust.

"Yes, you are." Owen appeared, angling between them until the man released her. Olivia hadn't even known he was here tonight.

Ryan approached from the other side. "Let's go. You're done here."

When the guy tried to argue, both men reached for him. He fought against them as they dragged him out the front door.

Becca moved closer and gently touched Olivia's wrist. "You okay?"

She stared in shock at her employees. The ones she always yelled at, who seemed to hate her. The woman who'd been her closest friend before Olivia destroyed everything. Nodding, she said, "Yes."

"Come on." Becca led her behind the bar again, where Wyatt immediately wrapped her in a hug. The bar had hushed with people watching the commotion.

"I'm sorry. I didn't see him until the others were already taking care of it," he said against her hair before he released her enough to look at her arm.

It was fine; she didn't think it would bruise or anything. Her heart still raced though.

"Here." Becca twisted open a water bottle and offered it to her.

Olivia took a sip, letting the coolness calm her. "Thank you."

The others returned with looks of concern aimed at her.

"I..." She didn't know what to say. "I thought you hated me. Why would you step in like that?"

Ryan's brow furrowed. "We don't hate you."

"You call me Ice Queen."

Wyatt chuckled beside her. Shawn, who'd come from the kitchen to see what the commotion was, said, "Yeah, but you're *our* Ice Queen."

Without another word, he kissed Becca on the cheek then returned to the back. She glanced around at the others. Ryan returned to work, and Owen gave her a smile with a nod toward Wyatt as he took over serving. As if it were that simple.

Only Becca and Wyatt remained with her.

"Come on, let's take a break." Wyatt held her hand and

led her to the office, with Becca following. He shut the door that muffled the noise. Her hands still shook, so she crossed her arms and leaned against the edge of the desk. He moved to stand in front of her. "Are you okay?"

"Yeah. He scared me more than anything."

Lifting a hand to her cheek, Wyatt brushed a thumb across her skin. "We'll make sure he never returns."

"Why?"

"What do you mean? The guy was a dick," Becca said, reminding them she was in the room. "And I didn't recognize him, so I don't think he's from around here anyway."

"No." She shook her head and stepped from Wyatt. "I mean, why did Owen and Ryan step in?"

Becca shrugged. "You heard Shawn. You're *our* Ice Queen."

"Okay, but why did *you* come to me?"

"I..." She glanced at Wyatt.

With a start, Olivia realized Becca didn't want to air out their dirty laundry in front of him. As if Becca wanted to spare her.

"Give us a minute?" Olivia asked him.

"Of course."

As soon as he left, she did the one thing she should have done eight years ago. "I'm sorry. About Kevin. About everything."

Becca stared at her for a moment before sitting on the arm of the nearest chair. "I don't care about Kevin. Before you moved back, I hadn't thought of him in years. Believe it or not, I got over him pretty quickly. What I couldn't get over was you betraying me, lying about it, and then running away."

"I'm sorry," she repeated.

"Why did you do it? You gave us your blessing to date

after the two of you broke up, so why did you start sleeping with him again?"

Olivia lowered her gaze to her feet. The truth was, there was no excuse for what she did. She knew that now. "It was the night of my mom's funeral the first time I went back to him."

"No, you don't get to do that." Becca stood with a huff. "You don't get to pull the dead-mom card to get out of this."

It wasn't funny. This was not a funny conversation. And yet, Olivia couldn't stop the laugh from bubbling up. She covered her mouth and looked at her former friend. "Sorry, I'm not—this isn't funny. I just... I worked so hard to be perfect my entire life, but the truth is I'm a fucking mess, Becca."

Becca's glare softened.

"I'm not using her death as an excuse. I just wanted to explain that my life was falling apart, and I had no idea what to do. We'd just buried my mom, my dad was basically a zombie, and my asshole uncle was making horrible j-jokes about the accident being her f-fault." She couldn't stop the hysteria at this point. "I took off. I had no idea where to go, and I... I made one of the worst mistakes of my life because I was desperate to feel something other than grief and depression. For one night, I didn't want to feel like it should've been me in that grave instead."

"Liv, what..." Becca grabbed her forearms, and Olivia realized she was picking at her fingers. "What are you talking about? Why did you think it should've been you?"

She couldn't breathe. It was too much. That day came flooding back, and she collapsed to the floor. Becca lowered with her, shouting something. She pulled Olivia into her arms.

No, those weren't her arms. Through tear-blurred vision, she met Wyatt's gaze.

"It was supposed to be me," Olivia managed to whisper.

"Why?" *Becca.* She was still here, holding her hand.

Closing her eyes, she said, "She was driving because of me. My dad was home and needed milk for his stupid fucking waffles, and I threw a fit when he asked me to run to the store to get some. I didn't even have a reason; I just didn't want to go. We started arguing about it, and all I remember is him yelling at me because he worked so hard to take care of us. He kept saying things about me being old enough to help out once in a while, but I kept fighting him."

Wyatt ran his fingers over her hair and pressed a kiss to the top of her head. She wondered briefly if he was thinking about how much the two of them fought when she first arrived. Somewhere in the back of her mind, she knew she should also be concerned about Becca seeing them like this, but she couldn't bring herself to care.

She swallowed past the lump forming in her throat. "My mom had been at the church, helping set things up for an event, and she came home to find us shouting. Of course, she stepped in and said she would run out and get it. She told me to go to my room until she returned, but sh-she..."

"She didn't return," Becca whispered.

"It was my fault." Olivia sobbed, pulling her hand away to cover her face. "I lost her, and I lost my dad because he blamed me. After the funeral, I took off. I drove around for a while until I ended up at ... the outlook point near Summersville."

"Olivia." Becca moved closer, hugging her even while she sat in Wyatt's arms. "Why didn't you call me?"

"Because I knew you'd talk me out of it." Remembering that night was more painful than anything. "But instead of driving over the edge like I'd considered, I drove to Kevin's house. I think a part of me hoped you would be there, but another part knew that by going to him, I would lose you. I lied to you because I... I wanted to be caught, to be yelled at."

Becca let out a breath. "You wanted to be punished."

Olivia nodded. "It's still not an excuse. I will never be able to apologize enough, but you deserved the truth."

"Does anyone know?" Wyatt asked in a hushed tone.

"Not all of it. Justin knows bits and pieces, but not the full story." She finally opened her eyes. To her surprise, Becca had tears running down her face too. Olivia sniffled. "I ruined my life because I didn't deserve to be happy."

"That is such... bullshit," Becca said. "Liv, it wasn't your fault."

"Yes, it was. If I hadn't—"

Becca lifted a hand to cover Olivia's mouth. "No, it's my turn. Your mom's accident was *not* your fault. I don't care if you specifically told her to drive down that road at that time; you did not *cause* the accident."

"She's right." Wyatt tightened his hold on her.

"But—"

"You couldn't have known," Becca continued. "If you had somehow been able to read the future and knew someone wouldn't stop at that intersection, you never would have let your mom leave, right?"

"Yeah, but—"

"No buts. You loved your mom. And she loved you more than anything in this world. Why do you think she insisted on going to end the fucking argument? She hated seeing you upset." Becca brushed Olivia's tears away with soft fingers. "What you did to me was shitty. What you did to yourself was worse. You asked why I came to you when that guy grabbed you?"

Olivia nodded, speechless.

"Because you were my best friend for most of our lives. If you would have just explained what happened, I would have forgiven you immediately." She rolled her eyes at herself. "Well, maybe not *immediately*. I mean, you slept with my boyfriend. But it wouldn't have taken long, especially if I knew why you did it."

"Livvy, did your dad actually say he blamed you?" Wyatt rubbed her back.

Sighing, she shook her head before resting it on his shoulder.

Becca's eyes widened as she glanced back and forth between them, the corner of her mouth twitching like she was fighting a smile. "He calls you Livvy." Only she would know how significant that was. Instead of commenting on it further, she said, "I forgive you, Liv. That's the other reason I went to you tonight. I... I'd like to try to move on. Maybe start over?"

Olivia could have cried again. She didn't deserve that.

"This asshole reminded me that it was a long time ago." She pointed at Wyatt. "Besides, I'm happy with Shawn and my life."

She didn't know what to say. "I... I'm not staying. Once I figure things out with the bar, I'm returning to Chicago."

Becca looked at her like she'd grown a second head. "So? That's only a couple hours away, and there is this crazy new thing called technology that makes it easy for people to talk while separated. We can still be friends."

"You're one of us now, no matter what." Wyatt kissed her temple. "We're a team here, a family."

Olivia clenched her jaw as the back of her throat

burned. She stared up at him, held his dark gaze. Why was he so infuriatingly perfect? Guys like this weren't supposed to exist in real life. Why did she have to find him now? Here?

"Livvy?" Wyatt whispered when she hadn't responded for a moment.

"I'd like that." She faced Becca again and took a deep breath. Blinking back more tears, she said, "It wasn't supposed to be like this."

"What?"

"I wasn't supposed to like it here." Olivia looked from Becca to Wyatt. His smile brightened, only intensifying the fluttering in her stomach.

TWENTY-FIVE

wyatt

The house was dark and quiet when Wyatt walked in. He toed off his shoes and bolted the front door behind him. Harper was asleep on the futon, sprawled out on her stomach with the blanket dangling off the side. He shook his head with a low chuckle as he moved closer. She slept like the dead, but he still tried to be silent as he pulled the blanket up. Out of habit, he brushed her blond hair out of her face. She might have been twenty-two, but she would always be his baby sister.

Heading into the kitchen, he thought about how much lighter he felt today. After his anxiety attack last weekend and then Livvy's breakdown a couple days ago, things have calmed down. They'd fallen into a routine, and everything went a lot smoother now that she wasn't holding all of that in. It still made him sick to think she'd considered ending her life. He never would have suspected she dealt with that.

She was fierce and brave, never taking shit from anyone, but the arrogance was just a front. She needed to talk to her dad. Wyatt was about ready to show up at the man's house and make them have a conversation himself. He also wanted to check on Jack, see if there was anything he could do for him.

Wyatt grabbed a bottle of beer from the fridge and cracked it open before going to his room. Though, he took a detour to poke his head into Elliot's room first. The boy was sound asleep with Zoey curled in a ball next to him.

In his own room, Wyatt took a long pull of his drink then set it on the nightstand. He stripped down to his boxers and sat on the bed with his back to the headboard and his phone in hand. There were two notifications from the Love Hunters app, and he knew both would be offers to hook up somewhere. Probably tonight, despite it being well after one in the morning.

Yet, he didn't open the messages.

He couldn't stop thinking about Livvy. Her confession about how she wasn't supposed to like it here still sat heavy in his heart. He knew she intended to leave, but it hurt all the same.

Everyone always left.

He scrolled through their texts instead of the app he had no desire to check. There weren't many between him and Livvy, mostly just about work, but they'd started becoming more personal the past week.

> Hey, get home all right?

He'd walked her to her car after closing, and then he waited to watch her take off, making sure that creep wasn't waiting to follow her.

ICE QUEEN

> Yep. At home, collapsed in bed lol

Smiling, he tapped her name to change her info before replying.

LIVVY

> You?

Also in bed

He knew that wasn't quite what she meant, but she'd thrown out that detail first.

Three little dots appeared and vanished. He waited, watching as they popped up again and went away. Why wasn't she responding? Or rather, what was she debating on sending?

A dozen ideas flitted through his mind, each dirtier than the last. He started rubbing his cock through his boxers.

The screen switched, startling him.

She was calling. He froze, his heart racing.

Straightening, he slid over the answer button and lifted the phone to his ear. "Hello?"

"Hey," she said in a hushed tone.

When she didn't immediately continue talking, he asked, "Is everything okay?"

"Yeah. Sorry. I just..." She sighed. "I... wanted to hear your voice."

He couldn't help but grin. "So, the bed comment *was* intentional."

"Maybe."

"Livvy."

"Fine, yes."

He lowered his hand to his crotch again. "What are you wearing?"

She snorted over the line. "I can't believe you actually asked me that, Mr. Cliché."

Wyatt groaned and leaned his head back. "I haven't done this in a really long time; I didn't know where to start."

A beat passed before she asked, "What happened with your ex?"

Letting out a long, slow breath, he stopped groping himself and grabbed his drink instead. He took a swig, needing the alcohol to get through this conversation. It was time though. She'd shared her tragic past. His paled in comparison. "All right, I met Loren in college. She was a year ahead of me, and when she graduated, she convinced me to leave school with her. I was three years into a political science degree, and I hated it, so it didn't take that much effort."

"You were studying political science?"

"Yeah. My parents are... to put it nicely, high society snobs."

Livvy made a noise like she was trying to hold back a laugh.

"They were very strict with high expectations." He set his drink aside once more. "I told them for three years that I didn't want to study that anymore, and each time, they said that my only other options were pre-med or pre-law. Otherwise, they wouldn't pay for college, and I wouldn't get the first half of my trust fund until I had a degree. The rest would come after graduate school."

"Oh my God. That's awful. Wait... you were a trust fund kid? Who knew?"

"Yeah, well, in the end, Loren asked me which was more important: love or money."

"And you chose her."

It wasn't a question, but he said, "I chose her. I quit school, and we moved here because she wanted to live in a cute little town—she'd grown up about an hour away. When I lost support from my parents, I had to get a job as quickly as possible. Your dad gave me a chance, despite how unqualified I was." He chuckled at the memory. "You thought *you* were bad the first few days? I was so much worse. I bet I shattered a dozen glasses within a month, but he kept me on, taking the time to teach me."

"I had no idea," Livvy whispered.

"He taught me so much more than how to be a bartender." Wyatt ran a hand over his hair. "I'd grown up extremely sheltered and didn't know how to do anything for myself other than bake, and that was only because I used to sneak into the kitchen back home and help our chef. When Loren decided a month in that this wasn't the life she wanted after all, she left me stranded and on my own. Without your dad, I wouldn't have made it. He literally taught me how to file taxes and do fucking laundry, Livvy."

Livvy was quiet on the other end. She sniffed once, and he wished they were together. He wanted her here in his arms.

"Loren packed up and left, and I waited around, thinking she would come back, but she didn't. And by then, my parents had practically disowned me. They even blamed Harper's pregnancy on my *rebellion*, saying she was acting out because of me."

"What the fuck?" Livvy breathed.

"Yeah," he said with another sigh. "I returned for Elliot's birth, and they were not happy about it. I actually ended up staying with the family of our old nanny. She let me stay in their spare room for a month because she knew I needed to be there for Harper. My parents call now once in a while to catch up—primarily because my mom wants to make sure I'm okay—but we're not close."

He cleared his throat, realizing just how much he was sharing. "But that's not the point of tonight's story. You only wanted to know about my ex. Long story short, I gave up everything only for her to leave me without any real explanation other than the fact that she wasn't happy here. She didn't even ask me if I was or if I wanted to go with her."

"And you haven't let anyone in since."

"Right..." *Until you*, he didn't say.

"Shit. That's... a lot. I'm so sorry."

"It was six years ago. It's stupid to hold on to something like that, but it really messed me up." After a minute, he said, "I know it doesn't compare—"

"No, don't do that. Your pain is valid, Wyatt. Don't brush it off because you think it's less than someone else's struggles," Livvy said, followed by an audible inhale. "God, we're sad."

He cracked a smile. "We really are."

They sat in peaceful silence, just as they had this past weekend in his room. It was crazy to think about it. A couple weeks ago, they were at each other's throat almost nonstop. She'd fired him at least two or three times. But now... "I wish you were here."

It took her a few beats to respond, and when she finally did, her words confused him.

"A big T-shirt and underwear."

"What?" His brow furrowed.

"You asked what I was wearing. A big T-shirt and underwear."

His grin widened; he loved that she knew he needed the subject changed.

"I understand why you're closed off," she went on. "We're on the same page with what we want."

He was starting to doubt that, but he asked, "And what's that?"

"Relief? Something fun without worrying that the other person will want more. I'm not sticking around here, so I don't expect anything you can't give. And you know upfront that I'm not staying, so you won't be hurt when I leave."

Swallowing, he whispered, "Right."

"Wyatt?"

"Hmm?"

"We're still on the same page, right?"

Everything in him screamed that he would regret this down the line, but he agreed. "Yeah. Of course. Just friends with benefits."

"Good." The relief in her voice made him close his eyes. "So... what are you wearing?"

"Only my boxers." Squeezing himself through the soft fabric, he tried to get back in the mood for what he'd started earlier. It wasn't difficult, not when he heard the sound of her shifting on the other end of the line. His lips curved into a smile once more. "Are you touching yourself?"

"Maybe..."

"*Olivia.*"

"Yes," she whispered.

He quickly got up to lock his door before kicking off his boxers and lying in bed naked. "Did you call me because you wanted to hear me while you touch yourself?"

Again, she whispered, "Yes."

But this time, he could hear the slight hitch in her breath. He could picture her rubbing along her slit, soaking her panties. Gripping his hard cock, he began pumping. "Take them off."

"What?"

"You know what."

There was another shuffling, then she returned, saying, "Now what?"

"Are you naked, Livvy?"

"Yes." She let out a breathy sigh. "I wish you were here, touching me, licking me... fucking me. I'm already wet."

A bead of precum appeared, and he swirled his thumb around his tip. Closing his eyes, he imagined it was her. Neither said anything for a minute. Only their increasingly ragged breath filled the silence. The tension built in Wyatt as he forgot about their prior conversation and focused solely on this moment. "God, I want that filthy mouth wrapped around me."

"Maybe if you behave tomorrow at work, I'll get on my knees for you again."

"Fuck yes," he hissed, pumping faster, harder. "Do those fingers inside you feel as good as mine, baby?"

She hesitated before admitting, "No. No one makes me feel like you do." She let out a gasping moan that nearly undid him right then and there. "Wyatt... Oh, shit. I'm so close."

"Me too." That coil inside tightened more and more, threatening to spring at any second. Shaking his head to himself, he said, "The next time I see you, I'm going to bend you over the nearest furniture and fuck you so hard."

"As long as..." She inhaled. "It's not at—oh, God. Just not in front of—Wyatt, I'm gonna come."

He was there too. "Do it. Let me hear you get off just from imagining me. From..." A grunt escaped his lips as his own orgasm built, nearly sending him over the edge. "Imagining my cock inside you, thrusting over and over."

There was a muffled cry, as if she'd covered her mouth with a pillow.

"Fuck." He groaned before releasing onto his stomach in long spurts.

His chest heaved as he slowly relaxed. Through the phone, Livvy's shaky breaths started to even out. He tucked his phone between his shoulder and ear so he could reach over and grab a tissue from the nightstand.

Cleaning up the majority of the mess, he said, "Livvy? You okay?"

"Perfect."

He could hear the smile in her voice, and it made him do the same. Getting out of bed, he slipped his underwear back on, grabbed a clean pair to change into, and headed across the hall to the bathroom. He tossed the tissue in the trash and turned on the shower.

"You know," Livvy started, "one of these days, we should have sex in an actual bed *together*."

Wyatt laughed then stilled. A year ago, if someone would have suggested that, he likely would have ended things right away. But when Livvy said it... he had no desire to call it off.

That alone probably should have terrified him. He knew they had no future, but instead of wanting to keep his distance, he wanted to take advantage of their time together.

"Wyatt?" she asked, clear concern in her tone. "I didn't mean to—"

"Yes," he said, cutting her off before she could backtrack. "We should definitely make that happen sometime soon."

He was done letting his shitty ex dictate his life. If this beautiful woman wanted to be with him while she was here, he was done fighting it.

He was done fighting his feelings for Olivia Cartwright.

TWENTY-SIX

Olivia

There was no way out of this. Olivia stared at the numbers, trying to make sense of them. Just as she had dozens of times over the past few weeks. They didn't add up though, no matter how hard she tried.

Running a hand through her hair, she sighed and rubbed at her throbbing temples. Numbers were her thing. She'd aced all of her econ and marketing classes, not to mention math growing up. It was the one thing she was really good at. So, why couldn't she figure this out?

A knock sounded on her open office door, and she glanced up to find Wyatt approaching. His brow furrowed at the sight of her. "What's wrong?"

He closed the door and crossed the room, setting a to-go cup of coffee in front of her. Bending down, he kissed the top of her head and put an arm around her shoulders. The sweet gestures surprised her, but it also felt natural. Since their phone chat a few nights ago, things had been good between them. There was no more denying they were friends. They still hadn't slept together in an actual bed, but she had held up her promise of getting on her knees again. She'd now blown him twice in this office. The possibility of getting caught turned her on more than she cared to admit.

"Thanks." She leaned into him. "It just doesn't make sense."

"What?" His thumb circled a spot on her neck that sent a shiver down her spine as he looked at the computer screen.

She pointed to one of the columns of the spreadsheet. "This is how much revenue we should have based on sales, expenses, and everything else."

"Okay."

"This," she pointed to a different column, "is how much money there actually is."

"What the hell? How is that much missing?"

"Exactly." Even considering the auto-withdrawal she'd put a stop to, it wasn't right. Sighing, she swiveled her chair to stand. She needed to move around. "When I first noticed a discrepancy, I'll be honest, I thought one of you were taking it."

Wyatt crossed his arms but didn't argue. "And now?"

"I know none of you would do that," she said without hesitation. "Which means something is wrong. I just need to figure out what it is. There are thousands of dollars disappearing. And if I don't fix this..."

"I know."

"No, you don't. This is bigger than keeping the bar open." She was tired of keeping this to herself, and now that she'd let some of it out, it was like she couldn't stop the rush of words escaping her lips. "My dad can't get proper care because he's pouring every cent he has into this place. I came back to help him, but it's so much worse than I thought. I never wanted to stay here in this tiny town where I lost everything and people think I'm some pretentious snob, but how can I leave when—when..."

Wyatt closed the distance between them and pulled her into his arms. "Shh. It's all right."

She hugged him back, resting her head against his shoulder as the tears finally fell. "I can't lose him too."

"I know," Wyatt whispered. He held her for a long moment before leaning back enough to lift a hand to her cheek. "We'll figure something out."

"*We?*"

The corner of his lips curled up ever so slightly. "Yeah, *we.*"

Her heart hammered in her chest as she held his gaze. He took her face in both hands and kissed her. His tongue brushed the seam of her lips, and she opened for him. When he guided her toward her desk, she finally pushed him away.

"Wait." She kept one hand on his chest. "I know what I said the other night, but after everything you've been through, I don't want to hurt you more. Are you sure about this?"

She barely had the words out before his mouth was on hers again. He lifted her to sit on the edge of the desk. One hand trailed from her knee, up her thigh, to her hip. It slid along her side toward her breast as he deepened the kiss.

"Wyatt," she tried again.

"I know you're leaving, but I'm tired of denying how much I like you. And the fact that you know my history and are so determined not to repeat it... that only makes me more positive that this is the right choice."

Olivia gripped his shirt and whispered, "I'm scared of falling too much."

"So am I." He brushed a thumb across her cheek. "But I really want to spend what time we do have together."

"You're sure?" She was terrified of how much she wanted that too.

He nodded with a smile, reaching for the buttons of her

suit jacket. Undoing one at a time, he leaned in to kiss along her jaw. "Very."

She let him remove her jacket. When he tossed it aside, she unbuckled his belt. His hand returned to her knee and slipped up under her skirt. Sucking in a breath, she guided his mouth back to hers. She cursed herself for selecting such a tight skirt today.

Wyatt pulled his hand out and blindly felt around for the zipper. She chuckled, hopped off the desk, and started to turn. "It's back—"

He was already unzipping her and lowering the skirt. With one hand, he pulled her hair over a shoulder before kissing the opposite side of her neck. His other fingers rounded her hip to brush her core through her thong.

Olivia melted into him. "We really shouldn't do this here."

"Do you want me to stop?" His knuckle pressed against her clit.

"God no. Just..." A soft moan escaped her when he rubbed harder. "Lock the door."

He nibbled on her ear for a second before releasing her to flip the lock. By the time he returned, his pants were around his ankles. He stepped up behind her to continue kissing her neck while grinding into her. His hand curled around her front once more, his fingers working their magic.

"This is probably stupid," he said, sliding her underwear to the side for better access, "but I want you so badly that I... I think it'll be worth the heartbreak in the end."

Olivia gasped as one finger slowly entered her. He continued grinding against her ass while working her up. She reached back to squeeze him through his boxers. "I do too."

She tugged the fabric down, wanting him bare. He was so hard already, and she swirled his precum around the tip.

"Wyatt?"

"Hmm?" He bit the side of her neck before licking the tender spot.

"More," she breathed. "I need more."

Against her skin, he asked, "How quiet can you be?"

"Let's find out." Grinning, she looked over her shoulder at him. "What are they going to do, fire me?"

He cupped her cheek and kissed her. His tongue brushed hers before releasing her to direct his cock between her legs, and she thought she might come undone right there. Moving back and forth, he teased her over and over, spreading her slickness along his length while kissing her shoulder, her neck, anything he could reach.

When he paused, she looked back one more time. The mischievous look in those dark eyes made her stomach flutter. He gently guided her to bend over the desk before gripping her by the hips. Ever so slowly, he nudged into her. Inch by inch, he slid farther and farther.

"*Fuck,*" she hissed as he fully impaled her, seated to the hilt.

Wyatt just stood there, filling her. She'd only had sex with a few guys in the past, but he was so much bigger than them. The delicious way he stretched her was the perfect balance between pain and pleasure, especially when he pulled out almost all the way and then slammed back into her.

She let out a moan, unable to stop herself.

He chuckled before doing it again. And again. She clenched her jaw, trying and failing not to make a sound. Reaching around with one hand, Wyatt slipped under her shirt to squeeze her breast and quickened his pace. When he pinched her nipple, she gasped. He did the same to the other side and didn't even give her a moment to recover before he moved south to flick her clit. It was like he knew exactly how to overwhelm her senses in the best way.

"Baby, you have to be quieter or they're going to know what we're doing in here," he said as she moaned more.

"I—" She breathed. "Don't. Care," she managed to say through gritted teeth between thrusts. It was the truth. At this moment, she couldn't care less who heard them. She just wanted him to fuck her. "Harder."

Releasing her hip, he tangled his other hand into her hair, making her arch toward him. She braced her hands on the desk as he pounded into her. Sounds of their skin smacking filled the small office. She was grateful for the music playing out in the main bar, and the fact that only Ryan and Becca were here. None of their usual patrons had arrived yet.

"You like that?" Wyatt circled her bundle of nerves. "You like when I take you hard?"

"Y-yes," she whimpered. "Wyatt, I... I'm gonna..."

"Not yet, baby. Wait for me." He slowed his finger work but not his thrusting.

Letting go of her hair, he pushed her down on the desk again. He gripped both of her hips hard enough that she wondered if there would be bruises later. She loved it. Every single second. He slapped her ass, eliciting a small cry from her. Someone was definitely going to hear them if they kept at it like this. He massaged the stinging skin before roaming toward her middle. His finger rubbed against her puckered hole, and she closed her eyes to fight off the orgasm just a little longer.

"Livvy?" he asked, hesitating.

She nodded. "Do it."

His thumb appeared in her face. "Suck."

She did, getting it nice and wet. Then, it was pushing against that tightness she had only ever let one man touch. Wyatt gradually worked his way inside. The feeling of both holes being used was too much. "Wyatt, I can't..."

Misunderstanding, he removed his thumb without question, instead returning to her clit. She'd only meant she couldn't last much longer. Thankfully, he said, "Come for me. Come on my dick, baby."

Covering her mouth with one hand, she moaned loudly as wave after wave of pleasure rolled through her.

Wyatt grunted and spilled into her a few seconds later. "Fuck, Olivia."

He slowed his rocking until stilling. His cock twitched inside her one more time while they both fought to catch their breath. Sliding his arms around her, he hugged her from behind and pressed a kiss to her hair.

As he softened, he slipped out of her. She grabbed a couple tissues from the desk to stop the mess leaking down her leg, realizing they hadn't used a condom. She was on the pill, and she trusted him, but she knew it was important to him. Before she could reassure him that everything would be fine though, Wyatt kissed her shoulder and said, "I know we said this is over when you leave, but damn. I will happily drive to Chicago for more of that."

TWENTY-SEVEN

wyatt

Why did he say that? Wyatt had no idea what possessed him to voice that thought out loud. He knew it was a mistake the second the words left his mouth.

"I..." He stood frozen, his pants still around his ankles, unsure how to fix this.

Livvy tossed the tissues in the trash, straightened her thong, and pulled up her skirt. As she tucked in her shirt, he tugged his own pants back up.

"I didn't... it was a joke," he tried.

She turned to face him with a look in her eyes that he couldn't read.

"I just meant that was really good." He could stop rambling. "*Really* good. Good enough that I'd drive a couple hours—"

"Wyatt." She cut him off, and her lips curled into an amused smile. "Relax, you're fine. I know what you meant." Stepping closer, she wrapped her arms around his waist and tilted her head back to stare at him.

He leaned down to kiss her brow, putting his hands on her sides. "So much for doing it in a bed next time."

Her soft laugh made him tighten his hold on her. He meant it when he said this time together would be worth the heartbreak, but damn was it going to hurt. Despite his best attempts, he actually enjoyed her company.

Pressing his lips to hers, he couldn't help but kiss her again.

Until someone knocked on the door. Hard. "Olivia Joanne Cartwright."

They jerked apart. Livvy's eyes were as wide as his. She visibly swallowed. "Shit."

Finger-brushing her hair, she rushed to the door. She glanced back while double checking her shirt and skirt. When she pointed to her jacket that had landed on the floor, Wyatt snatched it up and draped it over her chair. He made sure his own clothes were straight as she unlocked and opened the door.

"Uncle Gary," she said. "I didn't expect to see you today. Come in."

He eyed Wyatt and strolled inside like he owned the place. Though, Wyatt supposed he did own a share of it. The man crossed his arms. "Judging by your bartenders trying to stall me out front and your locked door, I don't think you were expecting anyone."

Livvy's face, which had still been slightly flushed, reddened more. Yet, that icy façade returned. Keeping her chin up, she rounded her desk to face them both, but she didn't sit. "Wyatt and I were just going over the numbers, trying to think of a way to save The Tavern. He's been here longer than most, so I thought his insight would be helpful."

"And the door needed to be locked because..."

She crossed her arms to mirror his stance. "To stop people from barging in and interrupting us."

"How *professional*," he sneered.

Wyatt took a step toward him, his fists clenching.

"Wyatt," Livvy said before he could do something rash, "could you please go check the orders for next week? Then, you can return to prepping for tonight's shift."

Taking a deep breath, he nodded. He wouldn't dare undermine her in front of her uncle. "Of course. Let me know if you need anything."

Her voice softened a fraction as she said, "I will. Thank you."

Reluctantly, he left the office, not bothering to shut the door behind him. He went into the bathroom to quickly wash his hands before running his fingers through his hair and walking down the short hall to the main room. Becca smirked when Wyatt appeared, but she didn't say anything as she continued stocking.

"So, that's why you two are getting along better," Ryan said, coming from the storage closet.

Becca chuckled, and Wyatt shot them both a scowl.

"How long has that been going on?" Ryan set a box of napkins on the bar top to refill low canisters he'd already brought over from the tables.

Wyatt unlocked the beer taps and made sure everything was functioning properly. "Please don't start. I know I shouldn't be sleeping with the boss."

Becca grabbed him by the arm when he tried to walk away. "No one was going to say that."

"Definitely not Becca, at least. She has no room to talk," Ryan said. "Do you know how many times I've caught her and Shawn going at it in—"

"All right, he gets it," she interrupted before turning toward Wyatt again. "If we were against this, why would we have tried to stop her slimy uncle from going back there?"

He huffed out a breath through his nose. "True. Thank you for that."

"I mean, he probably still heard you two," she said. "Did you even *try* to be quiet? I turned the music up after I realized that her shout wasn't you two fighting, but damn. If that's your idea of sneaking around, we really need to have a chat. I'll teach you the ways."

Ryan snorted. "Sucking off Shawn in the storage closet isn't any better. At least they did it in a room with a lock."

Becca balled up a napkin and threw it at him.

"We tried at first," Wyatt said with a chuckle, wanting to stop them before another ice incident started. "But then, we got carried away, and she said she didn't care, so..."

"So you plowed into her like there was no mañana." Becca helped Ryan finish the last napkin holder.

A throat cleared, and Wyatt decided it was time to go dig a hole to crawl into. He really didn't want to face Livvy's uncle, but he didn't want to show any fear toward this man who made her life hell. Gritting his teeth, Wyatt turned.

Gary looked as if he was about two seconds from beating the shit out of him. And Wyatt didn't blame him at this point. Livvy stood behind him, pinching the bridge of her nose and slowly shaking her head in clear frustration. Or exhaustion. He couldn't tell, but it was probably a combination of both.

"Real professional team you've got here, Liv." Gary glanced from Wyatt to her. "End this before your father finds out and it kills him."

Without another word, he stormed out of the bar. No one spoke for a long moment.

Breaking the silence, Ryan said, "I think that's my cue to go prep the kitchen."

Becca grabbed the napkin dispensers and went to place them on the tables.

But Wyatt was still watching Livvy. Something between grief and shame filled her gaze, breaking his heart. When she turned to head back to her office, he sighed.

"Go," Becca whispered, returning for the box of extra napkins. "It'll be slow tonight, so I can take care of the bar. Go take care of her."

He squeezed her shoulder. "Thank you. Come get me if you need help."

On his way toward the hall, he paused. Going behind the counter, he poured two glasses of tequila. Becca chuckled.

The office door was partially open when he made it there. Livvy sat at her desk, her face buried in her hands. Wyatt set the glasses down before moving to her side. He squatted next to her, reaching for her arm. "I'm sorry."

It seemed as good of a place as any to start.

Lowering her hands, she grabbed one of the glasses and took a gulp of tequila. "It's fine. My uncle and employees all think I'm a dirty slut now, and the guy I'm fucking has no problem talking about our sex life to his friends, but it's fine."

Guilt coursed through him. He wasn't that guy. He didn't usually share details about his personal life with anyone like that—except with Charlie when she'd ask about his occasional hookups—but he wasn't about to argue. Livvy had every right to be mad. Instead, he repeated, "I'm sorry. They were telling me about trying to stall Gary and reassuring me they didn't care if we were together, and I just... let something slip. I'm not used to opening up to people, and now I can't seem to stop. Not that I'm trying to come up with an excuse."

"Wyatt," she whispered, "stop."

His anxiety was building though, his chest tightening. "It won't happen again. I swear."

"Shh." Livvy pivoted her chair. "I know. I believe you. It's... I'm not mad at you." As if to prove her point, she bent forward to kiss him softly on the lips. "I'm just frustrated with everything. Mainly my uncle, who feels the need to continuously remind me how important it is that I save this bar, how my father needs it. Like I don't know. Like I'm not the one taking care of him and stepping up to do all of this."

Wyatt stood and leaned against the desk.

"God forbid he do anything to actually help out." She took another sip of the alcohol. "But now, he thinks I'm just sleeping with the staff and wasting time."

"There's nothing wrong with what we're doing," Wyatt said. "We're two consenting adults, and it's not like I'm sleeping with you for a promotion."

At that, she smiled. "You're not? And here I was thinking you wanted to be manager once I left."

His jaw dropped open. Fear coursed through him. Did she really think that was why he was doing this?

"I know that's why you were mad about me being here, Wyatt. I'm not an idiot."

"Okay, but that has nothing to do with screwing around. I swear." He lifted her hand into his. "I'm happy you're here now. You grew on me."

"Who knew all it took was me getting down on my knees?"

He let out a laugh. "Literally the entire world knows that's the quickest way to a guy's heart."

Grinning, she rolled her eyes.

"But that's not why you grew on me," he went on, needing her to hear this. "You're incredible, Livvy. You're so smart and strong. And contrary to popular belief, you can be kind, even sweet, when you stop hiding behind those walls protecting your heart."

"Wyatt..." She stood and put a hand over said heart. "Thank you. And thanks for following me in here."

"I couldn't let you wallow." Wrapping an arm around her, he added, "Besides, I'm not one to fuck a woman over her desk and leave."

She playfully smacked his chest.

Before she could pull away, he tightened his hold on her. He kissed her once, twice. "Seriously though, are you okay?"

"I'm... tired," she said. "I don't know how to make things better, and it's a lot."

"All right, let's look at this from another angle." He guided her to her chair and pulled another closer to sit with her. "Instead of solely trying to figure out where the missing money went or how to turn things around for the bar, let's come up with a way to raise money to save it and help your dad."

She looked at him as if he had offered her the world. "Like a fundraiser?"

"Exactly."

"But my dad doesn't want people to know he's sick."

Wyatt lifted the second glass of tequila to his lips and took a sip to give him time to think. "What if he knew it would make a massive difference? The people in this town love Jack. If he's struggling, they'll want to help."

"I don't know..." She drank from her own cup.

"We should at least talk to him."

Livvy smirked. "There you go with that *we* again."

"Jack has been my boss for years," Wyatt said. "More than that, he was my family when I had none, always making sure I'm doing okay. He cares so much about his employees and customers; let us show our love in return for once."

TWENTY-EIGHT

Olivia

The moment Olivia opened her eyes, she regretted it. Her head was splitting in half. That was the only plausible explanation for such pain. She rolled over with a groan, snuggling into the warm body beside her. A very naked warm body.

Ignoring the pounding headache, her eyes snapped open again and she pushed herself up. As the sheet slid down her bare chest, she gasped and tugged it up around her.

"Dammit," she whispered.

Despite looking like he was sleeping, Wyatt chuckled. His hand went to her back and began moving in soothing circles.

"It's not funny," she said, lying against him once more. "I didn't know where I was for a second."

His fingers stilled. "Did you think I could be someone else?"

Rolling her eyes at the clear jealousy, she kissed the underside of his jaw. "No. I'm just not used to waking up next to anyone."

"Me neither." Wyatt wrapped his other arm around her, hugging her to him. "I have to admit... I like it."

"It's not the first time we've been here," she reminded him.

He trailed a hand along her side. "True, but it's the first time we've been naked."

At that realization, she groaned. "Are you fucking kidding me? We finally made it to a bed, and I can't remember any of it?" She reached up to rub her temple, her eyes closing again. "This is why I don't drink tequila."

Wyatt pushed her hand away to take over, massaging the side of her head. "As soon as I don't feel like I'm going to spew my insides, I'll refresh your memory."

She couldn't help but laugh. "So sexy."

"I try."

She could feel his grin on her forehead as he kissed her. This was dangerous territory—cuddling in bed like this. It wasn't helping the growing feelings that were getting more difficult to deny by the day. She hooked one leg over his, letting his hardness brush her thigh, and encircled his waist with an arm as she partially laid on top of him. It would be so easy to let him into her heart.

Who was she kidding? He'd already burrowed in there, and she didn't think she would be getting rid of him anytime soon. Leaving was going to kill her.

"Stop," he whispered.

"What?"

"You're so tense. Stop overthinking this." He lowered his hand from her head, which had started to feel a little better.

She sat up again. "I need some water and ibuprofen."

Wyatt sighed. "Stay. I'll get it."

He climbed out of bed and slid into some shorts. Halfway to the door, he paused. Returning, he cupped both sides of her face to tilt her head back. He kissed her thoroughly, sending sparks through her entire body. She felt it all the way in her toes.

Breaking apart, he said, "We're still on the same page. Promise."

When he left, she lay down and clenched her jaw to fight the burning in her throat. They were definitely not on the same page. She was falling hard, and she had no idea what to do about it.

She probably should have gotten up and dressed. She should have gone home.

Instead, she waited for him to come back, praying for the pain to ease. By the time he returned with two glasses and a bottle of ibuprofen, she'd managed to push down the overwhelming emotions and lock them away. Just as she always did.

Tucking the sheet around her chest, she took the water he offered. She sipped on it, letting the coolness refresh her. He set his glass down and opened the ibuprofen. After they both took some, he drained his water and climbed into bed again. She slowly drank hers to stall a bit longer. Out of the corner of her eye, she saw him shuffling under the blankets. He pulled something out, and she finally looked over.

And choked on her water, spitting it across the bed.

It was his damn shorts. He'd whipped them off and now tossed them to the floor with a mischievous smirk.

Olivia covered her mouth and coughed. Setting her cup down, she shook her head in disbelief. "You're ridiculous," she said between coughs.

He patted her on the back. "Need mouth-to-mouth resuscitation?"

"You know," she turned toward him more, "I might." Two could play that game.

As Wyatt reached for her, she climbed over him to straddle his lap. The headache was still prominent, but his touch made it tolerable. He distracted her by sliding his hands up her bare skin, and she covered his mouth with hers. He gripped the nape of her neck and deepened the kiss. She didn't even have a chance to be self-conscious about morning breath. Not that he seemed to care. He began to harden once more beneath her as she rocked against him.

This was happening. They were finally going to have sex in a freaking bed.

She let out a moan as he shifted enough to grab a condom from the bedside table. When he froze, tensing beneath her, she lifted to see his face.

"Yesterday..." He raised with her, sitting against the headboard. "We didn't use one."

"No, we didn't," she said, stroking a finger down his jaw. He hadn't shaved in a few days, and she had to admit, the rugged, stubble look was really good on him. "I'm on the pill; I promise. We're fine."

Wyatt slowly shook his head. "It's not a hundred percent guaranteed."

"Neither are condoms." She took it from him. "Would you feel better if I took a morning-after pill? I can go get one later."

"That's your choice."

This man... She leaned in to kiss him. "I know you're scared because of Harper's past, but she was seventeen. We're older, a little better equipped to handle that if it happens."

His eyes widened, and she could see the fear churning in his dark irises.

"Not that I want it to right now. And if by some miracle it does happen, I don't expect you to jump on board and be a part of our lives. You'd be under no obligation." She tore the foil open with her teeth and scooted back.

"Livvy," he hissed when she wrapped a hand around him. She leaned down to take him in her mouth to speed up the process. It didn't take long to get him as hard as steel.

He reached between her legs, but she straightened, releasing his cock with a pop before shaking her head. She rolled the condom on. "I want to feel you. Now."

She lifted up and guided him toward her entrance, but he grabbed her hips to stop her before she could sink down onto him.

"I would never abandon you like that." He leaned in close. "If you had my baby, I would be there for both of you, however you needed or wanted me."

"I know." She had no doubts about that.

His gaze softened, as if he understood exactly how she was feeling. How real this was for both of them, despite their claiming otherwise.

"Slow," he said, guiding her onto him. "And we have to be quiet for real this time unless you want to be questioned by a kindergartener."

Olivia bit her lip as she smiled and nodded. Bracing herself with one hand on his shoulder, she slowly lowered, taking him in inch by inch. Once she was fully seated, she paused to adjust. But more than that, she paused to wrap her arms around him and kiss him again. His own arm tightened around her while his other fingers went to her hair. Just being held like this with him deep inside her was perfection.

Needing friction to sate the ache between her thighs, she began moving. Rising and falling, rocking back and forth, Olivia held on to Wyatt like her life depended on it. With a gasp, she broke the kiss and buried her face against the side of his neck.

"Yes, baby," he whispered. "Ride that cock. Take what you need."

She shook her head, not daring to lift it to look him in the eyes. "If you..." Her lips slammed shut as he shifted to lie down and hit a particularly deep spot, setting her nerves on fire. "*Oh fuck*. No dirty talk if you... want me to stay quiet. I... I can't."

His low chuckle tickled in her ear.

When he tried to slow their pace, she said under her breath, "More. Wyatt, more."

He stopped, and she opened her mouth to argue, but then he was gripping her and rolling her onto her back. Hooking his arms beneath her knees, he practically folded her in half to start thrusting harder. His kiss swallowed her moans.

Keeping a steady rhythm, he drilled into her, this new angle making her see stars.

Wyatt released one leg to circle her clit. He broke the kiss with a, "Fuck, I'm not going to last much longer. Are you close?"

She didn't respond right away. She couldn't. There were no words to describe how blissful she felt. How she never wanted this to end.

"Livvy." He slowed and released her other leg to bracket her face with both hands as he lowered his weight onto her. "Look at me, baby."

Squeezing her eyes shut, she shook her head. She wrapped her legs around him and dug her heels into his ass to get him to keep going faster, but he didn't.

His fingers brushed along her cheek, her jaw. "Olivia, sweetheart, look at me."

She relented and met his gaze, and it was exactly as she

had feared. Wyatt stared at her with so much love that she was certain her heart was going to burst. Her vision blurred with unshed tears.

"What happened?" Concern filled his voice as he stopped inside her. "Did I hurt you?"

"No! No, not at all," she said quickly. "Please keep going. I just…"

He started moving again. "Just what?"

Olivia was no stranger to making love. She hadn't slept with many guys, but none were as domineering as Wyatt when it came to sex. He'd awakened something in her she hadn't even realized she wanted—a carnal need to be taken in ways she'd never desired. She wanted the hot, animalistic sex. The reckless hard fucks at work or in his truck, where they could so easily be caught.

Being with him like this, when he was gentle and sweet… it was too much.

"Livvy?"

We never should have done it in a bed. But she couldn't say that to him. She couldn't shatter him that way, especially before they finished. Instead, she whispered part of the truth. "I really like you."

Wyatt stared at her with a sad smile, like he understood without her needing to explain. Because of course he did. He quickened the pace, once more reaching between them to bring her closer to the edge. They fell over it together, gasping and holding each other tightly.

As their breathing slowed, their pulses returning to normal, he kissed her temple and said, "I really like you too."

By some miracle, Olivia and Wyatt made it out of his house before anyone else woke up. Borrowing Harper's car, Wyatt drove Olivia to the bar to get her own. At least they'd had the sense not to drive home last night. She had a vague memory of him getting Charlie to come pick them up saying she owed him for the cat-man date. Whatever the hell that meant.

His truck was still in the parking lot too, but he assured her it was fine; he would make his sister help him get it later. He kissed Olivia goodbye, like that was a normal thing they did. She didn't comment on it though. She just got in and took off.

Now, she sat outside her dad's house, trying to get the courage to go inside. Her dad wouldn't care that she'd stayed out all night. He might have been concerned, or he might have teased her about it, but he wouldn't judge or lecture her.

Her uncle, on the other hand...

The moment she'd seen his car in the driveway, her stomach churned. And not just because the previous night's tequila was still making her a bit woozy. Her head ached, and she was trying to figure out what to do about Wyatt and the bar. She didn't want to deal with Gary again so soon.

Pulling down her visor, she checked the mirror to make sure she looked presentable. Her eyes were a little red with dark circles beneath. She sighed, knowing there was nothing she could do right now to fix it.

She grabbed her phone and purse before getting out then took her time walking to the front door. Entering her own home shouldn't feel like this. She shouldn't be terrified to face a man who was barely around when she was growing up.

Yet, as she walked into the living room to find him on the couch and her dad in his recliner, both with serious looks on their faces, her chest tightened.

Neither said a word as she hung her purse on the coat rack and removed her shoes. Wyatt had lent her a sweatshirt and pair of pajama pants she'd needed to roll up multiple times to keep from falling down, and she had put her hair in a messy bun when they reached her car.

She was unbelievably comfortable, but she also knew the men in front of her were accustomed to seeing her in professional wear most of the time. Even when not wearing a business suit, she usually wore slacks and a nice blouse or sweater. She always looked well put together.

Right now, she looked anything but.

"Nice of you to finally return home," Gary said with a sneer.

"We were worried." Her dad's tone was gentler. "You used to call if you were staying out."

Shit. She felt bad on his account. That worry was something she understood well. Even when they barely spoke during her last year of high school, they always told each other when they were leaving. After the accident, it had become an unspoken agreement. "I'm so sorry. I... forgot. I'm not used to telling someone anymore."

Her uncle scoffed. "You know, your neighbor was called into work. It was a good thing I was still in the area."

"How gracious of you to help your own brother," she said in a monotone voice.

"Liv," her dad hissed. "What's going on with you? You're never this reckless."

"I'm never this happy," she mumbled.

His eyes widened, mirroring her shock at the revelation.

That was it. For the first time in years, she was genuinely happy.

"Oh, yes, I'm sure screwing your employee and getting drunk at work is a blast." Gary crossed his arms. "I'd bet anything he's the one skimming money off the top and he's just sleeping with you as a distraction."

"Gary," her dad said, his tone growing firm. "That's enough." He only looked a little uncomfortable when he glanced at Olivia. "You're dating one of the bartenders?"

Her mouth opened then shut. Explaining friends with benefits was not a conversation she wanted to have with her father. It didn't matter though. Gary wasn't done.

"The one who thinks he's in charge of things," he said with a huff.

She clenched her hands into fists. "It's none of your business who I am or am not dating. I'm done with this conversation." She turned to storm to her room but paused. Facing her uncle, she said, "And Wyatt is a good man. He would never do that."

Not waiting for a response, she went to her bedroom and slammed the door behind her. Her uncle's words echoed in her mind. She didn't believe it, but for just a second, the fear of that truth crept in. Shaking it off, she pulled out her phone and texted Wyatt that she'd made it home safely. He replied immediately, as if he'd been waiting.

WYATT

Glad to hear it :)

Before she could respond, he sent another text.

WYATT

My bed feels empty without you... come back?

She smiled at the screen and sat on the edge of her mattress. They should slow down. This was getting too serious. But she still found herself typing back,

I need to stay with my dad for a bit, but soon. Promise.

TWENTY-NINE

wyatt

Wyatt was not an artistic man. He was not graced with those genes like his sister, or even his nephew, who was arguably better than him at just five years old. Elliot sat beside him at the short desk, fingers and arms covered in paint. His little smock only slightly helped keep it off his clothes. They'd learned by now to stick him in old clothes on painting days.

"That's so good, Elliot," Charlie said, standing behind them.

It was. Elliot had created a forest with what looked like a dragon at the center. And Wyatt could actually tell it was a dragon. There were wings and a long tail, nothing like the odd blob-shaped animals he'd seen in some of the other kids' paintings drying along the counters. The rest of the children had all left, but Elliot convinced Wyatt to stay longer while Charlie and Harper cleaned the classroom.

Wyatt looked down at his own art. If one could call it that. He'd copied Elliot's idea to make a forest, but it was rough, to say the least. And dark. Why was it so dark?

"Uncle Wyatt," Elliot leaned closer, "I think you're worse than Mr. Colby."

His sister snorted and slapped a hand over her mouth. Charlie managed to hide her amusement a little better. "Elliot, everyone has their own style and abilities. We don't tell them when they're... not super good. We just encourage them to keep practicing so they get better."

"*Ohh.*" He nodded and turned to Wyatt, laying a hand on his arm and getting green paint on him. "That's okay, Uncle Wyatt. You'll do better next time... probably."

"So encouraging," Wyatt deadpanned.

"Mom, can we go get ice cream?"

Wyatt laughed at the abrupt change in topic. He loved his nephew.

Harper shook her head. "It's too close to dinner time."

"Then, can we get pizza?" Elliot grinned. Sneaky little thing.

She glared at Wyatt, like it was his fault. It was, but still. He'd taught Elliot that trick a while ago. Ask for something more than he wants so when someone says no, the smaller thing he *really* wants doesn't seem like a big deal.

Wyatt nudged him in the side with his elbow. "Pizza sounds pretty good."

"Fine," Harper said, bringing Wyatt a paper towel to wipe the paint off his arm.

"Uncle Wyatt, are you bringing your new girlfriend?" Elliot asked.

He fought down his surprise at the question. "Um... no, I think she's busy."

"Aw..." The boy pouted. "I like her." He stood to take his painting to the counter.

That was when Wyatt realized how quiet the other two were. Both Harper and Charlie stared at him with wide eyes.

"What?"

"You didn't deny it," Harper whispered.

"I..." He glanced from her to Charlie to Elliot. "He's five. I didn't think trying to explain that she isn't really my girlfriend was a good idea, especially when he's seen her at the house and caught us kissing." That had been fun. Livvy had stopped by in the afternoon yesterday before they both went to the bar, and of course, Harper and Elliot came home earlier than he anticipated. Luckily, things hadn't escalated yet. They'd been kissing in his bedroom, but both were fully clothed.

Harper moved closer, her smile growing. "Wyatt—"

"Don't." He pushed to his feet. "Please, don't. I know, okay? But she's not planning on staying. As soon as she figures out how to save The Tavern and help her dad, she's heading back to Chicago."

"That's only a couple of hours away." Charlie joined them.

He sighed. The truth was, he had thought about it a lot recently. "Two hours and thirty-three minutes."

Both women grinned at him again. His sister said, "Which you know because you looked it up. You're considering this?"

"I don't know."

Elliot wandered back over. "Pizza?"

"Are we getting pizza?" a male voice asked from the doorway.

"Mr. Colby!" Elliot ran toward their friend. Ever since he started school, he'd started calling him *Mr. Colby* instead of just *Colby* like he had all summer, even though the man wasn't his teacher.

"Hey, buddy." Colby squatted down. "Wow, you are covered in paint." When Elliot laughed, Colby said, "Mom, do we want help getting cleaned up before dinner?"

Harper nodded with a smile. "Please and thank you."

As they went to the sink in the back of the room, Harper busied herself by picking up the paints and brushes. Wyatt smirked and lowered his voice. "Ready to admit something is going on there?"

"Nothing is going on there." She shot a glance over her shoulder at them.

"At least *I'm* no longer in denial," Wyatt said.

Charlie chuckled and grabbed the supplies from Harper, taking away her only means of distraction. She carried the brushes and palette to the sink.

"I'm not in denial," Harper whispered, leaning against the desk. "Nothing is going on. Colby is sweet, but we're just friends. I'm not ready for more yet."

Sighing, Wyatt draped an arm around her shoulders. It had been eight months since she and Elliot moved in with him. She'd left her piece-of-shit husband only a couple of months before that and then lived with their parents, but she needed more freedom. They were just as controlling and trying to get her to return to David. She had decided that she needed a way to find her own independence without them and their money, even if it meant crashing with her older brother until then. Not that he minded. Wyatt loved having her and Elliot here. And he *really* loved that she was no longer letting anyone control her.

But she and David had been together for six years, and Wyatt understood her hesitation to jump into another relationship so soon.

"I think I'm falling in love with Livvy," he confessed, knowing Harper needed a subject change. "It scares the shit out of me."

"She's not Loren."

"I know," he said. "She's nothing like her. Livvy is... She doesn't want to start anything real because she knows about my past and claims she doesn't want to hurt me... I believe her, which..."

Harper turned toward him. "Which just makes you want her more."

He nodded.

"You're really considering a long-distance relationship?"

Letting out a slow breath, he shrugged. "I don't know." Hearing it out loud sounded ridiculous. "Contrary to popular belief, I think they can work but on a temporary basis. There needs to be an end goal where the couple is together, and I just don't see how that's possible for us. She wants to build a life in Chicago, or another big city, and I really don't want that. Neither of us wants to ask the other to compromise, so where does that leave us?"

"But you love her," Harper said.

"Sometimes, that's not enough." His chest ached at the thought. "I know I'm going to lose her, but I can't stay away. I'd rather spend what time we *do* have together than apart."

Her gaze softened.

"Pizza!" Elliot rushed over, colliding with her legs. His smock had been removed, his shirt changed, and his arms cleaned off.

Harper scooped him up and kissed his cheek. "All right, all right. Let's go feed this hungry monster before he starves to death."

He giggled as she tickled him.

Before long, the group was heading down the street toward the pizza place. Wyatt pulled out his phone, debating on whether or not to text Livvy. He wanted to, but he also knew he was getting in way too deep. He'd meant every word he told his sister.

Charlie pulled the door open, ushering them inside, but Wyatt paused. The bakery across the road caught his attention like always. But this time, an idea struck him.

"Wyatt?" Charlie said.

He went into A Little Slice of Heaven while texting Livvy.

> I have an idea for a fundraiser. I'm about to get pizza with my sister and some friends. Care to join us so we can talk about it?

She didn't respond, so he assumed she was busy. He would see her tomorrow at work either way. Though, he had wanted an excuse to see her sooner.

They grabbed a table and ordered a couple of pizzas and drinks. While the others chatted, he started a list on his phone. He needed to get this idea written down so he wouldn't forget.

"Have room for one more?"

Wyatt's eyes snapped up. He all but jumped to his feet at the sight of Livvy standing there. Gathering his composure, he leaned in and kissed her on the cheek. "Hi."

"Hi," she said with a breathy laugh.

"I thought you said your girlfriend wasn't coming," Elliot said across the table.

"I guess she changed her mind." Wyatt pulled over an extra chair for her as the others shifted to make room.

Livvy grinned and whispered, "Girlfriend?"

As they took their seats, he said, "It was just easier not to correct him."

Her smile made his pulse race. He couldn't stop staring at her. She was so fucking beautiful.

"We ordered a cheese pizza and a pepperoni and sausage," Harper said, stealing her attention. "I hope one of those is okay."

Livvy nodded and gave her drink order to the waiter who came back around. Charlie dove in, asking about her day, but Wyatt couldn't hear the small talk. She was here.

And after his earlier confession to his sister, it was almost like a shock to his system. It overwhelmed him, sending him into anxiety-attack territory. He clenched his jaw and tried to focus on keeping his breaths steady. He twisted his hands together in his lap so no one could see him fidgeting.

As if sensing him, Livvy reached for his hand under the table. She didn't even look his way; she was still talking to his friends and sister. But she knew. Her fingers laced through his, giving a reassuring squeeze. Elliot started telling a story about something that happened at school, drawing the spotlight to him, and Livvy finally angled toward Wyatt.

Dropping her voice, she whispered, "Everything okay?"

"Yeah." He brushed his thumb over her knuckles. "Thank you. I didn't think you were coming. You didn't respond."

"I wasn't doing anything productive at work, so I thought I'd just walk down and meet you here. I guess I could've answered before showing up."

"You can always just show up." He probably shouldn't have said that, but he couldn't take back the words. Besides, it was the truth.

"So, this fundraiser idea..."

Wyatt nodded, letting her change the topic. He opened the list on his phone again and handed it over. "What if we had a big bake sale and competition?"

THIRTY

Olivia

A thump startled Olivia awake. She sat up and looked around her dark room, her head foggy from the strange dream she'd been having that involved dancing cupcakes circling Wyatt in his kitchen while he wore nothing but an apron. Actually, she'd enjoyed it quite a bit.

Grabbing her phone from a side table, she saw that it was nearly six in the morning. She sighed and leaned back against her pillow. Until reality set in and she remembered where she was.

Olivia all but jumped out of bed and ran to the door. She flipped on the hallway light, even though she knew this house like the back of her hand.

"Dad?" Her heart pounded in her chest as she opened her father's door. "Oh my God."

He was lying on the floor beside his bed. "I thought I could do it myself."

The sadness in his voice broke her heart. She turned on his lamp before kneeling. "Are you hurt?"

She didn't want to move him and make something worse. He shook his head though. "Think I'll be sore for a bit, but I'm fine."

"Okay, let's get you off the floor." She helped him roll to his back and sit up. Hooking his arm over her shoulders, she waited for him to slowly get his legs ready to help as much as he could. When he nodded, she lifted. Together, they managed to get him onto the edge of the bed.

She looked him over for obvious injuries. "Where were you trying to go?"

"My chair..." He sighed and ran a shaky hand over his thinning hair. "I can't sleep, and I thought it might be more comfortable. I'm sorry I woke you."

Waving him off, she sat next to him. "Don't. I'm here to help you, Dad. Wake me up as much as you need to."

"My sweet girl." He hugged her close to his side and kissed her forehead.

It was such an unexpected gesture that she couldn't hold it back anymore. She held on to him, missing the simpler days when he was perfectly healthy and her mom was still here. Tears started to fall before she could stop them. They soaked into his shirt, but he didn't seem to care.

He lifted a hand to her hair, not letting her pull away. "Shhh, what's wrong?"

Barely above a whisper, she asked, "Do you blame me? For the accident?"

"What? Why would you—" He pushed her back and put a palm to her cheek. "Olivia, why would you think that?"

"We got in that fight. It was my fault she went out, and then y-you barely talked to m-me after."

He brushed at the tears rolling down her face, but she saw he had his own too. When she tried to look away, he gently gripped her chin. "Sweetheart, I need you to listen to me," he said before visibly swallowing. "I *never* blamed you. I couldn't talk to you because I blamed myself."

Her stomach dropped. "What?"

"It was so painful to look at you, knowing I was the

reason your mother was taken," he whispered. "I didn't know how to face you. I'm a fucking coward."

"Dad."

"If I made you feel like it was your fault..."

As he trailed off, she leaned forward to hug him again. Together, they sobbed over the past, over their shared guilt.

"I felt like I lost you both," she whispered between sniffles.

"I'm sorry, Livvy," he said, stroking a hand along her back. "I'm so fucking sorry. I didn't mean to push you away. I just... She was the love of my life. It broke something inside me when she left, and I didn't know how to handle it on top of the guilt."

"Me too." Olivia turned to rest her head on his shoulder.

For several minutes, they sat in silence. This had been a long-overdue conversation, and now that it was out there, she felt like she could take a full breath for the first time in years.

Since they were opening up, she said, "I wish I knew how to help you more."

"You're doing so much, Olivia. Look at me." He tilted her chin up again. "Do you have any idea how proud I am of you? You went off to college, continued to get your master's, and were making it in the big city. You set goals and followed your dreams, yet the moment you heard I was struggling, you stopped to return home without blinking an eye. Even after our... falling apart."

Olivia took a shaky breath.

"I know you never wanted to return to this small town," her dad said, his sad tone pulling at her heartstrings. "It holds too much history, too many bad memories. If I could, I would go back and change things in an instant. I'll never be able to apologize enough."

"Dad—"

"All I mean is, I understand how much you don't want to be here, how much you hate it here. I'm so grateful you are though."

"I... don't hate it here." She lowered her eyes to her hands in her lap.

To her surprise, he chuckled. "Because you found someone who makes you happy."

It wasn't a question, but she nodded. She couldn't even deny it anymore, and that made her chest ache. Because she wanted Wyatt in her life. Despite her best efforts, she had fallen for the man. But she couldn't have him. She wouldn't ask him to uproot his life again. Not only because that wasn't fair to him but because she didn't want to face his rejection.

"You know, it's okay to let our dreams change and adapt over time—healthy even," her dad said. "You're not the same person as the eighteen-year-old Olivia who was desperate to escape this place. It's okay to stop running... if you're ready."

She clenched her jaw, trying to fight the returning tears.

"Have you gone to see her since returning?"

Olivia shook her head. She hadn't been to her mother's grave since the funeral, but she couldn't tell him that. It hurt too much to even think about going. It made it all the more real.

"Maybe it's time, sweetheart."

Another sob worked its way up her throat, and she clung to him. They still had a lot to work through. She wasn't sure how much to share about the last few years, but at least she could now. The guilt lingered. She wasn't sure it would ever fade entirely. However, it wasn't quite as heavy with another person supporting her.

Perhaps she'd been wrong. Cutting people out of her life, denying herself love and family, hadn't made her stronger. It hadn't kept her from getting hurt. The only thing it did was isolate her.

Her dad was right about visiting her mom. He was right about it maybe being time to stop running away from the past and head toward the future.

She just needed to figure out what exactly she wanted that future to look like and who she wanted to be there with her.

Olivia lowered the volume of the music when she heard the front door open and close. She set down the pot she'd been cleaning and went to see who was here. Expecting Angela, she was startled to find her uncle instead. "Hey. We didn't expect you today."

He glared at her. "First you get snippy with me because I'm not around enough, and now you don't want me here?"

"I didn't say that," she said at the same time her dad said, "Gary."

Her uncle had a way of making her feel about two inches tall. Especially when he brushed her off as insignificant, like he did now. He turned and headed to the couch near her dad's recliner. Dropping onto it, he sighed.

"What's going on?" her dad asked.

Gary leaned forward, bracing his elbows on his knees. "I got a letter from the bank. If we don't make serious changes very soon, we'll need to shut down and sell to keep from going under."

Olivia bristled at that. She might not have cared about the bar when she first arrived, but she did now. More importantly, she knew how much it meant to the others who worked there. It wasn't only their means of income; they were a family. She moved into the room to be a part of the conversation. "We're working on a solution. Wyatt and I are planning a fundraiser event that should—"

"A simple fundraiser won't be enough," Gary interrupted. "It will help, but we need to lessen our expenses too."

"We've cut down on a lot, making sure we're not ordering excess." She took a seat in the adjacent armchair. "Unless we stop offering certain things, I don't know what else to cut, and doing that means less sales, so it's a lose-lose."

"I'm not talking about inventory." His sneer made her stomach twist. "If you're growing too attached to these people—to your new boyfriend—to make the tough decisions, I'll do it for you."

"No." The last thing she wanted was for him to step in and do something drastic, like firing half the employees. "I... I'll do what needs to be done. I just need to figure some things out first. I'm not too attached; he's not my boyfriend. He knows as soon as I can, I'm moving back to Chicago."

She regretted the statement as soon as it was out. Especially with the way her dad's face fell. After this morning's conversation, she had started to consider staying, but she didn't want to voice that yet. Not if it would get anyone's hopes up. But she saw in his eyes that he'd already thought she made that decision.

Gary crossed his arms, his go-to stance of intimidation. She was surprised he didn't stand too.

"We're out of time," he said. "You don't have the luxury of sitting around, playing with that boy while you *figure things out*. Get it done."

"I will."

"You have two weeks or I'm taking control of the situation."

Her jaw dropped. Two weeks? How in the hell was she supposed to fix this in two weeks?

THIRTY-ONE

wyatt

A bell chimed as Wyatt opened the glass front door, the sound making him smile. He'd told Livvy he would meet her at The Tavern shortly, but first, he wanted to talk to Hank and Deena. He had seen the older couple through the window looking around their new bakery.

"Good morning," Deena said with a smile that looked a little forced.

Wyatt paused. "Sorry, is now a bad time?"

"No, you're fine."

Her husband, however, mumbled, "It might be the only time."

An ominous feeling settled over Wyatt.

"What can we help you with?" Deena asked.

Wyatt walked farther into the shop, his heart racing. "Um... well, we're planning an event—a fundraiser—to try to save The Tavern. It's going to be a bake sale and competition, so I thought maybe you'd be interested in participating or being a sponsor. I also wanted to ask if..." He swallowed and then took a deep breath. "If you were going to be looking to hire another baker."

Both of their gazes softened, but it did nothing to ease the tension. Normally, he would chalk it up to his anxiety making him uneasy. There was sadness in their eyes though.

"We appreciate you coming to us, but I'm afraid we're going to have to say no to all of that," the woman said.

"Oh." Wyatt nodded and pretended his heart wasn't breaking.

"Not that we don't want to do it," she added.

Hank sighed. "We're not opening the shop. Our loan didn't go through, but even before we found out, we were having doubts. We don't want to set up a whole business we're attached to so far from our daughter. She lives in Illinois with her family, so we're moving there and will try again after we get settled."

"I understand." Wyatt glanced around the empty space.

"You're a baker?" Deena asked.

He shuffled his feet, looking down. "Just at home."

She stepped closer and put a weathered hand on his arm. Waiting for him to meet her eyes, she said, "That's how we all start."

"Don't suppose you want to take over this project and open a bakery instead?" Hank asked.

Wyatt gave him a sad smile. He wished that was possible. That wasn't something he ever really considered, but now that it was out there, he wanted it. More than just about anything. "Even if I had that kind of money, I know nothing about running my own business."

"Shame." Hank leaned against the counter. "It's already pretty much set up for that. All new appliances and everything."

When Wyatt left, his chest was tighter than it had been in a while. Thunder rumbled above, and he quickened his pace. He'd said he didn't know how to run a business, but as he glimpsed Happily Ever Crafter on his way to the bar, he realized he knew a few people who could give him advice. Not only had Charlie and Vi successfully kept their shop open the last few years, but they had expanded it to include the classroom in the next-door building. And Aiden's mom had owned the store for a couple of decades before them.

Plus, the woman Wyatt was sleeping with had two business degrees. The bar didn't adequately reflect her knowledge or skills; she'd boarded an already-sinking ship.

It started to sprinkle just as he reached the front door, and he rushed inside. He spotted Livvy at one of the tall tables. It was early enough that only a few others sat at the bar and in one of the booths.

Wyatt nodded at Owen behind the bar as he went to Livvy. His heart beat too quickly, and he needed her to ground him.

"Hey." She grinned at him, and it eased some of that tension within.

He put a hand on her side and leaned in to brush his lips across hers. "Hi."

Casually kissing her in the middle of the bar probably wasn't the smartest move, but when she tugged on his neck to bring him in for another, the concern faded. She wanted this too.

"How did it go?" she asked as he pulled a bar stool closer to take a seat next to her. When he didn't respond, she groaned. "That bad?"

"That bad." He relayed everything the couple had told him, only leaving out the part where he'd asked about a job. That wasn't something he was ready to share with anyone. Admitting he wanted to follow those dreams terrified him.

"Well, shit... That sucks." Livvy tucked a piece of hair behind her ear—she had started wearing it down ever since he mentioned he liked it that way a few weeks ago. He loved running his fingers through the silky strands. "I mean, we can still do this without them, but it would've been awesome to have their help. Even if they were just judges."

"Yeah." He didn't know what else to say.

She reached for his hand. "Hey, look at me."

He did, realizing he'd been fidgeting and avoiding her eyes.

"Are you okay?"

He nodded.

"Wyatt." She stood when he still didn't talk. Lowering her voice, she asked, "Are you having an anxiety attack or just upset?"

Both. It was getting to be too much. All of it. For so long, he'd been content with his monotonous life. Now, he was attached to this woman and he had foolishly started to dream about a new career doing something he genuinely enjoyed.

"Breathe." Livvy stepped closer and placed a hand on his chest. "Do you want to go back to the office?"

He was so tired of losing control like this. It was beyond frustrating to understand what was happening and still not be able to prevent it. Not answering, he walked around her to the office. He braced both hands on the desk, hanging his head.

The door clicked shut behind him. A gentle hand landed on his back and rubbed soothing circles. "What do you need?"

"I don't know," he said. "It's just... I thought..."

Livvy waited in silence, letting him take the time he needed.

"Everything is spiraling, and I can't stop it. I can't do anything." He turned to drop into one of the chairs.

She moved with him, sitting on his lap. "What is spiraling? Is this about the fundraiser or something else?"

"Everything. The fundraiser. The bakery job. You." His words were barely more than a whisper by the time he finished speaking.

"Okay, let's take this one thing at a time," she said, not an ounce of judgment in her tone. "The fundraiser can happen without the bakery. We'll figure it out. Let me panic about that one; it's on me, not you."

"But I want to help."

She laced their fingers together on her lap. "And you will. But for the moment, set it aside if you can."

He nodded in agreement.

"Good. Now, what did you mean by the bakery job?"

Shit. He hadn't meant to let that slip. Keeping his eyes on their hands, he whispered, "I asked if they needed another baker while I was there."

Livvy tilted his face toward her and kissed him once. "I didn't know you were considering that."

"I didn't fully plan it," he said. "Charlie and I kind of talked about it, but I didn't know if I'd actually do it."

"I think that's great. I mean, it's horrible that it didn't work out with them, but do you want to pursue that?"

Some of the pressure on his shoulders lifted. "I don't know. Maybe? I guess I just... I got excited about possibly helping out there. But it doesn't matter now."

She lifted a hand to run along the stubble on his jaw. "It does though. If this is what you want to do, you should fight for it. What about starting your own business?"

He scoffed. "I don't have the money or knowledge to do that."

"You've practically managed things around here for years. You know the basics at the very least." She shifted on his lap to wrap an arm around his neck. "And I'm sure

Charlie and Vi could give you advice or help figure things out along the way."

Silence stretched between them at her lack of offering to help herself. Which brought him to number three on his list of things to spiral over. He brushed a thumb across her cheek,

But then, she whispered, "Plus, you have me."

He froze, his heart pounding away in his chest. "But for how long?"

"I... don't know, but even when I leave, we'll still be friends. Even if this," she kissed the corner of his mouth, "ends, you'll have me in your corner."

Clenching his jaw, he nodded again. He didn't miss the way she said *if* it ended.

"Wyatt, you knew what this was when we started." She stood from his lap, and he felt the withdrawal deep in his core. But she was right; he'd agreed to this. He had wanted this.

Wanting more was on him.

He gently grabbed her by the arm and tugged her to his lap again. She straddled his waist, and he hooked one hand around her thigh and the other around the swell of her ass. "I know. I'm sorry. It's just hard."

Her gaze softened. "It is for me too. I don't want to say goodbye."

Then, don't, he wanted to say. Instead, he kissed her, rubbing his hand along her leg.

"Wyatt," she said with a sigh as she leaned away. "If this is too hard for you—"

He pressed his lips to hers. There wasn't anything she could say that he didn't already know. This was going to hurt like hell in the end. It was way too late to change that. Even if they called it quits today, he would be miserable having to be around her all the time. At least if they kept going until she left, he wouldn't have to see her every day while not being able to touch her.

Not that it would make it easier.

Livvy's tongue brushed his as she parted her lips. She rocked her hips, and his grip tightened on her. But then, she broke the kiss with a knowing smile. "That's not fair. You can't just distract me like that when you don't want to talk about your feelings."

Chuckling, he kissed underneath her jaw. "But it's so fun."

"I'll make you a deal," she said, holding his face with both hands to make him look at her. "We won't talk about it right now, but we do need to get to work planning this fundraiser. I want it to happen next weekend, so we have to at least get the basics nailed down to start spreading the word."

He opened his mouth, but she cut him off.

"Do not make a joke about nailing me first." She pecked his cheek then stood from his lap. "If you're good and help me, we can play later."

Wyatt pushed to his feet, adjusting his pants that he was straining against. With a mischievous grin, he asked, "Are we playing here or at my house? Because I'll make Harper take Elliot out for dinner if I get to take you home and make you scream my name."

"Since when does the location make a difference?" she teased. "It's not like I haven't done that here before."

"True." He closed the distance between them to smack her curvy ass. "But at home, I have toys."

THIRTY-TWO

Olivia

There was a very high possibility that Olivia wouldn't have any hair left by the end of the week. She'd run her hands through it so many times, putting it up, taking it down, pulling out strands, that she was certain she would go bald soon if she didn't chill the hell out. She had also started chewing on her nails again, so that was awesome. That habit had been kicked in college, but apparently, it had returned.

"What do you mean they're not coming?" she asked, on the verge of screaming. The two people they'd lined up to judge the contest were both unavailable all of a sudden?

"Todd says he's sick," Becca said as they walked toward the armory. It was essentially just one big room—a gym mostly used for town events—but they wanted to see the space to get an idea of how to set up tables tomorrow. "And Stephanie had some vague excuse of being busy."

Olivia sighed. "Great. So, who else do we have who can be a judge?"

She'd been excited that the mayor was going to be one, along with a fireman.

"I'm sure Mrs. Davis would do it, and she might know someone else to join her."

The older woman who served as the town's biggest gossip would probably love to be involved. Honestly, Olivia didn't know why they hadn't asked her before. She liked to be in everyone's business, but she had the biggest heart.

"That's a great idea." Olivia nodded. "I'll see if Aiden can ask her when I call him about placing another ad for tomorrow morning."

They reached the armory just as a familiar truck pulled up beside them. She lifted a hand in a short wave at Wyatt and Shawn. Both got out and joined them, but her smile fell at the looks on their faces.

"What's going on?" she asked.

"We don't have the armory," Wyatt said.

Becca hooked an arm through Shawn's. "What do you mean?"

Wyatt held Olivia's gaze, as if worried to continue. He visibly inhaled. "There was a scheduling mix up. Someone else booked it for the same time, and they put in the request first, apparently."

"What? Who?"

"I don't know," he said. "A birthday party?"

She clenched her jaw, her chest heaving. "What do we do now?"

"We called the parks and rec office and reserved the park," Shawn said.

Wyatt took her hand in his. "The weather should be nice, so we'll just make it an outdoor event."

Olivia shook her head, reeling at this change of plans. She didn't handle last-minute changes well. The loss of control nauseated her. "Perfect. We'll serve baked goods where we can attract fucking bugs."

She pinched the bridge of her nose. Her temples throbbed.

"The competitors and volunteers will keep an eye on things. It'll be okay," Wyatt tried to say, but she was struggling to listen to reason. She took one step backward before his strong arm wrapped around her waist. He pulled her against his firm chest and lowered his voice. "Panicking is my job. Take a deep breath. Everything is going to be fine."

"Fine?" she nearly shouted as she ripped out of his arms, "This is a fucking nightmare, Wyatt. First, we lose our judges, and now, our venue?" She gripped the hair on top of her head. It wasn't his fault, but she couldn't help but take out her frustration on him. The day before had been so perfect. They'd spent it baking at his house, practicing his entries for the contest. She hated that she flipped on him so easily. "Someone is clearly trying to sabotage us! We have less than twenty-four hours to figure it all out."

"Baby, you need to calm down."

She dropped her arms and narrowed her gaze.

"Dude, never tell a woman to calm down," Shawn whispered, smacking him on the shoulder.

He was right. The phrase triggered her deep inside, making her want to do the exact opposite of its intention. She seethed, rage boiling to the surface. Before she could say something she would regret, she turned and marched down the sidewalk.

"Livvy!"

Ignoring him, she stormed toward where she had parked along the street. He ran after her though, blocking the door, reminding her of the first night they spent together.

"Leave me alone, Wyatt." She changed her trajectory; she would walk to the bar instead. It was only a few blocks. Hell, she could run home from here if she wanted.

"Not until you talk to me." He grabbed her hand, seemingly trying to get her to stop.

She did, but only to tell him, "I don't want to talk to you

—or anyone. This is a disaster, and I... I need some damn space to rethink things and *calm down*."

"I shouldn't have said that. I'm sorry. I know it makes things worse, especially for someone with anxiety." He inched closer. "Please let me help." When she didn't say anything, he whispered, "Olivia—"

"Don't." Hearing his genuine concern, seeing the love in his eyes... it was too much. She couldn't keep doing this with him. It was adding to the stress, knowing their demise was inevitable. She hadn't planned on breaking this off until she left, but she was already in a pissy mood, so why not add heartbreak to the day? Standing on her toes, she pressed her lips to his. She reveled in the way his arms instantly encircled her, held her like he never wanted to let go. Which was exactly why she broke the kiss and stepped away. "I can't do this anymore. It's too hard."

His brow creased. "What?"

Pointing between them, she said, "This. I'm calling it. I know we were going to wait, but the longer we do, the more painful it's going to be."

"Livvy—"

"This was supposed to be casual sex, nothing more. It can't be more, Wyatt. I'm not staying here."

Pain flashed in his eyes. He didn't bother trying to hide it. "Don't do this. Not now. Not like this, when you're angry and stressed."

"That's why it needs to happen now." Her voice shook as her throat tightened. "How the hell am I supposed to do it when we're happy together?"

His lips parted as understanding filled his gaze. He crossed his arms over his chest, and she wondered if it was to keep himself from reaching out to her.

"The last thing I want to do is hurt you," she whispered.

"But we both knew we had an expiration date, and I can't... I can't pretend I'm not falling in love with you anymore. It's going to kill me if we keep going and wait longer."

For once, Wyatt didn't argue. He didn't say anything, which hurt worse. She wanted him mad and yelling. She wanted him to fight.

With her.

For her.

It didn't matter so long as he did *something*.

Instead, he nodded and whispered, "Fine."

Then, he turned and walked away, leaving her gaping after him. She put a hand over her aching heart and continued to The Tavern. By the time she made it, she could barely see through the tears.

Owen stood behind the bar, which meant Ryan must have been in the kitchen.

"How'd it go?" Owen asked as she passed by him.

Shaking her head, she ignored him and made her way to the office. She slammed the door behind her before leaning against it. Only then did she let herself exhale as she slid down to the floor. She hugged her knees to her chest, grateful she'd opted for more comfortable clothes today.

She hadn't felt this much heartbreak since her mom died. Before returning last month, she hadn't cried this hard since moving away. There wasn't enough air in the room.

She didn't know how long she sat like that before a knock dragged her out of her pit of despair.

"Olivia?" Owen said through the door.

Taking a deep breath, she cleared her throat. "Yes?"

"Can I come in?"

She didn't want to face one of her employees like this. Yet, she didn't quite want to be alone either. Pushing to her feet, she wiped at her wet face but knew it wouldn't do much good. When she opened the door, Owen sighed.

He stepped forward, raising his arms, then hesitated. "Can I?"

A noise that was between a sob and laughter escaped her as she moved in to hug him. The man was only a handful of years older than her, but he had such a fatherly presence. They all joked about him being the dad of the bar, but it was true. Especially with her own dad's absence.

The thought brought on a wave of fresh tears. Owen rubbed her back, holding her close. "It's gonna be okay."

"No, it's not," she whispered. "Nothing is okay."

"What happened?"

And just like that, the walls came crumbling down yet again. The dam burst, and everything spilled out. She told him about her dad's health, the bar struggling financially, her dilemma with Wyatt, how much she missed her mom. She even let out her fears about the future because of her inability to figure out what career she wanted.

There was no holding back.

Owen listened without interrupting. At one point, he'd guided her to sit in one of the chairs while she rambled. He didn't say a word, just sat with her, holding her hand. By the time she ran out of things to vent about, she was exhausted, mentally drained.

"That is... a lot," Owen said after a minute of waiting to make sure she was finally done.

She let out a soft chuckle, wiping at her eyes and nose with a tissue. "Yeah."

"Well, I don't know what to tell you about Wyatt other than to follow your heart." With a smile, he added, "But that sounds cliché as hell." He pulled his phone out of his jeans' pocket. "As for the competition, I can call Mrs. Davis. She's friends with my mom."

"Really?" She sat a little straighter. "What about the bar and my dad? Any advice there?"

He lowered his phone. "I wish. You're right; it doesn't make sense. I've been here for years, and things do get slow from time to time, but we should be doing at least well enough to stay open." His lips pursed to the side for a second. "You said you felt like someone was sabotaging today's events? Could that same person be stealing money?"

Sighing, she slouched in her seat. "That's what I'm thinking, but how? Who? I've been monitoring things since I got here, and it's like it's vanishing straight out of our systems. And unless you have something to confess, I don't think it's any of you."

"No, I don't think it is either," he said. "So, the question is, who else has access to everything? Who could be taking it if it's not the six of us? It has to be going somewhere."

She started to shake her head, but a sinking feeling in her gut stopped her. Two other people had access to all the accounts. Her dad, who she knew wasn't taking it.

And her uncle Gary.

THIRTY-THREE

wyatt

The scent of chocolate, cinnamon, caramel, and apple drifted along the cool autumn breeze through the park. Wyatt stared around in wonder, marveling at how things had come together. His coworkers had really put in a lot of effort to make it happen, and they owed a huge thanks to Mrs. Davis, who hadn't hesitated to jump in and help however she could. She'd even recruited a couple of friends to spread the word throughout town. And she had agreed to be one of the new judges.

Aiden had run an extra reminder in the paper this morning. Charlie, Vi, and Harper plastered the town with flyers all week, and then they went around bringing participants' baked goods to the park. Colby had distributed the flyers at the schools as well.

Everyone had pitched in, and not for the first time, this small town amazed him. He'd grown up in a high-society community that was nothing like this. Back home, most people only looked out for themselves. Here, they supported one another, making impossible things happen.

Set up in a large square, contest participants stood at tables with their entries. Down the center of the space were two rows of more tables laden with all sorts of goodies to purchase. All donated to raise money for the bar. For Jack and Olivia. The townspeople didn't know about his illness, yet they still simply wanted to support them.

And despite her concerns about doing this outside, it had worked out well so far. It could be seen from the road while driving by, and since it was in the park, a lot of families lingered to let the kids play on the playground. They weren't only coming and going. Several people stayed to visit and continued to buy snacks and drinks. It had turned into a much bigger event than any of them expected.

Wyatt hadn't seen Olivia since she ran off yesterday. He'd wanted to chase after her so badly, but she had made a point, and if this was what she needed... he would let her go. Even if it felt like a thousand knives were piercing his heart.

But for her not to be here at all? He was starting to get really worried. This wasn't like her. She wasn't someone who blew things off, especially important work-related events. He was just about to give in and text her when a voice drew his attention back to the present.

"All right, what do we have here?" Mrs. Davis asked. She had convinced Colby to be a judge along with her, and of course, that meant Elliot was one too. He was practically glued to Colby's side whenever he could be. If that man wasn't so nice and good to Wyatt's sister and nephew, Wyatt might have been jealous. As it was, he was only concerned Elliot was growing too attached. Harper insisted nothing was going on with her and Colby, but he'd seen them together. It was only a matter of time. And if it didn't end well... Elliot already had to leave his father. To lose another person like that would devastate him.

"Uncle Wyatt made cake." Elliot grinned over the clipboard Mrs. Davis had given him to match their own. Not that he had any idea what he was doing beyond saying which treats were his favorite. Still, it warmed Wyatt's heart to see that they had included him.

"Chocolate and peanut butter mousse cheesecake." He lifted the cover off the cooler he'd brought to keep it chilled. As he set the dish on the table and pulled off the lid to slice the cake, he said, "I also made some gluten-free pumpkin sugar cookies for those with allergies."

He placed three pieces of cake on separate plates before passing them over, each with a plastic fork. Then, he opened the Tupperware container of cookies and pushed them to the edge of the table. More of his cookies and cakes were on the center tables to be sold as well. He'd spent the majority of the last three days baking, and he'd loved every second of it.

Elliot set his clipboard down to eat, smiling as he got chocolate on his face. It went along with the rest of the evidence from his tastings. The kid was so messy. He nodded as if considering the flavors. "Very yummy."

Chuckling, Wyatt said, "Thanks, buddy."

He already knew it was one of Elliot's favorites, so there might have been a little bias. Colby ate the entire slice and asked for a second.

"Save room for the rest," Mrs. Davis said with a laugh, even as she grabbed a cookie to try. "Wyatt, I had no idea you could bake like this. Both are delicious."

"He loves to bake." Elliot put his empty plate in the closest trash can before going for the cookies. "He does it all the time at home. Especially when in a bad mood or when he's sad. It makes him feel better."

Wyatt ruffled the little boy's hair with a smile as Mrs. Davis said, "Is that so?"

He nodded.

"You know, that bakery down the street is no longer opening. But the people of this town were excited about it."

"I did know that." He grabbed a napkin and tried to clean his nephew's face. The boy wiggled around, making it difficult, and Wyatt rolled his eyes. "But I don't have the means for something like that. Besides, I like my job."

"'Cause he gets to work with his *girlfriend*," Elliot said, singing the last word.

Harper approached with a laugh. "Stop teasing your uncle." She stood behind him and tilted his head back to kiss his forehead. Seeing the mess on his face and shirt, she groaned. "You're going to be so hyped up on sugar..."

"I'll take him to the playground to run it off when we're done." Colby pointed to the other area of the park where kids played.

"Thank you." She put a hand on his arm, but her eyes were on Wyatt. To the other three, she asked "You have a few more tables, right? Why don't you guys continue so I can talk to Wyatt?"

Elliot picked up his clipboard and scribbled something on the paper as he walked alongside Colby to the next table. Mrs. Davis followed, but not before snatching one more cookie. When it was just Wyatt and his sister left, he put another piece of cake on a plate before covering the dish and setting it back in the cooler. Harper took a bite, and he grabbed a second fork to eat some as well.

"How are sales going?" he asked.

"Fine." She narrowed her eyes. "Where's Olivia?"

He shrugged, staring at the cheesecake.

"Wyatt..." Harper sighed. "What happened?"

"She was stressed yesterday and took it out on me." He swallowed another bite. "Honestly, that was fine. I knew she wasn't really mad at me, and I was okay with her venting at me if that was what she needed, but then she broke up with me, saying it would be easier while fighting."

"Shit."

A breathy laugh escaped him. His sister never cursed. "Yeah, so, she stormed off to the bar, and I haven't seen her since."

"Wait." Harped put her fork down. "She broke up with you? I thought you said she wasn't your girlfriend?"

"Oh please, we all know I was lying. We might have said it was just casual sex, but it was more," he said before raking his fingers through his hair. "Sorry, I know that's too much info. You're my freakin' sister—"

She shook her head. "Wyatt, I know everyone sees me as the sweet, quiet one, but you do remember I got pregnant at seventeen, right? I'm not exactly inexperienced or naïve. I like—"

"Nope, not going that far." He laughed now, and it felt strange under the circumstances. "I love you, but I don't need to know the details of what you do or do not like in bed. Keep that between you and Colby."

"Oh my God. Keep it down," she hissed, glancing around to make sure no one was close enough to hear. "I told you nothing is going on there. He's just my friend; I'm not sleeping with him. I haven't been with anyone since..."

He hated reminding her of her piece of scum ex. "Okay, sorry. But yes, Olivia and I were together, even if we were both in denial. We spent all of our time together. We weren't sleeping with other people—or at least, I wasn't. I even deleted Love Hunters. And I'm pretty sure she wasn't either. She... she said she couldn't pretend she wasn't falling in love with me anymore. What the hell do I do with that?"

Harper's gaze softened. "Do you love her?"

"I..." Did he? "I don't know, but I was at least heading that way."

"Then, you need to go after her. Talk to her. You're both so stubborn; it's infuriating. Someone is going to have to compromise if you two want to make this work."

He understood that, but he'd changed his life for a woman before, and he had vowed to never do it again. Not after Loren had destroyed him so thoroughly.

"Look," Charlie said, running over to them. She pointed toward the entrance of the park.

Wyatt's breath caught in his throat. Olivia was here, and she was pushing her father in a wheelchair.

THIRTY-FOUR

olivia

Olivia hadn't wanted to come to the bake sale competition, but when her father said he *did* want to go, she couldn't say no. For weeks, she'd tried getting him out of the house. Asking to attend an event like this was a huge deal.

Though, she suspected he was doing it more for her benefit than his own. When she'd returned home last night, he had immediately known something was wrong. So, she was fairly certain his request for her to bring him to the fundraiser was part of a bigger scheme.

"It's my bar," he'd said. *"I should be there. Plus, I think you and Angela were right; it's time to quit hiding."*

She helped him out of her car and into his wheelchair then headed toward the clearing where everything was set up. They stopped at the edge of the sidewalk. It was going to be a pain in the ass pushing him through the grass, but she would do it.

"We can just stay on the cement," he whispered.

"Absolutely not." She took a deep breath and rolled him into the dirt. Pressing down on the handles, she used the leverage to lift the small front wheels slightly. It made it a little easier to get over bumps without the fear of tipping him forward. The man refused to wear a seatbelt, and the last thing he needed was to be dumped out on his face.

She'd only made it a few feet when her arms started to shake.

"Need a hand?"

Her eyes jerked up to Wyatt's. Without waiting for a response, he reached for the front of the chair and lifted to pull it along. Olivia continued pushing from behind, and he led them toward what appeared to be his table so that her dad could sit in the shade.

The event had already started; dozens of people mingled around the baked goods. A hush settled as they noticed his arrival. Some whispered, no doubt wondering why he wasn't walking, but more smiled and greeted him in passing.

It looked like the sale was going well. Someone had set up an area with lemonade and water too. It reminded her of how everyone gathered for the annual animal shelter event each spring.

"It's good to see you, Jack." Wyatt patted him on the shoulder when they reached their destination. "Glad you decided to join us."

"It was time," he said. "Are these yours?" He pointed to the cooler on the ground then the container of cookies on the table. Both of which Olivia had helped him pack yesterday morning.

Wyatt nodded with the rare shy smile she loved so much. The one that showed he was proud but embarrassed to take credit. He opened the Tupperware and set a cookie on a plate that he put on the corner nearest her dad.

"Holy shit," her dad said after taking a bite. "Where have you been hiding these all this time?"

Olivia couldn't help but chuckle, even while in pain from seeing Wyatt. "You should try the cheesecake."

Her dad's brows rose. "I definitely should." While

Wyatt got it out of the cooler, her dad asked, "So, you've already tried it, Liv?"

"She helped me make the first one earlier in the week to test the recipe." Wyatt froze, as if realizing what he'd said out loud.

"You convinced my daughter to help you bake?"

Olivia took a cookie to occupy herself. "I didn't do much. Just followed his instructions."

It was her dad's turn to laugh. "Do you remember the last time you tried to make cookies by yourself 'just following instructions'?"

The memory nearly made her choke. She didn't know whether to laugh or cry. "The first Christmas after Mom died."

"Her mom loved to cook and bake," he told Wyatt, whose gaze was on Olivia. "But my girl here can barely follow a recipe. My wife always had her mix things she measured for her ahead of time. Every year, they made dozens and dozens of cookies for Christmas. So, after she passed, little Livvy here tried to do it on her own."

At that, Olivia rolled her eyes. "You make it sound like I was a child making a mess in the kitchen." She stepped around him to grab a couple of waters from the cooler. Handing one to her dad, she told Wyatt, "I was *seventeen* making a mess in the kitchen."

Wyatt smiled. They were standing side by side now, and she knew she should move, step away, but she couldn't yet.

"She tried to start with chocolate chip because they're the easiest," her dad said, voice full of amusement.

It was the first time she'd seen him this happy in a long while. Sure, it was at her expense, but she would take it. Besides, it was the truth. She couldn't cook for shit.

"The first pan ended up completely burned to a crisp." She glanced at Wyatt.

"The second and third didn't burn, but they were inedible," her dad said. "I really tried."

Wyatt's brow furrowed. "What did you do?"

She bit at her lower lip before confessing, "I switched the measurements for salt and sugar... and read it wrong. I thought it said three-to-four cups, not three-fourths of a cup."

"They were disgusting," her dad added. "Like licking a salt block."

Olivia watched Wyatt clearly fighting back a laugh. It broke through, and he pulled her into his arms when she frowned. "Oh, *baby*."

They both stilled. His arms fell, and she stepped back, clearing her throat.

He looked between her and her dad uncomfortably. "You know what? I bet Mrs. Davis would love to have your help judging the competition. I'm just gonna..."

Pointing to the older woman standing at the next table with a clipboard, he rushed off. Olivia sighed and faced her father.

"I thought you said you weren't dating?" He set his now-empty plate down.

"We're not. Weren't." She crossed her arms.

"Obviously."

With a groan, she said, "Fine, yes, we were kind of together, but it's over now."

"Is that why you came home in tears last night?" He tilted his head. "Why is it over? It's as clear as day that you two care about each other. Liv, you baked with him. He came to help you pull me over here without needing to be asked, and he didn't seem surprised to see me like this. He didn't ask questions, so I'm assuming you told him what's going on. You let him in, and I saw the way you looked at one another."

"It's complicated."

"I'm old and deteriorating, but I think I can keep up," he said with a wink.

She leaned against the table. This wasn't exactly a conversation she wanted to have right now, let alone with her father, but maybe it would help to have his insight. "I broke up with him yesterday because we're getting too close. You know I'm not staying here, and he's had a horrible experience in the past with a woman asking him to uproot his life for her. I won't make him go through that again."

To her surprise, her dad smiled.

"What?"

"You said you won't make him, not that you won't ask him."

"So?"

He reached for her arms, uncrossing them to hold her hand. "So, that means you know what his answer would be if you *did* ask. You know he'd say yes."

She chewed on the inside of her cheek. Turning away from the event to hide her tears from the townsfolk, she said, "The people I love most always leave me."

"Olivia..."

She shook her head, not wanting to say more. But she didn't need to. Her dad knew her well enough to put the pieces together.

"That's why you left? Why you tried to disappear into a big city?" He squeezed her hand.

"After losing Mom, I couldn't... I couldn't face that again," she whispered. "I thought putting distance between me and this place... would help, especially w-with..."

"With me?"

She nodded, and he pulled her closer. Just as she had growing up, she sat on his knee and let him wrap her in a hug. She curled against his chest, crying into his collar. There were so many people around, but right now, she couldn't bring herself to care.

"I'm sorry I wasn't there for you," her dad said, rubbing her back. "I will regret that for the rest of my life. I thought you left because you blamed me, not because you were afraid of losing others. Death—loss—is a part of life, sweetheart. No one lives forever, and sometimes it doesn't work out with those you give your heart to."

"I don't know if I can live through that again."

"You can. You're the strongest person I know." He brushed a strand of her hair out of her face. "You can't spend what time you have on this earth fearing loss. It's the most painful thing in the world. It was agony when your mom died. But you know what?"

Olivia sniffled, wiping at her cheeks. "What?"

"I wouldn't trade our time together for anything. Being able to spend part of my life with her, having you, made the pain worth it. Love is always worth the potential pain, Olivia. You just have to be brave enough to take the chance."

She lifted her head and looked around, finding the man she loved without trouble. Wyatt balanced a handful of plates with different baked goods alongside Elliot, who carried two as well. They grinned and chatted on their way over. Mrs. Davis, Colby, and Harper followed.

Olivia stood and used one of the napkins from the table to dry her eyes. Based on the way everyone's gaze softened as they approached, it didn't help much.

"We brought over one of everything so you can pick a

favorite with us," Elliot said as he and Wyatt laid their plates out for her dad.

Mrs. Davis handed him a clipboard and started to explain their ranking system. While Harper stopped Elliot from grabbing more than one cookie, Wyatt moved to Olivia's side.

He didn't say anything, didn't touch her. He just stood beside her, silently supporting her despite her breaking up with him. Inching closer, she slipped her hand into his. He didn't hesitate to squeeze her fingers, and she let out a relieved breath, knowing they would work this out.

Together, they watched the crowds. They watched people greeting her dad and wishing him well. They watched him trying each entry with a smile, sharing them with Elliot.

For a while, Olivia let herself live in this moment and pretend everything was going to be all right. But deep down, she knew it wouldn't. This bake sale was a wonderful idea, and the donations would help a lot, but if her suspicions were right, it wouldn't be enough.

To make any real progress in saving The Tavern, she needed to prove her uncle was stealing the money. Then, she needed to find a more permanent solution to lower costs until they were back on their feet.

And the only way she could think of to accomplish that would leave someone hating her. She didn't know how to decide who that would be.

THIRTY-FIVE

wyatt

There weren't any leftovers. Not one morsel. Even the remnants of the entries for the competition had been bought up and distributed by Mrs. Davis. She had insisted no one went home empty handed.

"Congrats, again, Wyatt," Colby said as they put the last of Wyatt's containers and the cooler in Harper's car. "That cheesecake was delicious."

"Thanks." Wyatt couldn't fight the grin if he wanted to. He'd been happy just to participate; he hadn't expected to win.

As Harper and Elliot neared, the little boy started to jump up and down. "Playground?"

"How is he not miserable?" Colby whispered. "I feel like if I make any sudden movements, I'm going to be sick."

"Because he's a five-year-old boy," Harper said, steering Elliot toward him. "And you made a promise."

Colby visibly inhaled and looked up at the clouds rolling in. "I know, I know. Come on, buddy. Let's go before it starts raining."

"No swings!" Harper yelled after them.

"That's going to end so badly," Wyatt said with a smirk.

His sister chuckled. "I know, but the sooner he runs it off, the quicker the sugar crash will come."

He watched them walk to the playground, Elliot

jumping around and talking a hundred miles a minute. Before Wyatt could even comment on it, Harper did, as if reading his mind.

"It scares me how much Elliot likes him."

"I know," Wyatt whispered, bumping her shoulder with his arm. "But Colby is nothing like David. Even if you give him a chance and it doesn't work out, I don't think it would be remotely close to what happened. Colby seems like a genuinely nice guy. I know that's not your type—"

She elbowed him in the stomach and stepped away. "All right, I get it. My taste in men could use some work."

Wyatt raised a brow. "A lot of work, sis. David was a manipulative dick. And your boyfriend before that wasn't much better."

"David wasn't like that when we started dating."

"You mean when he was acting nice to get into your pants?" He crossed his arms and shook his head.

"Wyatt..."

"What? I'm right, and you know it." Wyatt loved Elliot more than almost anything in the world, and he knew Harper did, but he wondered what her life might have looked like if she'd never given in to that asshole.

Sighing, she said, "Stop going through the what-ifs. I see it in your face."

He tried to clear the thoughts from showing.

"My only regret is not divorcing him sooner," she said. "I will never regret the beginning of our relationship. Not only did it bring me the greatest little boy, but it led to me moving here, meeting new friends, and discovering my love of art. I did things out of order, but I made it here."

Wyatt opened his mouth. To say what, he wasn't sure. It didn't matter though.

Harper nodded toward the bar. "Go talk to Olivia. If

you love her as much as I think you do, you need to tell her. It might not change her choice, but you'll regret it if you don't at least try to fight for her. She's a good one. And Elliot likes her too now that he knows she's no longer being mean to you."

He couldn't argue with that. She was right about needing to talk to Livvy. Throughout the event, she had mostly stayed by his side, and she'd reached for his hand. Even if she truly wanted to stop seeing each other, he knew they would end on peaceful terms instead of in a fight. But the way she'd looked at him...

A sliver of hope dwelled in his heart. If she was willing to give him a chance, he would do whatever it took to make it work. He swore he would never give another woman control over his life, but she was worth it. Wyatt trusted Livvy with the heart she'd helped pieced back together.

With a new determination, he said, "I'll see you at home."

Harper grinned, and he took off.

The Tavern was crowded when he made it inside. Several people from the event mingled, ordering food and drinks. He wondered if they did it to help or if they weren't ready to call it a day. Either way, the sight eased his worry. Jack sat at one of the lower tables, catching up with people. The man had owned and worked this bar for over a decade; everyone had missed him. They would want to know why he'd been absent.

"She's in the office," Owen said when Wyatt approached the bar.

"Thanks." He headed down the hallway and knocked on the closed door at the end.

Her voice rang out from the other side. "Come in."

Wyatt entered, shutting the door behind him when he saw that she was alone in here.

"I can't believe you actually knocked." Livvy glanced up at him from her desk. Her long hair was up in a messy bun, and she looked exhausted, but she was as beautiful as ever. The cash box sat beside her, along with a calculator, a notebook, and her planner.

He moved closer and saw the spreadsheets open on the computer. "How's it going? Think it made a difference?"

"It helped, but not enough," she whispered, standing and shaking her head. "I think my uncle is taking the money. I'm working on proving it, but I doubt we can get it back."

As she began pacing next to her desk, he leaned against. "Shit."

"Yep." Her tone shifted into one full of anger. "The man who has been insisting I figure this out, putting all the weight on my shoulders and acting like it will be my fault if the bar shuts down."

"What do we do?"

"I'm trying to get him off of the accounts." She stopped to face him. "If I can stop him, we'll struggle but make it. But only if I..."

Wyatt didn't like the grief in her eyes. "If you?"

"Let someone go." She lowered her gaze.

He was sure he heard her wrong. She'd hinted at it before, but he thought they had decided against that. His chest heaved as he tried to come up with anything else. He looked down at her notebooks and spreadsheets to see the numbers. A list of their names was on a piece of paper, and one was underlined. He shook his head. "You can't."

"I have to."

"No." He knew his tone was harsh, but he couldn't let this happen. "You can't fire Ryan."

"Then, who?" She lifted her chin. "Who, Wyatt? I'm open to suggestions."

"He needs this job to support his little girl."

"He calls in all the time, shows up late—"

"So cutting out his pay won't make that much of a difference!" Wyatt was seething now. He stepped around her but stopped near the chairs, unsure where to even go.

Livvy's sigh rang through the room. "You're right."

He turned to face her.

"Which means I need to let someone else go," she said, crossing her arms. "Someone who gets paid more."

Her meaning hit him like a blow to the gut. He almost laughed. "You're gonna fire me again?"

She visibly swallowed. "Yes."

He let out a breathy laugh, but it wasn't because he was amused. Rolling his eyes, he moved toward the door and said, "Fine. I'll see you when it gets busy and you change your mind like usual."

"I'm serious this time, Wyatt."

He paused with one hand on the doorknob. Just by her voice, he knew she was. This time was different. Facing her again, he started to shake his head. "Don't do this."

"You have the highest pay and the most hours. It's the logical choice."

"Fuck logical," he said, stomping closer. "You know you need me here, and I need this job."

"You don't even *like* this job," she whispered. "This isn't what you want to do with your life."

"No, don't do that. Just because we're sleeping together doesn't give you the right to tell me what I want in life, Olivia." It was one thing to change his life for her, but for her to fire him? To take away his choice entirely? That was vastly different.

She scoffed. "We're not just sleeping together, you infuriating asshole. You know it's more than that. It has been for a while."

"Says the woman who broke up with me yesterday because she's scared."

"Because I'm fucking terrified!" Her voice rose. "You're not the only one here who's a mess with commitment issues. I know this isn't a surprise, but I don't like not having a plan, not being in control."

Understatement of the year.

"I told you that you weren't the only one with anxiety. Mine was bad before my mom died," she continued. "After? It got so much worse. Every second of my life had to be planned, and if something was off, I would have a full-on meltdown. And it still happens. You've seen it twice now."

"Livvy." His stance softened a fraction, but she wasn't done.

"I ran away from this town, wanting to hate it so that it wouldn't hurt as badly to lose anyone else. I went to a big university in a big city to disappear."

The tears lining her eyes broke his heart.

She swallowed. "But even with all of that schooling—two degrees and a mountain of debt—I couldn't figure out what I wanted to do with it. How do I plan my life if I don't even know what to do? And then, my dad... my dad called me—"

Her words cut off, and Wyatt stopped fighting it. He reached for her, wrapping her in a hug.

"You want to know the most fucked-up part?" she whispered. "My first reaction when he told me what was going on wasn't fear or grief. It was relief that I had a reason to put my life on hold. I thought it would give me time to think through everything, to plan. I was looking for jobs in the city, expecting to return. I told myself I could take any job while I figured out a career path." She pushed away from Wyatt. "But then, I met you and started questioning everything again."

He stepped back, knowing they both needed space. "What do you want me to do, apologize?"

Olivia groaned and pinched the bridge of her nose. "No. I'm just trying to explain."

"Explain what?" He was tired of these games, of the ups and downs.

It seemed she was too. Throwing out her arms to her sides, she shouted, "I love you, idiot!" She lowered her voice. "I love you. I'm choosing you. I'm not leaving again."

Wyatt stared at her, unable to breathe. He'd wanted this so much. He'd longed for those words, but hearing them now...

He started spiraling. Could he really let her give up everything to be with him?

"I love you, Wyatt. And I want you to see that you should grab on to this opportunity and go after your dreams," she said, reminding him of the real issues right now.

He gritted his teeth and backed toward the door, needing air. It was like his lungs didn't want to function anymore. Turning the knob, he said, "That wasn't your decision to make though."

Without waiting for a response, he left the office. He ignored the stares of his friends and the other townspeople who'd no doubt heard them over the music. It was raining when he made it outside, but he didn't care. Instead of going to his truck, he began jogging down the street.

For the first time in perhaps ever, he wanted his friends. Needed them. He didn't want to be alone, despite the anxiety coursing through him.

His feet pounded along the wet sidewalk, matching his racing heart. He barely managed to skid to a stop in front of Happily Ever Crafter before yanking open the door and praying to whoever might be listening that Charlie had come here instead of going home after the event. The bell ringing overhead as he stepped inside was muffled by the blood pulsing in his ears.

Looking down, he cursed. He didn't want to track in so much water.

Charlie appeared from the classroom side of the shop. Her smile fell, and she rushed forward with concern in her big blue eyes. "What's wrong?"

Aiden came out to see what the commotion was, but Wyatt focused on Charlie as he tried to even out his breathing.

"Wyatt?" She reached him and put a hand on his arm.

When she tried to lead him farther inside, he shook his head. "I'll get everything wet."

"I don't care." She led him toward the cash register. "Talk to me, please."

He lowered to the floor with his back against the white counter, pulling his knees up to his chest. He ran a hand through his hair while draping the other arm over his legs. "She..." There were so many things to tell Charlie—that Gary was behind the money disappearing, that the bake sale and competition hadn't been enough to save the bar, that he'd been fired to make up the difference—but he couldn't speak yet.

Charlie knelt next to him. "Can I touch you, or will that make it worse?"

He held an arm up, and she slid in closer to sit at his side and hug him.

The world was quieter down here, darker, calmer.

"Take a deep breath," she whispered.

Aiden appeared in front of them and lowered to the floor, offering a water bottle. When Wyatt didn't move, Charlie took it.

She opened it and held it up close to Wyatt's hand. "Drink."

He obeyed, gulping down some of the cool water. She didn't say anything else, just held him as he worked to steady his breathing and heart rate. Aiden never commented on the fact that his fiancée was curled up, hugging another man. They simply sat with him.

Eventually, he calmed down enough to whisper, "She said she loves me. Livvy is staying."

It was silent for a long moment. He lifted his gaze to find his two friends smiling at him. Though, Charlie's brow furrowed. "Then, why are you here? What made you have an anxiety attack? That was a bad one, Wy. You really scared me."

"Sorry," he mumbled. Taking a deep breath, he tried to figure out how to explain this. "There's so much going on; this week has been so stressful. It's been a roller coaster with Livvy from day one, and I... I think it all hit me at once. Last night, I thought I was losing her for good. The reason I went in to even talk to her just now was because I was willing to find a way to make things work. But she beat me to it, which threw me off. Right after firing me for good this time, I might add."

"Whoa," Aiden said. "Hold on. That was a lot."

Before Wyatt could try to explain better, Charlie said, "You were willing to make it work long distance or move.

So, why run away from her? Even if you don't feel ready to admit it's love, why are you here instead of with her? She was telling you she'd give up her life in the city to be with you. Don't run away from your happily ever after, Wyatt. Trust me."

That was the thing. He did love Livvy. He'd fallen so in love with her that it was almost painful. But he was still scared, and he was mad at her. Though, even as he thought it, he knew she made the right choice for the bar. He wouldn't hold that against her.

"But I don't want her to give everything up. I've been there, and I can't do that to her."

"You have to let her make that decision."

Closing his eyes, he nodded. She was right. Of course she was right.

Needing a few more minutes, he told Charlie and Aiden everything else. Then, he would go back to Livvy. He would make this work. If she was really staying...

She needed to know that he loved her too.

THIRTY-SIX

Olivia

He'd walked away.

Olivia told Wyatt she loved him and would stay for him, and he had walked away.

A band tightened around her chest, making it impossible to take a full breath.

But she couldn't wallow in her grief. Not right now. The Tavern was packed, and she was helping Owen and Shawn on the floor. Becca and Ryan were also around, stepping in here and there, but it was a calm atmosphere. She was pretty sure that was her father's doing. He sat at one of the tables, surrounded by people like he was holding court.

No one mentioned Wyatt, but she could see the concern in her employees' eyes.

"Can I get another beer, please?" Justin asked, approaching where she stood at the bar.

Knowing his preference, she turned and grabbed one for him, even though she wasn't on drink duty. It had been a unanimous decision that it was best if she didn't do that part of the job unless they really needed help.

Justin had missed most of the event because of work, but she was grateful he'd made it. He put a hand on her wrist before she could retreat. "I'm really worried about you, Liv."

"I'm fine," she lied, though she knew he could see right through her.

"Looks like your little event was successful," another voice said, sending a shiver down her spine.

Olivia glared at her uncle. "It was. Too bad you couldn't make it or, you know, help with any of the planning."

Gary shook his head as if exhausted by a petulant child. "Some of us have full-time jobs, Olivia. We can't all afford to come and go as we please."

"Some of us can't *afford* much of anything because of the funds disappearing." She was playing with fire, but for once, she didn't care. She was done letting him walk all over her.

"Figure out who was stealing yet?" He looked at Owen and Shawn. "Where's the one you've been sleeping with?"

She crossed her arms. "Not here."

He scoffed. "How convenient. Have you checked the money made from the event? Did you have a donation box? Maybe you should make sure he didn't take it with him."

"Wyatt didn't take anything." Only the shattered remains of her heart.

"Still, you should give it to me so I can go deposit it right away. It's not safe to leave it sitting around," her uncle said.

She couldn't believe this man. Then again, who knew how long he'd been siphoning money out of this place, slowly sucking it dry? "It's fine. I've put it in a safe spot. I'll deposit it Monday morning."

"Don't be foolish. I'm heading out of town. It's on the way."

Justin stepped aside, allowing her dad to roll his chair to the bar as he asked, "What's going on over here?"

Owen had joined them too, and she was thankful for his constant quiet support.

"Your daughter is being stubborn to prove some point about her being responsible or some shit," Gary said. "I told her to give me the money raised today so I can put it in the bank on my way out of town."

"Into whose account?" She couldn't stop the accusation from leaving her mouth. This wasn't the time or place to have this fight, but she wasn't going to let him touch that cash.

"What the hell is that supposed to mean?"

Olivia rolled her eyes. "You know damn well what I mean."

Her uncle's face reddened. He looked at his brother and back. "You think *I* took the money? From my own fucking bar?"

"All right, maybe we should—"

She interrupted her dad. "I know you did. And I'm not letting you take any more. I've already talked to a lawyer."

"You bitch," he seethed. "You have no right—"

"Enough," her dad shouted. "Talk to my daughter like that again, and I'll—"

"You'll what?" Gary asked. "It's not like you can fight me now."

"No, but I can."

Olivia's heart stopped.

Gary turned around, only to be met by Wyatt's fist. A collective "*ohh*" rang out through the room. The crowd had quieted, watching the situation play out. Her uncle stumbled, and Wyatt grabbed him by the front of his shirt to pin him against the bar. Olivia rushed around to their side, debating on whether to stop him.

"Talk to them like that again, and I'll be the one you have to deal with. Are we clear?" Wyatt said in his face.

"Okay, break it up," another voice said. A police officer

put a hand on Wyatt's shoulder, and Olivia realized it was Lincoln, her neighbor growing up.

"You're done here," Wyatt told Gary, ignoring Lincoln's tug.

Olivia stepped in, grabbing Wyatt's arm. "Stop, Wyatt. Please, stop. He's not worth getting arrested."

"He's the one who should be in jail," he hissed, but he released her uncle.

"I know." She pulled him away, trying not to get her hopes up that he'd returned for her. Especially when he put his arm around her. She didn't even care that he was wet from the rain.

Lincoln offered her dad his hand to shake. "Good to see you, Mr. Cartwright. Wanna tell me what's going on?"

Owen and the others had slowly ushered the crowd out, telling everyone they needed to shut down early. A few people mumbled complaints, but she was fairly certain it was only because they wanted to watch the drama unfold.

Gary pointed at Olivia. "She's accusing me of—"

"*She* has proof," Olivia said.

Wyatt's fingers dug into her hip, but he didn't give any hint that she was bluffing.

Her uncle's face paled. He sputtered, glancing around. He believed her; she saw the fear in his eyes. "You conniving—you are just like your mother, you know that?"

"Thank you." She stopped fighting her smile.

"She was always trying to push me out of the picture too."

"Maybe they were both right to do so," her dad said.

Gary's shocked face turned to his brother. "You believe her? Over me?"

Her dad didn't even hesitate to say, "Yes."

Olivia let out a breath.

"You're done here, Gary."

"You can't do this," he argued. "It's half mine."

"Actually, it's not." Olivia stepped forward, meeting her dad's gaze. "You own forty-five percent of the business, just like Dad. I own the other ten. It was passed on to me from my mother. Together, my dad and I own the majority."

Gary looked on the verge of screaming. He took one step toward her, and several things happened at once. Not only did Wyatt pull her behind him, but every one of her employees moved in front of her. All of them. It wasn't necessary because Lincoln was there to block him too, but knowing they would stand between her and a potential threat made her throat tighten. They really had become her family.

"What the hell did we miss?" Vi asked as she, Charlie, and Aiden walked inside.

WYATT TUGGED ON A SWEATSHIRT, COVERING HIS BARE chest, much to Olivia's dismay. He'd left it here and was now seemingly glad to have something dry to change into. Though, there weren't any pants for him. She almost joked that he could just take his off to let them dry, but now wasn't the time.

Her dad had Gary kicked out of the bar and then immediately called the bank to put a hold on the accounts. He was now sitting at one of the tables with Lincoln and Owen, going through the numbers himself. She'd told him the lawyer said they needed a court order to make Gary provide his bank statements to compare. It could take a while for this to be resolved, but so long as he couldn't take more from them, they would be okay.

That was an issue for later though. There was nothing more they could do about it tonight. And she needed to face the other elephant in the room.

The hot, broody elephant currently staring at her.

"I'm sorry," they both started at the same time.

She shook her head, waving a hand in front of her. "No, let me say this. I shouldn't have dumped that on you and then thrown in the L word. It was too much."

"Don't." He moved closer, stopping mere inches away. She curled her fingers into fists, resisting the urge to touch him. The corner of his mouth twitched as he glanced down. "Don't apologize for that. Unless... you didn't mean it. If it was said in the heat of the moment—"

"I mean it." She licked wet her lips. "I love you."

He ended her agony, cupping the side of her neck. "I love you too, Olivia. I only left because I was spiraling into a bad anxiety attack. Before any of that, I came to tell you that if you want to do this and still live or work in Chicago, we can figure it out. I don't want you to change your life for me."

"Wyatt." She put her hands on his chest. "I don't want to go back. I'm done feeling invisible. For the first time in years, I feel truly seen, and that's because of you. But I'm doing this for me too, for my dad, for this stupid bar and the people who've become my friends." She let out a soft laugh then sniffled as her throat burned. "You are not the only reason I'm staying. You just made me see all the reasons I had to stop running."

The words were barely out before his mouth was on hers. His hand slid into her hair as he pushed her against the desk. She gripped his sweatshirt, holding him tightly. As if there was any space left between them. His tongue brushed hers, sending sparks all the way to her toes.

A throat cleared, and they jumped apart, panting. Olivia's face heated as she found her dad and Charlie watching them from the door she hadn't heard open.

"I take it you two made up?" he said, amusement lighting his eyes.

Wyatt moved to her side and draped an arm around her shoulders. He kissed her temple. "Yes, sir."

"You told him?"

"Everything," Olivia said with a smile. She'd shared her plan with him earlier, before Wyatt arrived at the bar the first time.

"Then, this calls for a celebration. My girl is finally home to stay!"

THIRTY-SEVEN

wyatt

1 month later...

"You're going to be late."

Wyatt looked over his shoulder at his sister. "What time is it?"

"Almost two."

"Shi-crap." He corrected himself, glancing at Elliot. His nephew was already distracted by Charlie though, who was painting a small sign at one of the tables. Next to her, Aiden held out a hand for a high five before pulling the boy onto his lap so they could watch Charlie. Of course, she'd brought some extra paper for him to draw too.

Wyatt finished painting the portion of the window frame he was working on.

"Here, let me take over," Harper said. "You're already a mess."

There was light blue paint covering his hands, with splatters on his arms and clothes. He handed her the brush and went to the sink in the back corner to try to get at least some of it off.

"Wy, stop stalling," Charlie hollered over to him.

He dried off his hands with a sigh. "I'm not stalling."

She smirked as he neared their table to see how things were coming along. "Go to your girlfriend, Wyatt."

"Yeah, go to your girlfriend, Uncle Wyatt," Elliot echoed.

"I'm going. I'm going." He squeezed Charlie's shoulder as he headed toward the glass door. Grabbing his jacket from the old-fashioned rack, he turned and took another look around.

"We've got this," Harper said with an understanding smile. "We'll see you later."

"All right, we'll be back in a bit." He headed out to his truck, knowing they were right. It wasn't that he didn't want to go. He was just nervous.

The drive across town gave him enough time to calm down and then panic again, especially when he stopped at the florist. But as he pulled in beside Livvy's car, a sense of peace overcame him. For her, he could do this. She got out of her car while he climbed out of his truck and went to her.

"Hi." He kissed her once before drawing her into a hug. "Where's your dad?"

"I dropped him off at home. He said this should be my moment. I tried to tell him you were coming too, but he insisted he would return later."

Wyatt nodded and brushed his lips against hers again. "Ready?"

"Yeah," Olivia whispered.

Wyatt slipped his free hand around hers. Together, they walked across the cold hard earth. When they reached their destination, Olivia tightened her hold on him.

He released her only long enough to put the bouquet of colorful flowers against the dark headstone. "Happy birthday, Mrs. Cartwright." He returned to Olivia who'd lowered to the grass, and he sat next to her, wrapping an arm around her shoulders. "Happy birthday, Livvy."

Finding out they had the same birthday had broken his

heart almost as much as learning she hadn't been to the cemetery since the funeral.

"She would've hated you calling her Mrs. Cartwright," Livvy said in a hushed tone.

With a smile, he said, "Sorry. Happy birthday, Maria."

"Happy birthday, Mom." Livvy sniffled and brushed away the tears that began falling. Her voice shook as she said, "I'm sorry it took so long for me to get back here."

Wyatt kissed the side of her head. He didn't know her mom, but from what he'd heard, he could almost guarantee the woman would have understood.

"I was so mad that you were taken from me, and I didn't handle it well," she said. "It was too hard, and leaving seemed like the easier option."

He held her as she summed up her life for the past six years—everything from her guilt and that tragic night to leaving for college, her exes, and living in the city. Most of it, he already knew, but it still made his chest ache hearing some of it. Especially the parts about her running away so that she didn't grow attached to anyone ever again. She also talked about returning for her dad and the bar.

When she lifted her head to give Wyatt a sad smile, he wiped at her damp cheeks with his thumb.

"And this is Wyatt. He's a pain in my butt most of the time, but you would've loved him," Livvy said. "He was the one who initially made me want to stay. He's the reason I knew it was time."

Wyatt couldn't help but smile. "Your daughter is an incredible woman. You'd be proud of her. I definitely am."

She leaned up to kiss him. "Thank you."

"I mean it." He brushed a piece of her hair from her face.

She kissed him again before resting against his side.

They sat that way for a while, neither speaking. The cold from the ground seeped into him, making him wish he'd thought to grab a blanket, but he would sit here as long as Livvy needed. This was an important moment for her.

Eventually, she said to him, "The meeting with the lawyer went well."

"Yeah?" Wyatt hadn't wanted to ask until after they left. "What'd he say?"

"They finally received Gary's bank statements, which prove he was taking the money. It should be enough for the judge to rule in our favor," she said. "I doubt we'll get it back. Gary won't follow the payment plan we've proposed, but it's looking promising that we will at least get to take his share of the business."

"That's great. As long as the bar continues doing well, it should bounce back, right?"

She nodded. "Slowly, but yeah. It should be fine if we don't take any more hits. The anonymous donation helped so much."

He had a pretty strong feeling the *anonymous* donor was Mrs. Davis. After all, she'd bought out the newspaper to save it this past summer, and she was constantly supporting the town.

"How'd things go for you today?" Livvy asked.

"Good. We're almost done."

"I'm so proud of you too. You know that, right?"

He did. "I couldn't have done any of this if you hadn't fired me."

At that, she chuckled and shifted to her knees. "Come on, let's get out of here. It's freezing."

They pushed to their feet but stayed another moment. He hugged Olivia from behind and bent to put his chin on her shoulder. "Thank you for letting me come with you."

"I'm glad you're here." She leaned to the side and turned her head to kiss him. They stood together, staring at the headstone, for a couple more minutes before she said, "Love you, Mom. I promise to visit more often."

Olivia pulled out of his arms, taking his hand to head to the parking lot, but he said, "Hold on."

He went to kneel next to the headstone and lowered his voice. "I promise to take care of her, Maria." He glanced over at his girlfriend, who stood watching him with a sad smile and her arms wrapped around herself. Taking one of the pale blue flowers to give her, he added, "Forever."

EPILOGUE

olivia

3 months later...

The bell chimed as Wyatt opened the door, and the crowd outside cheered. Olivia grinned from her spot behind the counter as Elliot ran in first. Wyatt scooped him up and stood aside to welcome the others. Justin pushed Olivia's dad in, followed by Harper, Colby, Charlie, Vi, Aiden, Aaron, and Lars, as well as all their parents and a couple dozen other people who'd come out for the grand opening of Sugar and Spice. Of course, Mrs. Davis was right there with them, grinning and putting money in the tip jar before she could even order.

Wyatt thanked them for coming and rushed to join Olivia, setting Elliot on the stool they'd put by the cash register. He kissed Olivia on the cheek.

"How can we help you, ma'am?" Elliot asked Harper, just as they had practiced the day before.

She smiled. "I'll take a chocolate chip brownie."

Elliot looked up at Wyatt, who whispered, "Two."

"That'll be two dollars," Elliot said as he put his hand out.

"Actually, can I have two brownies?" She winked.

He held up his fingers and added two plus two. "Four dollars?"

She nodded and handed him four ones.

"Good job, buddy." Wyatt opened the cash register for him. Olivia plated two brownies and passed them over. Her dad watched them with a smile.

Harper took them and asked Elliot, "Want to sit with us and eat one?"

Elliot glanced at his uncle.

"Go. I'll take over until you're done."

The little boy jumped down and ran around to his mom. Justin pushed Olivia's dad up to the counter with a smile.

"Proud of you, boy," the latter said.

"Thanks, Jack." Wyatt plated up a piece of cheesecake for each of them. She knew her dad's words meant a great deal to him.

People continued ordering, filling up the tables quickly. Many stood around talking once there weren't any more chairs. They sold out of some treats just as quickly. It warmed Olivia's heart to see the townspeople come to support Wyatt, even with it being so cold and snowy outside. After the last customer ordered, she slid an arm around his waist.

"Hi, baby," he said, brushing his lips against her forehead.

Chuckling, she put a hand on his chest. "Congratulations, Mr. Baker. I'd say the opening was a success."

After the bank approved his loan request, he hadn't hesitated to buy the bakery from the couple who had changed their plans. They had been so happy to hear someone would still be opening such a shop. They'd even come today and now sat with Wyatt and Olivia's friends and family.

It had taken a while to come up with a plan, rebrand, and finally open, but he made it through.

"I didn't expect this kind of turnout." He released her to serve a few more customers who arrived.

They'd closed the bar for the afternoon, and Charlie and Vi closed Happily Ever Crafter, so everyone could make it. Mrs. Davis had helped encourage others around town to show up too. In the end though, most of the people still trickling in came purely to support the man who'd lived here the past six years thinking he hadn't made any friends. He didn't see how loved he was around here. He'd served half the town at one point or another, and they hadn't forgotten him.

When he passed over the last cupcake to a young girl, he looked at the empty glass case in awe. There was nothing left. Not a single cookie or scone or piece of cheesecake. All of it had been bought, and the tip jar was full.

Slipping her hand into his, Olivia led Wyatt to the tables their families and friends had pushed together.

"There he is!" Aiden patted him on the shoulder. He stood behind Charlie's chair, who got to her feet to hug Wyatt then Olivia.

Becca rounded the table to do the same. Since their heart to heart, the two had become friends again. Olivia loved working together now that they weren't at each other's throats.

For so long, she had pushed away everyone out of fear. She knew that letting them in gave them the potential to leave, to hurt her. But in trying to protect her heart, she'd only succeeded in making herself lonely.

Never again would she do that. She wanted to love and be loved in return by these people.

"So, is it everything you wanted today to be?" Harper

asked in a clearly staged voice, flicking her eyebrows up with a mischievous look.

Olivia glanced between the siblings in confusion.

Wyatt shook his head with a sigh. "Subtle, Harps."

"I told you I should be the one to ask," Justin said with a shrug before wheeling her dad backward to face them.

"What is going on?" Olivia's brow furrowed.

Elliot jumped up and down, clearly excited. "Do it!"

Taking a deep breath, Wyatt turned to the rest of the shop and cleared his throat. "Can I have everyone's attention please?"

The room quieted, all eyes landing on him. Hers widened. She had talked to him about giving a speech, knowing it would likely trigger his anxiety. They had agreed that it would be best not to give one, that he would thank people as they ordered and call it a day.

"First, I just wanted to thank everyone again," he said. "Most of you know me as a bartender, but baking has always been my passion, my first love after my family. I never dreamed this was possible. It only is because of everyone's support, but none more than my incredible girlfriend."

She laced their fingers together and stepped closer as he angled toward her.

"Thank you, Livvy, for fighting with me and firing me from the bar."

The crowd laughed, and she rolled her eyes but smiled.

"Thank you for believing in me. For encouraging me." He lifted a hand to her cheek. "For loving me." He kissed her once, twice. "You butted into my life like a thorn in my side, and I will forever be grateful."

Her stomach fluttered, her throat tightening as suspicion crept into her mind.

"We've both gone through so much, but I truly believe it was to bring us together."

"Wyatt..."

He smiled, his free hand reaching behind him. Tears blurred her vision as she spotted the small black box Harper put in his palm. He knelt, holding it out in front of him. "Olivia Joanne, beautiful, stubborn love of my life," he popped open the box to reveal a diamond ring, "will you marry me?"

Olivia was nodding before he even finished asking. Her heart had never felt so full. He pulled the ring from the box and slid it onto her finger as he stood to kiss her. Lifting her off the ground, he deepened the kiss while their friends and family clapped and cheered.

Eventually, he lowered her and cupped her cheek. "I love you, Livvy."

"I love you too," she said through the tears.

His hand swept into her hair as he kissed her again. And then, their friends were demanding their attention, offering their congratulations. She leaned into her fiancé, amazed at how much her life had changed in the past year. There was still so much to figure out. They were working on building the bar back up, and after moving in with Wyatt, they realized the house was way too small for the four of them, so Harper was looking for a new place. But for the first time in almost a decade, Olivia was happy.

She looked around at the people she loved and knew that losing any of them would hurt like hell. But living without them was so much worse. As Wyatt once said, it was better to spend what time they did have together. Otherwise, what was the point?

"How long before we can sneak away?" Wyatt whispered into her ear.

Olivia laughed. "This is *your* shop. We can't leave."

"Who said anything about leaving?" He kissed the side of her neck. "I installed a lock on the office door yesterday." His hand slid low on her back then moved lower to squeeze her ass.

She bit at her lower lip and glanced around, wondering if the others were occupied enough not to notice. They had mastered the art of quiet sex from living in close quarters with his sister and nephew. Right now, it was just a matter of discretely slipping away from the party.

Standing on her toes, Olivia said, "Meet me there in a couple minutes."

The End

Did you miss Aiden and Charlie's story?
Check out The Wrong Brother today!

More stories are coming soon! Harper's book will kick off
the new Single Parents' Club series, and we'll see what
happens to Aaron and Vi later in the Love Hunters series
(hint: their respective love interests have been briefly
mentioned in these first two books)!

If you enjoyed this book, please consider leaving a review!
Even just a sentence or two really helps authors get their
stories seen by more readers.

also by cm haines

LOVE HUNTERS

The Wrong Brother

The Right Man

Book 3 (TBA)

Book 4 (TBA)

VEIL OF MOONLIGHT

A Crimson Fate (Fall 2024)

A Cursed Slumber (Fall 2024)

Book 3 (TBA)

Book 4 (TBA)

STANDALONES

Cursed by Darkness (Fall 2024)

acknowledgments

This book started as sort of a fun side project, but with the help of some incredible people, it became one of my favorite books I've ever written.

First and foremost, thank you to my beta readers— Jennifer Gardner, Jessi Penhorwood Hoffman, Allyssa Painter, Arceli Firage, Cassandrah Woyak, Jenny Elliott, and Mariah Brown. Your feedback not only helped me expand this story but grow as a writer. With your guidance, I was able to dive deeper than I initially planned, and it made all the difference. I hope you like this new version of Olivia and Wyatt's book.

A huge shout out to my editor Heather Dowell. Your reactions meant everything to me, and I loved working with you on this book.

The biggest thank you ever to Leah Miller, who proofread the entire book in less than 48 hours and put up with my panicking. More than that, you encouraged me through every step of this process, and I honestly don't know what I'd do without you.

Of course, I also want to thank my family (even though I hope they never read this book). Their constant support is why I get to follow this dream.

And last but absolutely not least, thank you to all of my readers! I'm so grateful to have each and every one of you.

about the author

From steamy romance to fantasy to dystopian sci-fi, CM Haines simply loves stories. In fact, her entire life pretty much revolves around them as she continues book blogging and works to provide a variety of freelance author services. She also writes young adult/new adult fiction under Cait Marie.

CM lives in Indiana, spending most days in her home office that's slowly becoming her own library. She has a BA in forensic psychology and an MFA in creative writing, both from Southern New Hampshire University. When she's not working with books in one way or another, she enjoys music, bullet journaling, and Disney movies.

Find CM Haines online:

Facebook Group
facebook.com/groups/caits.reading.bandits
Newsletter
caitmarieh.com/newsletter
Website
caitmarieh.com

facebook.com/cm.haines2

instagram.com/c8_marie

tiktok.com/@cait.marie.h

x.com/c8_marie

amazon.com/stores/CM-Haines/author/B0BSSHJ1BN

Made in the USA
Monee, IL
20 August 2024

64175187R00164